The Enigmatic Door

A Florian Fooks Murder Mystery

The Enigmatic Door

Shirley Arnham

First edition.

A CIP catalogue record for this book is available from the British Library.

Ebook ISBN 978-1-7399186-0-6
Paperback ISBN 978-1-7399186-1-3

Table of Contents

CHAPTER ONE 1

CHAPTER TWO 9

CHAPTER THREE 21

CHAPTER FOUR 31

CHAPTER FIVE 39

CHAPTER SIX 49

CHAPTER SEVEN 59

CHAPTER EIGHT 69

CHAPTER NINE 81

CHAPTER TEN 91

CHAPTER ELEVEN 99

CHAPTER TWELVE 115

CHAPTER THIRTEEN 123

CHAPTER FOURTEEN 133

CHAPTER FIFTEEN 143

CHAPTER SIXTEEN 155

CHAPTER SEVENTEEN 163

CHAPTER EIGHTEEN 167

CHAPTER NINETEEN 175

CHAPTER TWENTY 187

CHAPTER TWENTY-ONE 197

CHAPTER TWENTY-TWO 207

CHAPTER TWENTY-THREE 223

CHAPTER TWENTY-FOUR 233

CHAPTER TWENTY-FIVE 241

CHAPTER TWENTY-SIX 253

CHAPTER TWENTY-SEVEN 259

CHAPTER TWENTY-EIGHT 269

CHAPTER TWENTY-NINE 281

CHAPTER THIRTY 291

CHAPTER THIRTY-ONE 299

EPILOGUE 305

ABOUT ME 311

ACKNOWLEGMENT 313

IN THE PIPELINE 315

CHAPTER ONE

Bronze Canyon, a small town in the territory of Wyoming, early May 1884

"What do y'mean, busting into my home in the middle of the night?" Fooks said, struggling into his pants and flicking his unruly hair away from his eyes. *Really must get that cut when I get time.*

They'd prodded him from the deep sleep which had claimed him. Though it was dark, recognizing his two nocturnal visitors was easy. Their builds and hushed voices were distinctive, but the clincher was their smell, a mixture of musty canvas jackets, stale tobacco, and unwashed bodies, not a popular scent yet all too familiar at Guardian Wall. Dismayed at finding them in his bedroom, he urged them into the living room before they woke his wife.

"Well? Why are you here?"

After a hard day, the last thing he wanted was nightly visitors, especially these two. Florian Fooks stood with arms akimbo, fixing the two shadows with a baleful glare. He looked every inch the leader of the notorious Guardian Wall Gang he'd used to be.

The taller of the two struck a match and lit the nearest lamp, illuminating the grinning face of his smaller companion, who raised a full bottle of whiskey. "We brung us a party."

The taller hissed at him, "Hush up, Sid."

Sid's face crumpled, and he bit his bottom lip at the rebuke. His shoulders drooped.

"You were hard to wake, Fooks. Sleeping like that'll get ya killed."

"Been working all day in the hardware store, Brad. Something you wouldn't understand."

What would Brad know about hard work? He'd never done an honest day's work in his life. Sure, both he and Tobe, his partner, had found the honest life hard at first, after all those years of easy money, but they'd stuck at it. Fooks, at least, was much happier being law-abiding. He had a good business, a nice home, and a wife, the ideal life for a young man.

Brad snorted. "No call to take that tone Fooks."

"I've every right." Fooks tossed his head. "What d'you want?"

"Jus' looking up an old friend," Brad said with a nonchalant shrug.

Fooks scowled. Typical of Brad to think breaking into a man's house and waking him wasn't anything out of the ordinary.

"Couldn't ya have done it in daylight?"

"Couldn't take a chance of running into that sheriff." Brad regarded his companion. "Could we, Sid?"

Sid shook his head.

"How did you find me?"

Brad swelled, pleased with himself and cocky. "Well, now, Fooks, I worked it out."

"Yeah, Fooks. Brad was real smart. You'd be proud of him, the way he figgered it." Sid's eyes sparkled.

Fooks faked a smile. "Yeah, I'm real proud."

"See, I told you he would be." Sid nodded to Brad.

Fooks pulled a face at the excitement in Sid's voice and motioned for him to be quiet.

"Keep it down, will you? Mary's asleep." He growled when they snickered. "She's my wife!"

"Your wife? Why, I figgered she was..."

When Brad went no further, Fooks smiled. *Seems my glare hasn't lost its touch.*

"You's married, Fooks?" Sid's eyes widened.

"Yes, what's wrong with that?" He was offended that they both thought he wouldn't marry, so much so that he'd forgotten his own admonition to be quiet.

"Oh, nothing," Brad said. He shook his head. "Jus' never figgered you for the marrying kind, is all."

"I told you what my plans were."

The bedroom door opened, interrupting him.

"Joseph, what's happening here? Who are these men?"

Mary stood in the doorway, her face kneaded into a frown. How to explain their presence? Mary knew his past, who and what he used to be. Gaining her trust had been difficult, and until now, she'd had no cause to regret her faith in him. The two men here might make her rethink that, something Fooks was keen to avoid.

Sid whooped. "Whoo-ee, Brad! Look at what Fooks has been doing."

Fooks rolled his eyes at the ceiling and smacked his lips.

Mary was late into her third trimester.

Brad grinned and punched Fooks on the arm. "Fooks, you ol' son of a gun."

"Ow!" Fooks rubbed his arm and glowered at Brad.

Mary stepped further into the room. "Joseph, aren't you going to make the introductions?" She raised an eyebrow at him.

Fooks didn't want to do anything of the sort. With a sour expression on his face, he opened his mouth to reply.

Before he could say anything, Brad doffed his hat. "Brad Coleman, ma'am. That there's Sid Murphy."

Sid snatched off his hat, held it to his chest, and nodded. "How do, ma'am."

"We're old friends of Fooks and Swan."

Brad grinned, but his expression sobered when Fooks gave him a withering look. "Not exactly friends. And they are just leaving." Fooks narrowed his eyes at Brad.

"We're in trouble, Fooks," Sid said with a gulp. "Real big trouble." His grip tightened on his hat.

"We came 'cause we need your thinking," Brad said.

Fooks cocked an eyebrow in his direction. Of all the gang members, Brad was the one who'd always questioned his plans.

For a moment, Fooks and Brad locked eyes. Running his fingers through his hair, Fooks glanced at his wife. "Mary, please go back to bed. I don't want you involved in this."

Mary sniffed and ignored him. She turned to their two unexpected guests. "Have you two gentlemen eaten recently?"

"No, ma'am," both said in a rush.

"Well, then—"

"Mary—"

Mary continued to ignore him, and he shook his head. Her own woman, that's what she was, the reason he loved her.

"I'll fix you something while you talk." With a slight smile on her face, she added, "With Fooks."

She disappeared into the kitchen.

Fooks turned to Brad and said, "How did you find me, and what d'you want?"

"Well, now, Fooks, those are two questions with answers long in the telling. Best we make ourselves comfortable while the little woman—"

Fooks gave Brad's shoulder a hard prod, and Brad yelped in pain. "Ow!"

"She isn't a little woman. She's my wife. Have some respect."

"So? She's..." Just as Fooks hoped, Brad's bravado crumbled again under the intense stare Fooks hadn't used for over three years.

Brad glanced around. "As I was saying, thems two long stories."

Fooks moved to his desk and picked up yesterday's newspaper. He pulled out several pages and placed them on the chair Brad threatened to sit in and then a few more on the sofa behind Sid. He growled at both to take the places he'd prepared.

"Well, now, no need to—"

"SIT!"

Brad and Sid sat in smart unison.

His lips tight, Fooks remained standing until he was sure they wouldn't dirty the furniture. Then he sat on the other sofa and leaned forward, his elbows on his knees. "Okay, how did you find me?" Best to go with this now. Wrap things up as fast as possible.

"In the newspaper, Fooks." Sid's eyes glowed.

"What?" Fooks stared, open-mouthed. His whereabouts being widely known was the last thing he wanted.

"Yeah, a few months ago. A story 'bout how we done got that old pocket watch of yours back for yous. Course, I realize it was only a made-up story, but I knowed straight off. Didn't I, Sid?"

"Yeah, he knowed straight off." Sid's features creased into a frown. "What did you know, Brad?"

Brad clenched his jaw.

Fooks rubbed his eyes and shook his head, smiling. Sid never changed.

"That although it said Florian Fooks wrote it. Y'know, to add to the drama of the piece an' all, but I reckoned old Fooks hisself wrote it." Brad chortled. "Fooks, you sure got the details right." He reached over and slapped Fooks on the back.

"What details?"

"'Bout you pacing about outside the cabin and Swan rocking in the chair." Brad snorted. "Nobody else but you would a remembered. Why, I'd forgotten it myself till that piece reminded me."

Fooks groaned and put his head in his hands.

He shook his head. How could he have been so stupid? Writing a story for the newspaper. Sheesh. Hadn't reckoned members of the gang would remember the details and track him down, had he?

"So?" Fooks shrugged. "It's a story in a newspaper. Why come here?"

"Go on, Brad. You tell him how you figgered out the rest," Sid squealed. "Brad was real smart." A moment later, Sid's expression sobered under the stares his current and former bosses gave him.

Fooks pulled his gaze from Sid and returned it to Brad for an explanation.

"Well, story was in the *Bronze Canyon Bugle*, and I knows Wash Turner is here."

Brad and Sid's visit sure was a complication, and Wash had better not find out, him being the sheriff an' all. Fooks rubbed his forehead, unsettled at Wash finding out. *Oh, this night was just getting better and better.*

Fooks rolled his eyes. "So?" He motioned for Brad to carry on.

"Put two an' two together, didn't I? Figgered here'd be the right place to seek you out. We'd only been watching the town for a day. Ain't we, Sid? Afore we spotted you coming out of that hardware store. Followed you back here, and we figgered we'd wait till nightfall afore we come talk to you."

"You still Joseph Crane, Fooks?" Sid asked.

Fooks glowered. "To the town, yeah."

Sid's eyes widened and he pointed over his shoulder at the kitchen. "Does she know?"

"Yes. What d'you take me for?"

"But she called you Joseph."

"Yes. It's my middle name, if you recall. She can't call me Fooks, can she? I'm living under an assumed name, and only Ma ever called me Florian." His voice rose an octave at the same time his head jerked up.

"Swan called you Flo," Sid said.

"Only occasionally." Fooks gritted his teeth. Swan called him Flo to get a rise out of him. He much preferred Fooks.

He took a breath and calmed. "You aren't here to discuss my domestic arrangements. You've told me how you found me, so why are you here?"

"Fooks, we're in a powerful lot of trouble."

"I know." Fooks' eyes widened. "I led you for most of it."

"You're the smartest man we know, Fooks." Sid swallowed hard. "Folks are saying you're some kinda criminal genius."

"Yeah, Fooks, so time to stand up and prove it," Brad said.

"Fellas, I can't get involved with anything you're up to. I'm making a new law-abiding life for myself here right now."

Fooks rubbed his thumbs, undecided. He opened his mouth to tell them to be on their way, but their concerned faces took the fight right out of him. He rubbed his forehead and then his eyes. Oh, boy, was he tired.

"What's happened?" he asked. He'd regret this.

"Murder," Brad said, clenching his jaw.

"Huh?" Fooks' head snapped up in surprise. Definitely not the kind of trouble he'd expected.

"They done accused us of murder, Fooks," Sid said with an audible gulp.

CHAPTER TWO

Fooks' eyes grew wide. "What have you done?"

"Nothin', Fooks. Honest." Sid gave his head a vigorous shake.

"Then why've they accused you of murder? And who's they?"

Brad squirmed. "Angelworth," he mumbled.

"Excuse me?" Fooks said. He'd heard right, hadn't he? Brad had said murder.

Brad cleared his throat and said in a louder voice, "Angelworth."

Fooks spluttered and rubbed his forehead. "Angelworth? They know you in Angelworth. Why would you go there?"

"Well, it's like this, Fooks..." Brad cleared his throat, glancing at his companion for help. "Y'see, Sid—"

Sid's head snapped up in alarm.

"Brad wanted to visit his..."

Sid grinned, but then, unable to carry on, his face fell.

"Sick aunt," Brad said. He smirked. "We's went to visit m' sick aunt." He chewed his lips, holding Fooks' incredulous gaze.

"What. Sick. Aunt?" Fooks asked through gritted teeth. "This sick aunt wouldn't just so happen to go by the name of Lively Layla, would she?"

With a snort, Brad dropped his head low so he wouldn't meet Fooks' eye.

Fooks rocked back. "How can you be so..." An appropriate word escaped him, and he gave up with a groan. He held his head in his hands and shook it.

Brad and Sid sat in uncomfortable silence, waiting for Fooks to compose himself.

"All right," Fooks said finally. "You went to Angelworth. You went to visit your sick aunt. What happened?"

"Well, while I's was with m' aunt, y'know, taking care of her, Sid was in the saloon. He gets word Sheriff Bennett is on his way round town an' he's looking for two dangerous owl hoots. Sid figgers it's time we oughta go, so he comes and gets me. We's sneak round the edge of town and skedaddle so nobody sees us getting to the livery. We's gets our horses an' rides out."

Brad shrugged and pulled a face. "Didn't think nothin' of it until a few days later when we're back at the Wall. Lucas went into Burton Wells for supplies, usual like, but he comes tearing back. Left the horses and buckboard right in the middle of the street. Hope Clara and Rosie are okay." His concern for the two horses did him credit, but not right now.

"Why did Lucas come back in such a hurry?" Fooks asked, mastering his patience.

"He ran into Sticky, hoping someone from the Wall would come into town." Brad went to his inside jacket pocket. "He gave Lucas this." He held out a folded newspaper page.

Fooks unfolded the newspaper with care, wondering what he was about to read. The headline was uncompromising:

COLEMAN AND MURPHY: WANTED FOR MURDER:

We regret to inform our readers of the closure of Mersham's livery until further notice. This is because of the conflagration last Tuesday night. Two men, alleged to be Brad Coleman and Sid Murphy, rode away in some hurry moments before the blaze started. A quick-thinking passer-by raised the alarm. All livestock was safety led away, and the damage was limited.

Amongst the debris, the clean-up crew discovered the body of Stephen Mercer, a distinguished lawyer in the territory who made many enemies during his career, none more so than in his judicious pursuit of the Guardian Wall Gang and their undertakings. Coleman and Murphy are members of this gang.

Reliable witnesses have put the two men in Angelworth that night. All local and federal authorities are on high alert for their apprehension, dead or alive. Information that leads to their capture may result in a reward of $10,000.

Fooks opened his hands and let the newspaper drop. He raised his eyes first to Brad and then to Sid.
"What did you do?" he asked with a hard overtone.
Sid shook his head. "Nothin', Fooks, honest."
"No one but us in the livery," Brad said.

"How can you be so certain? Liveries are dark places, and there's lots of corners to hide in."

Sid and Brad swapped glances.

"Why should there be? It was two o'clock in the morning. Most decent folks like Mercer woulda been in bed," Brad said.

"Obviously not."

"'Sides." Brad continued. "We's had to break in."

Fooks continued to stare hard at Brad. The uncomfortable silence broke when Mary pushed open the kitchen door.

"Would someone help me with this heavy tray, please?"

Fooks stood.

"I'll help ya, ma'am," said Sid, jumping up.

Fooks shot Brad a warning glance. Brad gave him a brief nod, and Fooks returned to the sofa.

Mary smiled at Sid. "Thank you."

In the kitchen, Mary smiled at the strange, diminutive man. He'd unwittingly prevented her from having a private word with Joseph. She pointed at the tray piled high with sandwiches and cups. A coffee pot stood waiting next to it.

"It's Sid, isn't it?" she asked when Sid went to pick up the tray. Perfect time to find out who they were.

"Yes, ma'am."

Sid picked up the tray, intending to make his way back with it. Instead, he found his way blocked.

"I take it you've known my husband for some while."

"Yes, ma'am," Sid said and swallowed hard.

Yes, that's what she'd thought. "How long, exactly?"

"Waal, I can't exactly tell ya how long, ma'am. All I remember is Fooks came to Guardian Wall in high summer. I don't recollect the year."

Mary was satisfied. He'd told her what she wanted to know. The two men were members of the outlaw gang Joseph had led until three years ago, when he and his partner had given up that life. But what did they want? Were they going to entice Joseph back into the Gang?

"Joseph left the gang. Why do you need him now?"

"Waal, ma'am, we's kinda in trouble, Brad and me. An', waal, I don't think I cen say no more, ma'am. Begging ya pardon, I mean no offense."

Mary inclined her head. "Very well." She stepped aside.

Sid glanced at the coffeepot and began to let go of the tray, intent on grabbing the pot. Mary realized some inexpert juggling was about to take place, no doubt resulting in her china in pieces on the floor.

"I'll bring this, Sid," she said. She snatched up the coffeepot.

Sid gave her a grateful grin. "Thank you, ma'am."

In the living room, Fooks reread the newspaper, this time taking in every word.

"Still say the same?" Brad asked with a smirk.

Fooks gnawed at his thumbnail. "I remember Stephen Mercer. He was a good guy."

"He made a lotta enemies amongst the outlaw fraternity."

"He did." Fooks studied the newspaper again. "Still no reason for him to die like he did. Horrible way to go." His eyebrows squashed together into a curious frown. "It says there was enough time to get all the animals out and damage to the building was minimal." He raised his head. "Don't that strike you as odd?" He collapsed the newspaper when Sid reached across him to set the laden tray down.

"How so?" Brad asked, reaching for a sandwich before Sid could set the tray on the table.

"If he was in the livery, why didn't Stephen come out when the fire started? I don't understand. The newspaper says they rescued all the animals."

"Mebbe 'cause he couldn't," Sid mumbled around a sandwich.

Fooks quickly picked up a plate and thrust it at him. Sid stopped chewing. Only when Fooks insisted did he take it. Fooks shook his head when Sid set the plate on the sofa beside him. *Someone needs to teach Sid a few manners.* He shook his head. *Not now.*

He had a more pressing matter. "Yeah, I'm thinking along those lines, too." Fooks threw his hands in the air. "I dunno, fellas." Seeing the disappointment in their eyes, he realized they wanted more from him. "There's gotta be more to it than this." He handed the newspaper back to Brad.

Licking his lips, he said, "You look tired, Mary. Why don't you go back to bed?"

"Oh, I'm not in the least bit tired." Mary appeared wide-awake and eager.

He rubbed his eyes. Delivery day in the hardware store was always exhausting. The monthly delivery required a lot of unpacking and putting away. Some customers wanted their deliveries on the same day. A steady stream of customers came in, wanting to pick through fresh stock. He and his two assistants had been on the go since early morning.

"Thank you for bringing the boys food and coffee, Mary. Go to bed now." This time it was a command, not a request.

Mary scowled and stood.

"Very well. Goodnight, gentleman."

"'Night, ma'am, and thank you."

Mary smiled at Sid and acknowledged Brad's nod before retreating to the bedroom.

"The safest place for you fellas right now is to go back to the Wall," Fooks said. He rubbed his forehead.

"We can't do that."

Fooks glanced first at Sid and then at Brad. Both squirmed under his gaze. Neither would meet his eye. Fooks was unsure for a moment about their reaction. Then he had it, and he let out a short, husky chuckle.

"The boys staged a coup!" he said. "They kicked you out."

"Said we was giving the gang a bad name," said Sid, crumbling under Fooks' scrutiny.

"Naw, they didn't kick us out. Me 'n' Sid left on our own account."

Fooks pressed his lips into a thin line. He knew Brad of old, always making out something wasn't his fault when, usually, it was.

"To preserve harmony in the gang. That's a good leadership quality. Ya ought to know that, Fooks. Might come in handy for you one day."

Fooks looked daggers at Brad. *Leadership? What does he know 'bout leadership?*

"Jus' till ya clear our names, Fooks. Then we can go back," said Sid.

"Clear your names? Me?" Fooks stared wide-eyed from one to the other. "What are you expecting me to do?"

Sid shrugged. "That's why we come, Fooks. Thought you might have an idea. If anyone can do it, you can."

Fooks groaned and put his head in his hands.

"Fellas," he said when he emerged, "I'm not in a position to help you right now." He tossed his hand at the bedroom door. "You can see my wife's about to have a baby any day. Not to mention I've got a business to run."

"If you can't help us, who can?" Sid asked, his brow knitted in concern.

Brad said over him, "Where's Swan? Mebbe—"

Fooks shook his head. A stab of pain shot through him at the mention of his partner. "Swan isn't here."

"Where is he? Get him back pronto. This is more urgent than anything he can be doing," Brad insisted.

Fooks shook his head. "I can't. He's in Boston. Dunno where, exactly."

Sid's eyes widened. "You two fallen out?"

"Not exactly." Fooks swallowed hard.

Brad huffed. It was obvious to Fooks he didn't believe a word.

"How long's he been gone, Fooks?"

Fooks grimaced. "Since Mary and me married." He rubbed his forehead.

Brad and Sid swapped glances.

"But she's a nice lady, Fooks. How can Swan not like her?"

"Not why he left, Sid," Fooks snapped.

"Then why? You two are so tight. I thought mebbe—"

"Nothing like that," Fooks said before Brad could put into words the direction he was going. "I think Swan wanted some time alone and to give me and Mary a chance." He wrung his hands. "I don't wanna say no more about it. He's not here, and that's an end to it.

"Fellas, go to Ruby Rock. Check into the Astoria Hotel for a few days. I'll scout around here and find out more. If I can." He pulled a face. "Best I can do for now. Sorry, fellas."

Fooks took his time sliding his legs under the bed covers. Beside him, Mary appeared to be asleep on her back. He mirrored her position, one hand under his head, and stared at the distant ceiling. No doubt, sleep would elude him for the rest of the night.

"Who's Sticky?"

"I thought you were asleep."

"Baby's been kicking for a while." She fumbled for his hand and pressed it to her bump.

Fooks beamed into the darkness when he felt his baby moving, and he smiled in Mary's direction.

"Wriggly little thing."

"Yes, she is."

Fooks laughed. "Oh, you're so sure it's a girl."

"It is. I know it."

"Mary, don't get your heart set on a girl. Babies have a way of surprising everyone."

"Janet Turner says so by the way I'm carrying. Most of the Women's Committee with girls think so, too."

Fooks chuckled. "Hardly scientific. Just a coincidence."

"And then there's Ted."

Fooks frowned. Ted was the younger of the two boys who helped in the hardware store. "Ted? What does he know about babies?"

"He's the eldest of seven. Every time his mother complained about the baby wriggling, she would have a girl."

"Ah! Proof, indeed," Fooks said.

"Yes, you'll eat your words. You'll see. I'll be glad to be rid of this lump, whoever they are." She paused. "Wonderful job, by the way."

"For what?"

"Distracting me. Who's Sticky?"

"You were listening?"

"Of course. Until the coffee bubbled and I couldn't hear anymore."

Fooks hesitated. "Sticky was someone I paid for his eyes and ears. Brad musta kept that up."

"Why is he called Sticky?"

"He had sticky fingers."

"And what does that mean?"

Fooks found talking to Mary about his criminal past difficult. He stumbled over his next words. "He's a pickpocket and observant. He can get close enough to folks to overhear conversations with no one noticing. Useful guy to have on board. I paid him to bring me anything he heard about the Guardian Wall Gang, its members, or..."

"Or?"

Fooks considered.

"Or anything that might be a potential job," he said in a whisper.

Mary grunted, and he glanced in her direction. "You did ask."

"So, the two men who came tonight? They're members of the Guardian Wall Gang, aren't they?" Mary crept closer and rested her hand over the open neck of his henley.

"Yes."

"And they're in trouble?" Mary's fingers smoothed the small patch of chest hair she found.

"Yes."

"Not your kind of trouble. More serious than that?"

"Yes. They're wanted for murder."

"What happened?"

Fooks raised his arm for Mary to snuggle underneath. Once she settled, he summarized the details for her.

"Did they do it?"

"No."

"How can you be so sure?"

"We're talking about Brad and Sid. Neither of them is smart enough for murder."

"So? People change."

"Not that much. 'Sides, there's no reason for them to murder the man who died. The evidence is circumstantial at best."

"Why did they want to find you?"

Fooks hesitated. "They need help. They can't go to the law now, can they?"

He almost caught Mary's thinking beside him. He wasn't surprised when she spoke again.

"So, what do Brad and Sid want you to do?"

Fooks took a deep breath. "I'm not sure, exactly, but they asked for my help."

"Are you going to help them?" Mary stroked his cheek. "Can you help them?"

Fooks enclosed her hand in his and shook his head. "I don't know. I shouldn't have spoken to them."

"You didn't have much choice, did you? Turning up the way they did."

"No, I guess not."

"How did they get in, anyway?"

Fooks put his hand over his eyes. "It's been a long day, Mary. I musta forgotten to lock the back door," he said, ashamed to be admitting to the lapse. "I won't make that mistake again."

"They're wanted outlaws."

"Yes, but this time, they're wanted for murder. Someone is framing them, and that isn't right."

"Who would frame them?"

"The actual murderer of Stephen Mercer might."

"Do you really believe it's murder? He didn't die by accident in the fire."

Fooks shuddered. "Aw, the more I go over it, the less it makes sense. Too many unanswered questions. In my mind, at least. I'm gonna have to find out more."

Mary looked over at him. "What will you do?"

"I'll speak to Craig and Wash tomorrow. They might know more than what's in the newspaper. Depends on what I learn if I do anything more." He snuggled his head against hers. "Get some sleep, huh? Morning is not far away now."

"And you must sleep, too." She accepted his kiss. "Things will look better in the morning."

"Yeah."

He wasn't convinced.

CHAPTER THREE

Craig Carmichael, editor-in-chief of the *Bronze Canyon Bugle*, glanced up at the sound of the tinkling bell, signaling a customer entering the newspaper office. He sighed. Printing day was always the busied day of the week. He didn't have time to stand and chat today, especially when he saw who it was.

Joseph Crane walked to the counter, folded his arms, and leaned on it, beaming in that infuriating way of his. The slightly lopsided mouth hinted at a steely determination.

"Hi, Craig."

Craig raised his eyebrows. Used to Joseph's manner by now, he could tell by his demeanor that he was after something. This usually required him digging about in his archives for hours on end, searching for an old news story.

"Joseph. What can I do for you today? I am rather busy. Printing day, 'n' all."

"Oh, oh, no, I want nothing old." Joseph nodded with a grin. "This is current affairs."

"Hmmm, makes a change."

"About a week ago, there was a fire over at Angelworth. I heard they found a man dead. I may have known him, and I wanna check the name."

"Yes, I remember. Okay, shouldn't be too hard to find. Take a seat, and I'll have a hunt now."

Joseph grinned. "Thanks."

As Joseph took a seat, he slid yesterday's *Cheyenne Daily* from the coffee table. Craig watched him for a moment before disappearing out back.

Craig called Joseph back to the counter before he was barely halfway through the front page.

"Here you are. Is this it?"

Joseph studied the cutting Craig had placed on the counter.

"Stephen Mercer, that's the one." Joseph gnawed at his thumbnail. "So, it was him."

"You knew him?"

"Not well." Joseph sniffed and wrinkled his nose. "I worked on a case with him a few years back."

"Didn't know ya'd been a lawman, Joseph," Craig said with a faint smile.

Joseph's background had intrigued Craig ever since he and his partner, Sam Martin, had come to Bronze Canyon. Craig took any opportunity to find out more about these two mysterious old friends of the sheriff. It had almost become a hobby. His pet theory was that Joseph might be Florian Fooks. Every clue helped him expand this idea.

"What?" Joseph grinned. "Oh, you'd be surprised at the strange jobs Sam and me had afore we came to Bronze Canyon." He gave Craig a wink. "Thanks."

Craig watched him go and then studied the cutting. The wanted men were two of the Guardian Wall Gang. Could that be the real reason Joseph was asking, because they were members of the gang formerly led by Florian Fooks? No one had heard anything about the outlaw leader for three years. Rumors circulated that he'd gone straight and was living a life of obscurity and respectability. Might that place be here in Bronze Canyon? Craig added the information to his collection.

Washington Turner, sheriff of Bronze Canyon, narrowed his eyes as Florian Fooks closed the newspaper office door. *Now, what was Fooks doing in there?* He watched Fooks run his fingers through his long brown hair and position his hat with precision. Fooks' tongue curled around the corner of his top lip, and his brow creased into a frown, a sure sign he was up to something. Wash growled. Fooks set off across the street towards the jail. *Now what does he want?*

"Hiya, Wash," Fooks said, entering the office.

Wash recognized the wide, mischievous grin, the one that always presaged trouble. *What am I in for today?* Wash was proud of his law-abiding and peaceful town. Allowing Fooks and Swan to settle in his town stretched his professional bounds. There were days when he questioned his wisdom. Today might be one of them.

Wash glanced sideways to the back room to show he wasn't alone.

"Joseph."

Fooks came to stand before the desk, his hands clasped in front of him. He peered down at Wash with a tight-lipped smile.

Wash leaned back in his chair. He regarded Fooks with a look that was a mixture of indulgent parent and long-suffering teacher. Keeping a close eye on Fooks, and his partner, Swan, before the latter had gone to Boston, had proven to be a challenge at times.

"Something I can help ya with? Or are ya hiding from someone?"

Fooks pushed back his hat and put his hands on his hips. A grin spread over his face. "Now, who would I be hiding from?"

Wash smirked. "How long ya got?" he muttered under his breath when his deputy came out of the back room.

"Howdy, Joseph," the deputy greeted.

Fooks tipped his hat before turning back to Wash.

"What d'you know about a livery fire over at Angelworth a while back? A man died."

"Probably not much more'n Craig has already told ya."

Fooks frowned. "You were watching me."

Wash grinned. "My job is to know about all the comings and goings in this town."

Fooks' frown deepened, and he pursed his lips. He glanced at the deputy, whose back was turned to them while he added posters to the wanted display. Satisfied the deputy wouldn't overhear them, Fooks pulled out the chair in front of Wash's desk and sat. He raised his eyebrows and nodded in the deputy's direction, tapping his fingers on the desk.

On the other side of the room, the deputy dropped the pile of wanted posters on the floor.

Wash closed his eyes and shook his head. The deputy he'd had foisted on him would be the death of him. From the spluttering, Fooks was trying to stop from laughing aloud. Wash opened his eyes and shook his head in disapproval. Yep, Fooks always found the situation funny.

Fooks cleared his throat and sobered. "Well?" he said, leaning forward and keeping his voice down. "You know what I'm referring to and why."

"Yes, and I'd counsel ya not to get involved," Wash said. He gave Fooks a hard stare. "Unless, a'course, ya already involved."

Fooks met Wash's eyes. Wash couldn't discern exactly what he read in them. Fooks was a complex character. Might be anything.

"I'm not involved. Just wanted to find out a little information about a man I worked with a few years back, that's all." Fooks slapped the desk and stood up. "Well, if you can't help me, I'd best be getting along now." He smiled and tipped his hat.

He glanced at the deputy, and his smile faded. He gave Wash a meaningful nod and left.

Wash contemplated the exchange. Fooks had a reason for asking. He wasn't a man who engaged in idle chitchat. The reforming outlaw was up to something, but what? Wash resolved to find out.

Later in the evening, as Fooks and Mary did the dishes from supper, a knock on the front door interrupted them. Fooks, preferring to wash, was up to his elbows in soapy water.

"I'll go," Mary said, throwing down the drying cloth.

"Er—" He didn't like Mary opening the door after dark. Too late. She'd gone.

Moments later, she returned with Wash, who had a rueful grin on his face. Doing dishes seemed far too domestic for a notorious outlaw like Florian Fooks. Caught at such a mundane task, he made a wry face.

"Sorry to interrupt. I figgered we needed to continue our conversation from this morning," Wash said.

Mary's gaze flicked from one man to the other. "What conversation?"

Fooks glanced at her and took a deep breath. "Remember how I told you about the death of a man I knew over at Angelworth? I asked Wash if he'd heard any more."

Wash finished the explanation. "Difficult to talk when Fooks came in earlier, Mary. My deputy was there. Need to finish the conversation here in private. Could be murder, and Fooks knows the wanted men."

"So, do you have any more information?" Mary asked.

"Not a lot more, no."

"Then why are you here?" Fooks asked.

"I want to know what you know. How did ya find out about this? Weren't in the *Bugle*, 'cause I checked. And how did ya meet Stephen Mercer? He was a high-flying lawyer. Making a real name for himself in certain influential circles."

"Long story," Fooks murmured. His eyes flicked between the two. He ran a hand through his hair.

Wash grinned. "I got time."

"So have I," Mary said.

"Mary—"

"No." Mary was firm. She raised her chin in defiance.

Fooks puffed. Neither would let him off the hook. "Best go take a seat." He gestured to the living room, aware he needed to do some fast thinking here.

As Wash and Mary settled, Fooks poured two whiskeys. He took a big slug of his before presenting the other to Wash.

"Will I need this?"

Fooks twitched his head. "Possibly."

He paced.

Wash and Mary swapped glances. Pacing didn't bode well.

"How are ya, Mary? You're looking well."

Mary smiled and ran a hand over her bump. "Thank you. Not long now. Dr. Albright thinks two or three weeks to go, but you never can tell with babies."

"No, they come when they're darn well ready."

Fooks faced them.

"Wash, you ever come across an outlaw by the name of Quinn Mooney?" he murmured, staring into his glass.

"Quinn Mooney?" Wash frowned. "Yeah, name rings a bell. Tell me about him."

"Did most of his outlawing in Nebraska. Had a small gang. Did a few successful bank jobs. Was making a name for himself, kinda like ours."

"Were you acquainted?"

"No." Fooks shook his head and took a drink. "I kept an eye on him when he drifted into Wyoming a time or two, pulling jobs here and there."

"What do you mean, you 'kept an eye on him'?"

"He was encroaching on my turf. First rule of business, Mary, check out your competitors. I put the word out, looking for information." Fooks peered into his glass. "When he began announcing they were the Guardian Wall Gang, I became really interested."

He set his glass on the coffee table and sat next to Mary.

"What did ya do?" Wash's voice had taken on a hard note.

"I let it go at first. When I learned more about the jobs he'd pulled in our name, I realized I couldn't let it continue. I didn't like his methods. He was rough. No one was getting killed or seriously hurt, but I figured it was only a matter of time. I couldn't dare take the risk. Quinn Mooney and his gang were impacting negatively on our reputation.

"The first time I came across Stephen Mercer, he was whipping up a storm against us 'cause of Quinn Mooney. He had the ear of men in some prominent places, which coulda gotten very bad for us. Very bad indeed.

"Mooney's crimes were nothing to do with us. I wasn't prepared to take the fall for things he'd done in our name. I had to make him see the error of his ways." Fooks let out a small, mirthless laugh.

"Who do you mean? Stephen Mercer or Quinn Mooney?"

"Stephen Mercer." Fooks twitched his head. "So, I hatched a plan to put Stephen straight on a few things. Figgered it would be easier to get him on our side than go after Mooney." He downed the rest of his whiskey and washed it around in his mouth before he spoke again. "First outing for Joseph Crane." He set down the empty glass.

"That's the name you're using now," Mary said.

Fooks smiled at her. "Joseph Crane isn't the first time I've used this name, y'know."

Mary rolled her eyes. "Go on."

"Not much more to tell."

Fooks walked to the table where the whiskey sat. "Joseph Crane." Bottle in hand, he glanced back ruefully. "Attorney at law." He offered the bottle to Wash, who shook his head. Fooks refilled his own glass.

"Joseph Crane has a way with words." He grinned back at them. "You might even say he has a silver tongue."

Neither appeared particularly amused, and he sobered quickly. He flopped onto the sofa.

"Joseph Crane went to Angelworth, posing as a special agent of the federal government."

Wash let out a growl of displeasure. "Fooks."

"What? I was an outlaw, protecting my livelihood and reputation." When Wash sniffed, Fooks continued. "I worked with Stephen Mercer for a few weeks. Pointed out which heists were down to me and the gang and which ones were Mooney's jobs, outlining the differences. I impressed upon him that the Guardian Wall Gang were gentlemen robbers. We treated folks with courtesy and respect, unlike the Mooney Gang.

"Didn't matter none, though. Quinn Mooney disappeared." He pursed his lips. "Dunno what happened to him. Last I gathered, he pulled a bank job in Nebraska and shot the sheriff, and the posse chased him and his gang outta town. Gang split, and Mooney headed into Wyoming."

"Is that true?"

"I tried to find out more." Fooks shook his head. "Most of the gang were killed or captured. What happened to Quinn Mooney is a mystery. All I learned were rumors. A bounty hunter said he was on his trail. Claimed he shot him, but he couldn't back up his story. What's more plausible is Mooney dying in a barn fire while rescuing his horse. Something I admired 'bout him. Quinn Mooney always took care of his horse. Mighta hightailed back to Nebraska, settled down, and become a farmer, for all I know."

He shrugged. "He dropped outta sight, and nobody ever heard about him again. Dead, probably."

He took a sip of whiskey. "At least the Guardian Wall Gang didn't have to take the credit for his crimes. That was the key thing."

"Were his methods really so different?" Mary asked.

"Yeah," Fooks said. "Hate to admit it now, of course, but I took real pride in the jobs I planned and executed. Quinn Mooney was sloppy and amateurish in his execution. Did things I wouldna done." Fooks wrinkled his nose. "He came up with some excellent ideas. I'll give him that."

"If his methods were so different, why did the Guardian Wall Gang get the blame?"

Wash sat back and awaited the answer to Mary's question with interest.

Fooks licked his lips. "I never met him. Never even saw him. But I spoke to men who had. He'd started announcing himself as me."

He swallowed. "Apparently, he coulda been me. A few years younger, perhaps. Enough like me to be convincing. It was eerie, and it made... Well, I felt uncomfortable. And I didn't like that."

Silence descended on the room.

"Did Stephen suspect anything? Given you and Mooney looked alike?" Mary asked.

Fooks pulled a face and shook his head. "He hadn't seen Quinn Mooney, and he'd certainly not met me before. Our resemblance to each other wasn't common knowledge. Yeah, I suppose he mighta figured it out later."

"Weren't you taking an enormous risk?"

Fooks inclined his head in agreement. "I had to do what I had to do." He brightened. "'Sides, Tobias was in town, watching my back."

Wash grunted. "Okay, you've told me how you become acquainted with Stephen Mercer. Who told you about his death? And don't lie to me, Fooks."

Fooks swallowed. "I still hear things. Lotta gossip in a hardware store."

"I don't buy it."

"All right!" Fooks snapped. He calmed, running a hand through his hair. "Look, if you ask me outright, I'll tell you." He rubbed his forehead. "But none of us will feel good with the outcome." He flicked anxious glances between Wash and Mary.

CHAPTER FOUR

Fooks looked at Wash in trepidation. Here was a tricky situation. What would Mary do? If Wash asked her about Brad and Sid, would she lie for him? Fooks remained in this town under several conditions, one being no dealings with criminals.

Wash would arrest him if Mary told the truth. Yet Wash must know how successful he was, building a fresh life here in Bronze Canyon. The hardware store was in much better shape now than it had ever been before.

Fooks groped for Mary's hand on the sofa. He knew when her eyes were on him, but he deliberately didn't return her gaze. *Wash musta figured on the possibility Brad and Sid would pay me a visit.* Fooks resisted the temptation to smile when Mary squeezed his hand, letting him know she wouldn't say anything.

"Any possibility Brad Coleman and Sid Murphy coulda done it?" Wash asked.

"No."

"Why are you so sure?"

"Come on, Wash, you know them. Sure, Brad's a career criminal, but he's not always smart enough to be a good outlaw, let alone murder someone. And Sid..." Fooks stumbled for something to say about his hapless former colleague. "Sid's just Sid. You know neither are murderers. Someone is setting them up because they were there. Convenient, is all."

Wash nodded. "Yeah, I kinda figgered the same thing."

"So, d'you have any more for me?"

"Some. The town doctor said Mercer died from smoke inhalation."

"But why was he in the livery at two o'clock in the morning?"

Wash glared at Fooks. "How d'ya know the time?"

Fooks shifted uneasily in his seat. "Well, it stands to reason the fire occurred late at night. The newspaper said it was pure chance someone spotted the flames and raised the alarm." He shrugged. "During the day, more folks would be around." He downed his drink. The strong liquor burned all the way down. With a grimace, he got up.

Even with his back turned, Fooks could feel Wash's eyes on him. He refilled his glass once again.

"Is the Angelworth sheriff looking into it?" Fooks asked over his shoulder.

"Bennett?"

Fooks nodded, and Wash pulled a face.

"Dunno."

Fooks turned to face him fully. "But someone has to, or else Brad and Sid are wanted for murder."

"Livery owner said he locked up about ten and all was peaceful. No one about." Wash shook his head. "Bennett posted the murder warrant. I probably woulda done the same given the circumstances."

Fooks walked back to the middle of the room, rubbing his forehead. He was tired, and he chose his words carefully. "Can you find out any more?"

"Not without Bennett asking me a whole load of questions 'bout why I'm asking." Wash hesitated. "The only way you're gonna know more is to go to Angelworth."

Fooks shook his head. That was the last thing he wanted to do.

Mary opened her eyes. She needed the bathroom yet again, one of the many drawbacks to being pregnant, nor was she surprised at being the bed's sole occupant.

She threw on her robe and went into the main room. As expected, she found her husband pacing. He had his back to her.

"Might have known," she said, crossing her arms. She smiled when he jumped.

"Mary, don't do that," he snapped at her. And then he asked more quietly, "Did I wake you?"

"No." Mary rolled her eyes. "You can tell me what's keeping you up in a moment. I've an appointment elsewhere."

He was pacing again when Mary returned, but he stopped when she walked over to him.

"You're worried, aren't you?"

"Yeah." He nodded. "You met Brad and Sid. Do either of them strike you as the murdering kind?"

Mary smiled. "Not sure about Brad. Sid seemed a sweet man."

Fooks grinned. "Yeah, he's pretty harmless." He ran his fingers through his hair. His hair needed cutting. It needed cutting now. He always left it for as long as he could get away with. He turned away. *Probably not much longer now though.*

Mary smiled. She went to him and ran a hand across his shoulders. His muscles were taut under his henley undershirt.

"Joseph?"

He peered at her over his shoulder, and then he turned and pulled her close.

She looked at him, opening her mouth to speak before collecting her thoughts.

"You don't believe there'll be a proper investigation, do you?"

He shook his head. "Not with suspects served up neatly on a plate," he said quietly. "And if they catch Brad and Sid..." He shook his head. "I wouldn't bet on them reaching trial."

Mary put her hand flat on his chest. "Joseph, go to Angelworth."

"How can I? You're gonna have a baby any day. I need to be here. And then, of course—" He stopped. *Then, of course, there's the danger a person might recognize me. If that person is a bounty hunter, one who shoots first and asks questions later... Sheesh, what a dilemma.*

"And if you don't go and you can make a difference?" She stroked his cheek. "You'd never forgive yourself if anything happened to them. Especially if they're innocent."

Fooks closed his eyes and shook his head.

"You must at least try. There're a few weeks left. You'll be back in plenty of time."

"I don't know, Mary. I don't know what to do."

Mary watched as his emotions flickered across his face, the agony of indecision.

She slipped her arms around his waist as far as they would go. "Look at me, Joseph. Please."

When he did, he stroked her cheek. "I don't deserve you, Mary." He touched his forehead to hers and let out a long, shuddering breath. "Will you be all right if I go?"

"Yes. I've plenty of friends who will come and stay. I won't be on my own."

"And what about your father? How are you gonna explain to Luke why I upped and left at a time like this?"

"Let me worry about Papa. The sooner you go, the sooner you will be back."

"What about the store?"

"Ted and Russ can cope for a short while. You said yourself, Russ is itching to have more responsibility. Well, now is his chance."

Fooks rubbed his cheek. "Angelworth is three days' ride from here."

"You won't go on the train?"

He shook his head. "The Guardian Wall Gang held up that line several times. Can't take the risk someone might spot me."

Mary nodded.

"I dunno how long it'll take to clear this up. I could be two, three weeks." He shook his head. "I can't leave you for so long."

"Joseph, this won't wait."

"Neither will the baby."

"Oh, I'll cross my legs until you get back." She laughed and gave her bump a fond rub. "We'll have words. Baby will understand."

Fooks grinned and pressed her palm to his lips. "Mary. I love you." He pressed his forehead against hers. "Even riding, you know there's a possibility someone might recognize me?"

"I know." Mary stroked his cheek. "You'll be careful, and it's been a while. Grow a beard, and you'll cover these." She pressed the two creases on either side of his mouth and smiled when they deepened into dimples.

"Easier said than done." He tightened his grip on her. "You're right. I have to try, don't I?"

Mary nodded. "You'll never settle otherwise."

"Well, if you're sure, then I'll go first thing in the morning."

"Yes, I'm sure."

Fooks slipped an arm around her shoulders and led her back to the bedroom. "If I've got a long ride ahead of me tomorrow, then I oughta get some sleep." He pressed a kiss to her forehead. "Thank you, Mary. I'll make this up to you, I promise."

Early the next morning, Fooks stuffed his saddlebags full and fastened them closed. His hand hovered over his gun belt. Earlier he'd cleaned his gun. Swan would have been proud of how thorough he'd been. This time he'd had to be. Rarely did he have cause to wear a gun these days, let alone use one. To say his gun had suffered from neglect was putting it mildly. He needed to prepare properly for this trip, yet he still lingered. Strapping on a gun brought a reminder of the old days, when wearing one had been a normal occurrence.

With reluctance, he buckled on the gun belt. He smiled in satisfaction when he could still use the same well-worn hole. Mary's good home cooking hadn't increased his girth. As he bent to secure the thongs around his thigh, the kitchen door opened.

"Seems strange to see you wearing a gun," Mary said.

"Yeah. Feels strange, too." He straightened and faced her. The flicker of confusion crossing her face gave him a moment's concern. "What's the matter?" he asked. "Have you changed your mind about me going? I don't have to go, y'know."

"No, I haven't changed my mind. You look different, that's all. Something I wasn't prepared for."

"Huh?"

"You're not Joseph Crane."

Fooks winced. *I know what's coming.* He asked anyway. "Who am I, then?"

"Florian Fooks."

Yep. Fooks sighed. "Mary, if anything happens... If you need me, send a telegram to Angelworth, to Joseph Crane."

"Yes, got it." She smiled as she smoothed his shirt collar over his vest. "Don't take any risks, Joseph. Someone may—"

Fooks put a finger to her lips. "Mary, I promise I'll be careful. I know how to take care of myself. I did it for a lot of years."

"You had Tobias with you."

"I know, and I'm not going into this alone."

"You're not?"

"Nope." He grinned the full double dimple at her. "I have a plan."

Mary smiled. "Yes, of course you do." She rolled her eyes. "A Florian Fooks plan?"

"They're the best kind," he said, heaving his saddlebags over his shoulder.

He kissed her quickly, knowing that if he tried for anything longer, he would never leave. Mary didn't protest. "Don't worry 'bout me. I'll be fine. You concentrate on taking care of yourself and our baby."

He paused beside the hat stand, on which hung two dark gray hats. He reached up and took down the more battered, the one he'd not worn for three years. Mary watched as he flipped it over in his hands for a moment before settling it on his head. When he turned back, the transformation was complete.

He was no longer Joseph Crane. In his place stood the notorious outlaw leader of the Guardian Wall Gang, Florian Fooks.

CHAPTER FIVE

First, Fooks went to the Astoria Hotel in Ruby Rock, where he'd told Brad and Sid to wait. He hoped, given their increased wanted status, they might heed his advice and lie low. He briefly considered checking the saloon first, knowing their habits all too well. Living in hope rather than expectation, he went to the hotel. No surprise to find two highly distinctive names in the hotel register. Jared Reinhardt and Cornelius Sylvester had checked in.

Fooks gave the agreed-upon knock on their door, two soft knocks, a pause, and three more knocks. He didn't get further than the pause when a chewing Sid opened the door. Fooks slipped in quickly.

"How did you know it was me?" he hissed.

"Oh, we done see you ride in, Fooks," Sid said with a grin.

Fooks sucked his teeth. "Couldn't you use less obvious names?"

"Well, Brad—"

"'Bout time ya got here. We're jus' 'bout gone plum crazy in here," Brad grumped immediately.

"It was for your own good," Fooks snapped back.

Brad growled. "Yeah, well, you try living with him in close proximity for three days," he mumbled, loud enough for the others to catch.

Fooks grinned.

Sid stopped chewing and was about to protest when Fooks touched his arm.

Fooks sat on the edge of the bed, the others across from him.

"What ya found out, Fooks?" Sid asked.

"Not much more, I'm afraid." When he saw their disappointed faces, he added. "However..." He swallowed. "I'm..." He took a deep breath. "I'm gonna go to Angelworth."

"Whoo-ee."

"Find out what I can."

Sid was one enormous grin, and even Brad appeared more cheerful.

"I can't promise anything, fellas. You're not off the hook yet. You do know that, don't you?"

"Yeah, yeah, we's knows, Fooks."

"I knew ol' Fooks wouldn't let us down."

Brad leaned forward, ready to talk business. "Now, let's get down to cases. What d'ya want us to do? Ride in and read that sheriff his fortune?"

Fooks eyes widened.

"No."

"Rough him up a little?"

"No."

"Well, then we—"

"Brad, whatever you're thinking, I can tell you it's not gonna happen that way. Here's how it is gonna work. I'm going to Angelworth. Alone. You two are going back to the Wall."

Sid squirmed. "But we can't, Fooks. Lucas done kicked us out."

"Yes, you can." Fooks raised a hand to still any further protest. "You tell Lucas you've seen me and I'm taking care of everything. He'll be all right once you explain things to him. Is Rev at the Wall?"

Rev's occupation at the Wall varied, depending on how close to God he felt at any given time. If in trouble or suffering from lack of money, he often "popped" in to visit with the fellas. He'd stay for a while, perhaps go on a job or two, until he had the urge to go out again.

Brad shrugged. "Was last time we's there."

Fooks pulled a face. "Okay, well, let's hope he still is 'cause I need him to meet me in Angelworth."

"You gotta plan, Fooks?"

"Yep."

Brad and Sid rode back to Guardian Wall, in trepidation of a frosty reception, while Fooks set out for Angelworth.

Fooks climbed out of the valley that Ruby Rock and Bronze Canyon called home. He tugged on his red and green plaid coat and hunched his shoulders. *Why didn't I get a new winter coat back in the fall?* Not looking forward to the next two days of riding. He planned to camp out, but the ground still had snow in places. A glance at the mountains ahead did nothing for his sense of foreboding.

Two uncomfortable days later, he came within sight of Angelworth. Then the rain began. So much for this being the driest part of Wyoming. Soaked and miserable, he rode into the busy town.

Putting up his horse at the Anderson's livery because Mersham's was still closed, he squelched along to the hotel. Pedestrians going about their business at full tilt forced him to slalom around them. He sidestepped all manner of merchandise left on the boardwalk. A ladder blocking his route obliged him to step out onto the street.

"Hey, watch where you're going, fella," a man said as he climbed down.

Fooks blinked at the rebuke. *Why is it my fault?* He swallowed the acid-tongued reply about to spring from his lips. Instead, he politely tipped his hat in apology. He glanced at the poster the man had pasted up. An advertisement for soap covered last year's rifle-shooting contest. The winner was L M. The billposter had smoothed the new publicity over the top, covering the rest of the name. Fooks smiled. He loved these small towns and what constituted news.

Aware he didn't present a wholesome image, he dinged the bell on the reception desk of the Grand Trail Hotel. The desk clerk appeared from the backroom. He sniffed with disapproval as the hotel's newest guest dripped water and mud on the carpet.

Fooks assured the clerk he had money, and he swallowed his pride when asked to pay in advance anyway. He signed the register. The clerk swept it around fast in case he tried to steal it. Fooks waited for his key.

"There you are." The clerk glanced at the register. "Mr. Crane? Oh, Mr. Crane." Now the clerk was all smiles. "How nice to see you again, sir. I'm sorry I didn't recognize you."

His last visit to Angelworth had been five years ago. Hadn't occurred to him the town would remember him after all that time. Fooks smiled, pleased. *Musta left a more lasting impression than I thought.*

"Been a long time." He spotted the nameplate, and his bright smile showed through the dirt and stubble. "Alfred."

"Yes, sir, sure has. Anything else I can do for you?"

"Yes." Fooks now knew his next request wouldn't be met with horror. "Could I have a bath sent up when it's convenient?"

Fooks sighed as he hung his suit over the closet door. He should present a smart image in the morning.

"Guess my packing isn't as good as it used to be," he mumbled while sadly eying his brown number. "Hope those creases drop out by morning."

He turned back to the rest of his luggage, and then a knock came at the door. The expected bathtub.

"Thanks," he said, his eyes glowing at the pails of boiling water the two housemaids poured in.

He hadn't been this dirty for a long time, and he'd forgotten how uncomfortable it could be. The generous tip reflected his delight at immersing himself in the warm, sudsy water. He wasted no time in stripping. In bliss, he allowed himself to soak for a while. He was drifting off when he heard another knock at the door.

"Yeah?" he called in disgust.

"Telegram, Mr. Crane."

Fooks groaned. He sure hoped this wasn't from Mary. The few minutes it'd take him to get dressed wouldn't make any difference.

"Leave it with the desk clerk, please. I'll be down in a while."

His curiosity would now cut short his soak, yet he allowed himself longer to wallow than he should have. He reluctantly climbed out of the tub. The convenience of having a bath anytime had become a luxury he reveled in. He shaved, put on clean clothes, and presented a much more savory image at the front desk sometime later.

"You have a telegram for me?"

"Yes, sir."

A grinning Alfred found the envelope in the pigeonhole. Fooks walked a few feet away from the desk before tearing it open. He grinned as he read the few words. *Not from Mary. Phew.* Right now, the next best thing.

He read:

To Joseph Crane, Grand Trail Hotel, Angelworth. Will arrive on 7:00 pm stage tomorrow. J.

Short and to the point, telling him exactly what he wanted to know. He turned back to Alfred, who looked curious.

"Good news, sir?"

"Yes, very good. Even better news would be you telling me the dining room is open."

The next morning, Fooks walked into the Angelworth sheriff's office with purpose. Today he appeared and felt the consummate professional. The creases had dropped out of his brown suit overnight. He'd also stopped at the barbers on the way.

The latent outlaw in him automatically took in the floor plan, always looking for ways to make an escape. They formed in his mind even when he didn't want them to. He noted the rear door bolted from the inside. He almost ran when he saw the notice board. There, front and center, were posters for Florian Fooks and his partner, Tobias Swan. He sighed inwardly. Why were their prices so high? And why dead or alive? Neither of them had shot anyone, let alone killed someone.

Sheriff Bennett glanced up from the newspaper he was reading. He was a dark-haired man of middling years who looked comfortable in his job. Fooks remembered him from the last time he'd been in Angelworth. Dealings with him then had been, by necessity, brief. If he recalled correctly, though, Bennett was a competent small-town sheriff, providing he had nothing more onerous to deal with than drunken cowboys on a Saturday night.

"'Morning, Sheriff," Fooks said.

Bennett frowned the do-I-know-you question.

Fooks' eyes continued to flick around the office. He remembered the cells being in the corner. They were gone, and a new door had been inserted in the back wall. *Must be through there now.* His eyes lit up as his gaze settled on a small safe. *Hudson 105, three-digit combination, audible clicks. Five minutes. Piece of cake.*

He mentally shook himself and turned a dazzling smile on the sheriff.

"Joseph Crane." Fooks stuck out his hand.

Bennett scraped back his chair. "Yeah, I remember you," he said. He took the offered hand with caution.

"Do you, Sheriff?" Fooks sounded surprised. He was alarmed by this but also pleased.

"Yeah, you were the lawyer sent by the federal government a few years back."

Fooks grinned. With hands on hips, he nodded. "That's me."

"'Cept, when I checked up on ya after ya'd gone, no one had ever heard of you." Sheriff Bennett retook his seat.

"Ah, 'course not, Sheriff. I was working undercover. No one would admit to knowing me." Fooks settled on the edge of the sheriff's desk. Bennett glared at him hard, and Fooks stood, feigning an innocent expression.

"Ya had a partner. Marlin or something? Is he with ya?"

"Sam Martin," Fooks corrected. "No, he's working on a case back East right now. It's just me." He scanned the room again. "Have you remodeled, Sheriff?"

"Had an extension built for the cells." Bennett flicked a finger at the rear door. "Four shiny new ones, jus' waiting for some occupants." His hand closed over a set of keys on his desk.

Fooks noted where the sheriff's hand lay and laughed. "Oh, I suspect they'll come in handy before too long for a diligent man like you."

Bennett grimaced. "Well, what d'ya want?"

"Read 'bout Stephen Mercer. Sounds a mite suspicious, if you ask me."

"You here in your official capacity, Mr. Crane?"

"Nope." Fooks gave the sheriff a tight-lipped smile. "I'm here on my own account. I liked Stephen Mercer. He was a good man, and well, I can't get it outta my head that something don't seem right. I thought I'd come along here and take a look for myself." He finished with a friendly smile.

Bennett grunted. "There isn't anything suspicious. He died from inhaling the smoke from the fire. All there is to it." He dropped his eyes to his beckoning newspaper.

Fooks pursed his lips and, with a thoughtful look on his face, settled back on the edge of the desk. "It was late at night. Why was he in the livery then?"

"His wife says Stephen often worked late. Pulled all-nighters. Especially if he was working on something important. His office is a little way down the street. I dare say he heard the alarm and went to help. Like a lot of us did. Unfortunately, smoke overcame him. Doc treated several folks for smoke that night. Just bad luck, is all."

"Did anyone see him?"

"Things were pretty confused, Crane. Running back and forth. Getting the animals out. Organizing a bucket chain. Beaters. Most folks were too intent on what they were doing to notice who they were doing it with."

"Hmmm." Fooks crossed his arms as a perplexed frown creased his forehead. "Don't it strike you as odd, though, that Stephen should work late the very night Coleman and Murphy are seen in town?"

"No, it doesn't," Bennett said with a scowl. "Told ya, nothing unusual about him working late."

"So, you think it's just a coincidence?"

"Bad luck, is all."

Fooks pulled a face
"But why Sheriff? What motive did Coleman and Murphy have for setting the livery on fire and killing Stephen?"

"Men like that don't need motives!"

"There's always a motive, Sheriff," Fooks said in a low voice, "even if it doesn't make sense to anyone else."

Bennett stared hard at Fooks. "If ya want a motive, I'd say mischief."

Fooks bit his lip as he considered Bennett's explanation. "Mind if I poke around a little?"

"What for?"

"To satisfy m'own curiosity."

"There's nothing to satisfy. I'm telling ya, Stephen Mercer died of smoke inhalation after Coleman and Murphy set the livery on fire."

"No harm in me taking a look, is there?" His face a picture of innocence, Fooks sat with arms folded on the edge of the desk.

"If ya find nothing, then will ya go away?"

"You have my word, Sheriff."

Bennett drew himself up. "All right. If ya wanna ask questions, try in the livery. Jerome Mersham's the man in charge."

Fooks smiled inwardly and rose from the desk. "Thanks, Sheriff"

He left with a grin. He just might have sown a seed of doubt in the sheriff's mind.

CHAPTER SIX

Down at the livery, work on repairing the fire damage was well underway. The damaged cladding had been removed from the backside of the structure, and an untidy pile of it lay to one side. The structural timbers were still in place, but many showed signs of charring. Scaffolding allowed for their replacement one at a time.

Inside, someone had removed the bedding and swept the hard-baked earth floor. Salvaged timbers from the stalls on the burnt side lay ready for re-installation. Others had joined the discard heap.

Fooks asked a stable hand where he might find Jerome Mersham and then walked over in the direction indicated. He studied a man in his late middle years: slender frame belying strength, brown hair receding at the temples, several days' growth on his chin.

"Mr. Mersham? I'm Joseph Crane." Seeing Jerome's doubtful expression, Fooks added, "Sheriff Bennett sent me." Not exactly, but he'd come directly from there. "I'm gonna be looking into the fire as a second pair of eyes in case he mighta missed something."

Jerome's face brightened, and Fooks smiled. That had gone down better than he'd hoped.

"Pleased to meet you, Mr. Crane."

"Likewise, Mr. Mersham." Fooks stood with arms akimbo and surveyed the scene. "My, my, it sure is a mess."

"Aw, it mighta been worse, I suppose. The whole lot mighta gone up. As it is, we can get away with repairing just this one side." Jerome flicked a hand toward the burnt section of the building.

"Lucky, indeed." Fooks took a step forward. "Where and how did the fire start?"

"Best guess, over here." Jerome indicated a structural timber burnt most of the way through. "Reckon Coleman and Murphy must've knocked over a lantern on their way out. This is about where they stabled their horses."

Fooks went for a closer inspection, crouching at the spot. He "hmmed" for some time. Behind him, he was aware of Jerome watching him intently. Finally, Fooks straightened.

"Satisfied, Mr. Crane?"

Fooks gave his head a non-committal twitch.

"Not much to see, is there?" Bennett asked from the door.

Fooks spun around, surprised to see the sheriff. He bit off the flippant remark he was about to make. Instead, he continued his inspection, conscious of the sheriff's eyes on him.

"Where was Stephen found?" he asked, joining Bennett and Jerome in the center of the livery.

"Right here in the aisle." Bennett pointed to the exact spot, a few feet from where they stood.

Fooks walked over and inspected the roof. Above, blackened timbers showed, but they appeared intact.

"Hmmm. Anything fall on him?"

"Nope, sure didn't look like it."

"How was he found, exactly? I mean, in what position?"

"Flat on his back."

Fooks didn't seem convinced. "Facing which way?"

"Up," said Jerome in a bid to appear helpful.

Fooks mastered his patience. "This way?" He swung a hand, suggesting the length of the building. "Or that way?" His hand swung across the aisle.

"This way." Bennett pointed down the aisle. "Head this end, feet down the other end."

"Uh-huh." Fooks glanced at the fire-damaged section. He assessed the distance from there to where the body had lain. "And in what sorta condition was the body?"

Bennett shifted uncomfortably. "Ah, well, ya'll have to ask Doc Sullivan."

"I will," Fooks assured him. "But your general impression, Sheriff."

"Waal, fire burnt his hair and clothes."

"All over?"

Bennett winced. "No, mainly on this side." He pointed towards the fire.

"Hmmm."

Fooks slowly scanned the livery again, taking in everything. In particular, he noted the fire's reach. He was also interested in the extent of the major damage. He scanned the opposite wall. After glancing at the spot where the body had lain, he walked over to the wall. A back way out always piqued his interest. Reaching up, he ran his hand over the structure.

"There's a door here?" He looked back at them.

"Ah, yeah, but it ain't never used. Not in the sixteen years I been here," Jerome said.

No door handle existed. The only sign that the pedestrian door had been there at all was the arrangement of the timbers. Fooks' hand dropped to finger for the keyhole. With a sigh of irritation, he stripped off his right glove for a better feel of the surface. The sensitive touch of a master safe breaker came in handy for other things sometimes. He found the keyhole and peered at it, determining the type of lock. Satisfied, he reached up and felt around for the extent of the door. He gave it a rattle. Locked.

"D'you have a key, Mr. Mersham?"

"Nope. Never had no key. Never needed one." Jerome sought reassurance from Bennett, who gave him a nod.

Fooks pulled his glove back on as he walked over to join them.

"Do you own the building, Mr. Mersham?"

"No, sir. Rent it from Alan Long."

Fooks turned his attention to Bennett for an explanation.

"He's the local realtor. Buys and sells most types of property hereabouts. Owns and rents several buildings. He even has the lease on the sheriff's office."

"So, he's a prominent businessman?"

"Yes, I'd say. Seen enough here?" Bennett asked, moving away.

Fooks grinned. "For now. Take me to the doc, Sheriff."

Ignoring the sheriff's scowl, he held his hand out to Jerome. "Thanks for giving us your time, Mr. Mersham."

Fooks, deep in thought, lagged behind Bennett as they left. Outside, he glanced back at the building and then put a hand out to stop the other man.

"Wait up, Sheriff."

Bennett sighed. "Something wrong, Crane?"

"Hmmm. Mebbe. Where d'you think that door goes?"

Bennett shrugged. "Mebbe to the alley between the buildings? I dunno."

"Let's go take a look-see before we visit the doc."

Fooks set off in the obvious direction, Bennett at his heels.

"Got an idea?"

"Mebbe. Wanna check on something, is all. Probably nothing."

Fooks and Bennett went to the side of the livery. The building next door stood close, only allowing one of them through at a time. The ground was a thick carpet of weeds, signifying a path rarely traveled.

Not a cut-through into Main Street either. The stables doglegged across the end. A route to nowhere. No use for the door anymore.

By the time they reached the door, the light receded into a pale gloom.

"Don't look as though anyone's been through here for years," Bennett commented.

"Uh-huh." Fooks struggled to peer at the lock. "Hmmm." He stripped off his gloves and reached into his pocket. Finding a white handkerchief, he shook it out and gave the corner a twist.

"What are you doing?"

"I'll show you in a moment. If I'm right."

Fooks poked the twisted end in the lock. Taking the handkerchief out, he pulled it flat. "Interesting," he murmured.

"Got something?"

"Yeah. C'mon, Sheriff, let's get out of here, and I'll show you."

Back in clear daylight, Fooks showed Bennett his findings. The areas where he'd poked the twisted handkerchief in the lock were now stained brown.

"What am I looking at?" Bennett asked.

"Oil. Someone's oiled this lock recently. Seems odd that someone would go to all that trouble for a door that's never used."

Bennett held Fooks' eye for a moment and then glanced back at the handkerchief.

"Yeah. It does," he conceded slowly. "But no key. You heard Jerome say so."

"Just because Jerome doesn't have a key, it doesn't mean there isn't one," Fooks said. *And some people don't need a key.*

Bennett nodded. "No, true enough, but I don't—"

Fooks touched his arm and gave him a tight-lipped smile. "We're gathering pieces of a puzzle, Sheriff. We're just getting started. It's bound to not make sense yet. Which way to the doc? He might have some more pieces for us."

At the doctor's office, Bennett made the introductions. Doc. Sullivan, in his early fifties, had graying, streaked hair and a mustache. It reminded Fooks of the awful one Swan had flirted with once.

Ignoring the distracting mustache with difficulty, Fooks lost no time in asking questions. The discoveries in the livery had his mind racing with possibilities. He was in a hurry for something to make sense. He already suspected this would take him a while. *Oh, how I'm longing to get back to Mary.*

"You examined Stephen, Doc?"

"I did."

"What did you conclude?"

"He was pretty burnt up, and in my opinion, the smoke overcame him."

"Sheriff Bennett tells me you treated others for smoke inhalation that night. How is it Stephen was the only person to die?"

Doc Sullivan let out a short, mirthless laugh. "If you can answer why some folks succumb and others don't, we would hail it as a medical miracle. The town rang to the sound of coughing for days after. No one else was in the fire like Stephen."

Fooks rubbed his chin. "Well, that's where he was found, sure." His hands went to his hips. "Any marks on the body suggesting something hit him and stopped him from getting out?"

"From what I could see, he had a cut to his left temple."

Fooks glanced at Bennett. "Bad enough to kill him?" he asked.

Sullivan winced. "Nope. Can't say that. Might have knocked him unconscious, though." He shrugged. "Hard to tell. Didn't appear to bleed much, so he musta died shortly afterward."

Fooks regarded the doc with interest. Nothing Sullivan had said so far helped him connect the pieces.

"The way they found him, Sheriff," Fooks said deliberately, "on his back, face up, doesn't suggest to me he was trying to get out." He regarded Bennett meaningfully. "Does it to you?"

Bennett exhaled a long breath. "It doesn't."

"Any other injuries showing?" Fooks asked.

Sullivan shook his head. "Nope."

Fooks smiled and held out his hand. "Well, thanks for your help, Doc."

Handshaking and goodbyes over, Sullivan saw them out.

"One other thing," he said, holding the door open. "Dunno if this is significant."

Fooks and Bennett, now in the street, glanced at each other. "Anything, Doc," Bennett said. He glanced at Fooks again. "That might help our investigation."

Fooks' eyes widened in surprise, but he declined to comment on Bennett's choice of words. He waited for something further from Sullivan.

"Stephen had a cut across the top of his left palm." Sullivan pursed his lips. "Not deep. Short. 'Bout an inch. Almost overlooked it 'cause of the burning to that side of his body. Might have happened in any way."

"Recent?" Fooks asked.

"Yeah, I would say so. Might've happened in the office. Binders, filing, one of those new typewriting machines. Who knows?"

Fooks grinned. "Yeah, offices can be dangerous places. Well, thanks again, Doc."

Bennett and Fooks walked along the boardwalk, the latter deep in thought.

"That was something I didn't know before," Bennett ventured.

"Uh-huh."

Bennett shook his head. "The facts still suggest Coleman and Murphy for Stephen's murder. They probably hit him over the head when he discovered them breaking into the livery. Knocked over the lantern, setting the fire that killed him."

"Sheriff, I'm not disputing the facts," Fooks snapped, interrupting the sheriff's flow. "I'm just not convinced by your interpretation of them."

The two men halted in the middle of the boardwalk and faced each other. Other pedestrians veered around them.

"What's Coleman and Murphy to you, huh?" Bennett jabbed a finger at Fooks. "Why are you so convinced they didn't kill him?"

Fooks swallowed. He fixed Bennett with a glare, aware this was out of character. Up to now, he'd presented a mild-mannered countenance. Bennett shifted, uncomfortable under his gaze.

"I don't know who killed Stephen Mercer," Fooks said in a low voice, trying not to sound too menacing. "I'm trying to find that out." He mastered his patience. "If Coleman and Murphy are responsible, then they weren't acting alone. Something clever is going on here, but I can't see it right now." He shook his head. "Too many unanswered questions. I seriously doubt if either of those two men is smart enough to come up with the answers I'm gonna find."

Fooks walked away, leaving Bennett standing on the boardwalk, undecided. He hurried to catch him.

"Okay, Crane," he said, pulling Fooks to a halt. "Have it your way. There are questions to answer, but I'm not changing my mind. Coleman and Murphy are responsible until the facts can prove otherwise."

Fooks considered this before nodding. Better to have Bennett on his side than working against him. The two men walked towards the jail, having reached an awkward understanding.

"So, what's the next step?"

"Mrs. Mercer told you her husband often worked late, especially if he was working on something difficult."

"Yes."

"What was he working on?"

Bennett shrugged. "I don't know, but Tubby will."

CHAPTER SEVEN

Fooks' eyes widened. "Who's Tubby?"

Bennett gave him a curious, rueful grin. "Theodore 'Tubby' Wilson. He's Stephen's clerk. He'll know about the cases Stephen was working on."

Fooks nodded. "Okay, let's pay him a call."

At the lawyer's office, Bennett introduced Fooks to Stephen's clerk. He shouldn't have, but along the way, Fooks had formed an image of the man. With a name like Tubby, how could he not? He couldn't have been more wrong. "Tubby" definitely wasn't the adjective for the man.

In reality, Tubby Wilson stood tall and painfully thin. Fooks wondered how he'd come by the misrepresenting appellation. Politeness stopped him from asking on so brief an acquaintance.

"How are you, Tubby?" Bennett asked, not at all perturbed by using the nickname.

"Oh, fair to middling, I would say, Sheriff. Just about finished the letters informing all Mr. Mercer's clients of the sad news."

"Yeah, can't be easy," Bennett said. "What me and Crane here need to know, Tubby, is what Stephen was working on. Can you help?"

"Sure can, Sheriff." Tubby stood and went to the other desk. "Mr. Mercer was particular with his files. Kept current files right here on his desk." He laid a hand on a pile containing about ten files, some a lot thicker than others.

Fooks rolled his eyes. "Busy man."

"Yes, sir. He liked busy. Always on the go." Tubby appeared distant for a moment and then brightened. "He was training me on most of 'em. Should keep me occupied until Mrs. Mercer decides what to do with the office."

Fooks and Bennett swapped glances and sympathy. The young man would likely lose his job soon.

"Mind if I look through those files, er, Tubby?" Fooks asked.

Tubby sought approval from Bennett before answering. Receiving a nod, he grinned. "Sure, as the sheriff says yes."

"Well, I'll leave that part of the investigation to you, Crane. My deputy is away, so I'm the only law in town. Be sure to let me know if you find anything interesting."

"Sure, Sheriff," Fooks said. He waved Bennett off and tried not to show his relief at the sheriff's departure. "Thanks for your help," he said with a pleasant smile.

Bennett regarded him doubtfully before taking his leave.

Fooks spent the rest of the morning going through the files. Most were routine and straightforward. Fooks set aside the three files he wanted more information on. The ones he'd decided upon were the more interesting, complex, or long-standing ones, and they were also the thickest.

"Can you tell me about these cases, Tubby?"

"Sure can. I've done most of the administration." Tubby moved from his desk and retook a seat nearer to Fooks. "Looks like you have the complicated ones," he said, eying the pile.

"Probably." Fooks picked up the first. "Woodward versus Thompkins."

"Emmett Woodward buys and sells old Spanish colonial furniture. Lots of heavy black wood, intricate carving. Y'know, that kinda thing."

"Yes."

"Some things he buys need parts repaired or replaced. You know, rusty ironwork for the hinges and clasps and things. Preston Thompkins is a blacksmith, but not the kind you'd take your horse to for a new shoe or if you wanted a repair to a broken plowshare. He's more on the decorative side of things.

"Anyway, Emmett is suing Preston for causing damage to a valuable piece of furniture. He says he asked Preston to fit new hinges to a cupboard. He did, but the doors were so far out of alignment they didn't fit. Instead of re-sighting the doors, he says Preston hacked away at the edges of the doors to make 'em fit. Emmett says the cupboard coulda been worth hundreds of dollars. On account of its providence, y'see. He said it came from a Moorish castle. All the way from Spain. Imagine. Now it's not worth more'n the price of kindling.

"Mr. Mercer didn't think Emmett's case held up. Sure, the providence checked out. The value of the cupboard Emmett claims is subjective. Worth what a buyer would pay for it. Nor is there proof Preston did the damage to the cupboard. He's claiming Emmett coulda done the damage himself. Yet Emmett insisted that the case go to court." Tubby shrugged. "Mr. Mercer kept telling him he stood little chance of succeeding."

"Then why did Stephen agree to take on the case?"

Tubby pulled a face, reluctant to speak ill of his late employer. "The cupboard wasn't the main issue. A while back, there were rumors about Preston and Mrs. Mercer. Died out quick enough, but, well, Preston wasn't Mr. Mercer's favorite person, if you get my meaning."

Fooks' eyes widened. Seems unlikely that Stephen Mercer would stoop to something as underhanded as professional humiliation. *A likely motive of sorts, of course, although I doubt a strong enough reason to kill Stephen. At least, I hope not.*

Fooks picked up the next file.

"Thorold versus Callaghan."

"Ah, now this one has been running for a long time."

"So, I see," Fooks said, noting the file's thickness.

"Mrs. Thorold fenced off a sizable area of land Tyler Callaghan said belonged to him. It's clear on Tyler's deeds. Mrs. Thorold said the land belonged to Charlie, her late husband. She had the bill of sale, but Tyler didn't accept it was genuine. They went to court. Mr. Mercer unearthed proof the land did belong to Charlie. Court dismissed Tyler's claim. Tyler is now appealing, alleging Mr. Mercer fabricated the proof."

"Did he?"

"No, sir. I dug around in the Land Office records for days on end. Found it dog-eared and faded. Mr. Mercer had no doubts it was correct. And the court agreed with him. Tyler is a hard man to convince. Mr. Mercer didn't think the appeal will fly." He shrugged. "You never can tell."

"Okay, and the last case, Pickering versus Long?"

"Alan Long is claiming unpaid rent on the property Martha Pickering rents from him. She says she didn't agree to the improvements Alan insisted upon. He put up the rent anyway, but no sign of the improvements. He's claiming he needs the increased rent to pay for the improvements."

Fooks grunted. "Chicken and egg."

"Yes, sir. Mr. Mercer tried to mediate, offered a compromise. Neither would give in. They both want their day in court."

Fooks tapped his fingers on the top file. He grinned when a thought came to him. "I noticed you called all the men by their first names."

Tubby appeared embarrassed. "Sorry, sir. That was unprofessional of me. Known them all since childhood. Went to school with 'em. Emmett, Alan, old Charlie

Thorold, Tyler, Preston. Oh, and Martha. We all sat in rows in the tiny schoolhouse here." He smiled as he reminisced.

Fooks blinked in surprise. "So, you grew up in Angelworth?"

"Yes, sir. Lived most of my life here. Apart from the time I spent in Philadelphia, where I studied for my law exams."

"Ah, and you qualified?"

"Yes, sir. Two years ago."

"And you came back here?" Fooks' eyes widened. Usually, newly qualified lawyers went to larger towns to work after graduation.

"My parents live here. I came back to Angelworth after I qualified. While visiting, Mr. Mercer wanted a clerk." Tubby shrugged. "He was a brilliant lawyer, Mr. Crane. One of the best, I'd say. I figured I wouldn't do any worse than to hitch my cart to him for a spell. Learn the ropes from a master."

Fooks smiled, liking the young man. If Fooks were any judge of character, Tubby Wilson would go far.

"And Tubby?"

Tubby flushed. "Oh, it's a name I got at school here. Ma is generous with her portions, and I was a kinda big kid, if y'know what I mean. Name stuck even though I'm no longer tubby. I've learned not to fight it, and I like to think it's said with affection now rather than to be mean."

Fooks' smile broadened. "Good for you..." He paused. "Tubby." He rose. "Well, thank you for letting me look through these. Given me a lot to ponder."

Fooks held out his hand. Tubby gaped for a moment, and then he grinned and took it. He seemed more used to being part of the furniture than the purpose of the visit.

Fooks was about to leave when he spotted something in the corner that appeared out of place, a hefty, ornate chest. He frowned with curiosity.

"That's rather unusual," he said.

"Oh, yes. Mr. Mercer always admired it when he visited Mrs. Thorold. He was pretty pleased when she gave it to him for winning her case. Woulda taken it home, but, well, he didn't get the chance."

"Hmmm." Fooks crouched and examined the chest more closely. It was made of slatted wood stained a black oak color, about three feet wide, a foot deep, and two feet high. Each plank was ornately carved with a Spanish Moorish design. The edges were bounded by black wrought ironwork, and in the center was an oversized antique padlock. Fooks gave it a rattle. Locked, as he'd suspected.

"Is there a key?" he said, giving in to his secret passion. He grinned at Tubby.

"Well, there was," Tubby said, leaning against a desk and folding his arms. "I found it on the doorstep."

"You found it on the doorstep?"

"Yes, sir. A huge one. Probably got knocked out of the lock during delivery. Dunno where it is now. I guess it'll turn up, eventually."

"Pity."

It was human curiosity, well, Fooks' curiosity, at least, to know if there was anything inside. He gave himself a shake for allowing himself to go off course. He mustn't get sidetracked. Fooks straightened before the urge became overwhelming. *Thought that sorta temptation had long gone. Must be something that never leaves you.*

Fooks returned to his hotel room. He hung up his suit jacket and removed his tie, shirt collar, and boots before lying on the bed. He stared at the ceiling, his head abuzz with ideas and possibilities. None of the many pieces collected so far seemed to fit together. The one thing he was sure about was that Brad and Sid weren't deliberately responsible for the death of Stephen Mercer. He'd come to Angelworth with that thought, though, so he was no further forward. At every turn, more and more mysteries had sprung into view.

He sighed and rubbed his hands over his face. "What have you got suckered into this time?"

More thinking didn't produce any answers. Going around in circles wasn't accomplishing anything. Frustrated, he sat up and threw his legs over the side of the bed.

"It won't come to you if you think about it too much. Do something else to take your mind off it."

But what? In the past, he would have lost himself in a game of poker. Not anymore. Any card game for money, he now avoided. He was all too aware of how easily betting would carry him away and unwilling to risk his marriage, new life, and livelihood on something as short-lived as a poker game. No, he had a self-imposed embargo on poker playing these days.

He needed someone to talk to, someone to work through his thoughts with, to bounce ideas off. He sat on the side of the bed, with shoulders slumped. Never had he missed Swan more than now. He hugged himself. The moment of vulnerability made him uneasy.

He lay on his side, curling into a fetal position. He allowed himself to remember his closest friend, thousands of miles away. What was he doing there? There was an ache, and he didn't know how to soothe it. After his baby came, he vowed he would go to Boston and find answers. He was acutely aware that he'd made this promise several times before and never fulfilled it. Things kept getting in the way.

Thinking about the baby, he wondered if Mary was okay. She'd said she would be, but that was not the point. He should be there at a time like this. What sorta father would he be if he weren't around from the beginning? Should he send a telegram? Find out what was happening?

He almost convinced himself to do that, but then his practical side kicked in. He shook his head. What if a problem occurred? He was too far away to do anything, help, or just be there. And nothing would change the situation. No, he must tuck his personal circumstances to one side while he dealt with this mystery.

Before he knew it, sleep claimed him. He awoke hours later, feeling refreshed and hungry, which wasn't like him at all. When he looked at his pocket watch, he found he'd slept the afternoon away.

"No wonder I'm hungry. It's nearly suppertime."

Still drowsy, he stumbled to get dressed. Clothes fought him all the way. He gave up when he fumbled with his tie. He tore off his dress shirt. A clean, light blue range shirt would do instead. His suit pants, he swapped for light tan ones. Stomping into his boots, he hesitated over his gun belt.

With a growl, he ignored it. What would he face in the dining room? Marauding Indians? Wild animals in the lobby? No, not needed. He picked up his dark gray hat and settled it on his head. Eying himself in the mirror with satisfaction, he felt ready to face the world again. Florian Fooks? He grinned. More like Joseph Crane at ease.

He went in search of something to eat.

Swan would emphatically approve of his choice of main course: a big helping of steak pie, mashed potatoes, and string beans, washed down with a bottle of claret. When the stage pulled up outside, Alfred sprang into action to help bring in bags and check in guests.

Fooks attended to his meal, untroubled by the to-ing and fro-ing from the lobby, until a loud voice boomed, "Reverend Josiah Wedgwood is my name, spiritual adviser to princes, presidents, and paupers. My card, should you have need of my services. A room at the back. Oh, no, no, no. A room overlooking the street, if you please, where I can keep an eye on all the Good Lord's creations. Please have my bag taken up; I will go straight through to the dining room."

Fooks glanced up when Rev appeared in the doorway, but he showed no sign of recognition. Rev stopped and took in the dining room, letting his eyes wash over the diners. He, too, didn't give any sign he recognized anyone. Yet each had seen the other. Rev sat at the table offered and took out a Bible.

Sometime later, his meal finished, Fooks folded the newspaper he'd purloined from the front desk. He placed his key fob on top so the room number showed and walked nonchalantly past Rev's table. From the corner of his eye, he caught Rev glancing at the number.

They would meet later. Should be interesting. They hadn't met since Fooks had gone straight.

When the soft knock on the door came, Fooks was lying on his bed, reading the newspaper. He padded across the room in his stockinged feet, taking his Schofield from its holster as he went. He hid behind the door and peeped around as he cracked it. Once certain that it was Rev, he opened the door fully.

"It's good to see you, Fooks." Rev shook Fooks' hand enthusiastically. He was a dark-haired man with more than a suspicion of a six o'clock shadow, dressed in a long black tunic and a wide-brimmed hat.

"You, too, Rev. Thanks for coming."

"Waal, Brad said you can get him 'n' Sid off this murder charge they done stuck on 'em. But you need my help to do it."

Fooks rolled his eyes. "That's putting it a little strong, Rev. Need proof." He walked away. "From what I've seen so far, proof might be hard to find. Enough to convince the sheriff here, anyway." He sank onto the bed. "I'm glad you're here. I can sure use a friendly face to bounce ideas off."

"Sid told me 'bout Swan. Gone to Boston?"

"Yeah." Fooks rubbed a hand over his face. "I keep meaning to go find him, but, well, one thing and another."

"Don't let it slide too long. You need him, boy."

"I know." Fooks nodded. "I miss him. That's why you're here. I need to wrap this up quickly, Rev. I'm needed at home. My wife's about to have a baby any day now."

Rev grinned, revealing nicotine-stained teeth. "Yeah, Sid said she was about to burst. What d'ya want me to do?"

"Ask around. Keep your ears open. Probably best if we don't let on we're acquainted. Once word gets around, I'm here asking questions about Stephen Mercer, I reckon folks will clam up. Won't find out anything. You, on the other hand, well, being a man of God an' all."

"You're putting a lot of faith in me," Rev said doubtfully.

Fooks pulled a face. "No one else, Rev. I considered Lucas, but he's not exactly subtle. Folks will tell you things. Open up." He smiled knowingly. "You have ways."

Rev cheered up. "Tell me more."

CHAPTER EIGHT

Fooks froze.

About to go into the sheriff's office, his hand was already on the door handle when he glanced through the window. Bennett stood in front of the notice board, studying the wanted posters, especially the one for Florian Fooks. *I've gotta get him away from there.*

Taking a deep breath, Fooks entered. "Morning," he said, giving the sheriff his most cheerful of greetings, coupled with his full double-dimpled grin.

Bennett looked around when Fooks walked into his office. "Thought you were coming to see me yesterday, Crane."

"So did I, Sheriff."

"Then what kept ya?" Bennett sat behind his desk.

"Well, you won't believe this." Fooks helped himself to a cup of coffee, knowing Bennett's eyes were on him. "After I'd finished in Stephen's office, I took myself back to my room at the hotel and lay on the bed to do some contemplating, and d'you know what happened?"

He settled on the edge of the desk.

"No. Do tell," Bennett said, flashing a sarcastic scowl.

Fooks sipped his coffee, unconcerned. "I fell asleep. Musta been plum tuckered out with the ride the day before and all the discoveries we made." He shrugged. "Didn't wake until nigh on suppertime. By then, I figured you wouldn't take kindly to me interrupting your family time, so—"

"Okay, Crane. What did you discover in Stephen's files?"

"Nothing concrete, but some details are interesting." Fooks took a sip of coffee before Bennett irritably flicked him off the desk.

"In what way?"

"Of the cases Stephen was working on, three stood out in my mind. There's something strange about all of 'em."

"What?"

Fooks gave a slight laugh and shook his head. He took a long pull of his coffee before answering. "Well, that's what we need to find out, Sheriff. I'd like to talk to all the parties involved." Her smiled pleasantly. "It'll be easier if you make the introductions for me. But first, a few questions, if I may."

Bennett glared at him. "I'm not here to run around after you."

"No, but you are here to uphold the law, and investigating the murder of one of your town's citizens is a fundamental part, I should say, especially when he was such an influential man." Fooks expected a response. Bennett continued to stare at him, so Fooks added, "Didn't anything we discovered yesterday raise a doubt in your mind?"

"Everything has a reasonable explanation."

"Like what?" Fooks sipped his coffee, expecting interesting answers.

"Mercer coulda hurt his hand in the office, like Doc Sullivan said."

Fooks nodded. "Yes. I asked Tubby. He doesn't recall."

Bennett shrugged. "Don't mean he didn't."

"Nope, but I would figger he would mention it. Tell Tubby to be careful." Fooks sniffed. "Then there is the oil on the lock of the side door. What's your explanation?"

"Coleman and Murphy broke in."

Fooks pulled a face. "Never heard either one of 'em being good with locks." *Careful, Fooks, inside knowledge.* He pulled a face and shook his head. "Nope. Don't sound like their style to me."

"Then they learned."

"They just so happened to have a can of oil on them?" Fooks shook his head at Bennett, and before the sheriff could reply, he asked his first question. "Who tipped you off that Coleman and Murphy were in town?"

"Alan Long."

"Uh-huh, and did he say how he knew Coleman and Murphy?"

Bennett squirmed. "No, he didn't," he said through gritted teeth.

"And you didn't ask," Fooks said, cocking his head in surprise, "how a respected businessman in your town would know two outlaws?"

"No reason to disbelieve him. 'Sides, he can be a mite scratchy."

"Scratchy?"

"Prickly. Have to be careful how ya speak to him sometimes."

"Hotheaded, y'mean?"

"No, not exactly. Jus' prickly," Bennett said with a splutter. "Look, I didn't have time to stand and chat, with two desperados loose in town."

"So, you immediately went off to hunt for 'em?"

"Yes." Bennett waited for Fooks to say more.

Fooks pursed his lips before settling back on the desk and folding his arms. "Who raised the alarm that the livery was on fire?"

"Tyler Callaghan."

"Uh-huh. Hmmm, interesting."

"Why?"

"'Cause both men you've mentioned are in two of the cases Stephen was working on. In fact, they're both the other party."

"Probably about time you told me more about Stephen's work."

"Hmmm, and afterward, we'd best go see Stephen's widow. Lucinda, isn't it?" When Bennett nodded, Fooks went on, "tell her we're looking into her husband's death in more detail."

"Yeah, I guess we are after all."

Fooks resisted the urge to grin in triumph. "Does she live in town?"

"On the edge. It's not far. Walkable. Who's on the list?"

Fooks took from his pocket the piece of paper on which he'd written all the names, and he read them out. He gave Bennett a summary of each case.

"Some are a way outta town, like the Thompkins place. Alan and Martha are both here in town."

Fooks tucked the paper back. "Let's go see Lucinda first. I'll tell you more on the way, and we can decide who else afterward."

It took several loud knocks on the Mercer front door before Lucinda Mercer appeared. Although it was late morning, she was still in her robe, and her blonde hair still hung loose, although she'd made some effort to corral it into a braid over her left shoulder. She appeared pale and tired, exactly the countenance you would expect for a grieving widow.

"Sheriff, I wasn't expecting visitors. I'm sorry; I can't seem to get myself together very early these days. Please come in."

"Sorry to bother you, ma'am. This is Joseph Crane. He worked with Stephen on a case a few years ago."

Lucinda blinked. "Mr. Crane. I remember Stephen mentioning you." She unconsciously tightened the tie of her robe. The gesture didn't escape Fooks' notice. Something else attracted his eagle eye: she wore nothing underneath.

"He did?" Fooks grinned, pleased Stephen had mentioned him to his wife.

"If you've come to offer your condolences, then thank you. Stephen's death came as a great shock. Not only to me, but the entire town. He was well thought of."

Lucinda took a seat and sat with her hands in her lap, making sure the robe was wrapped tightly around her legs. She directed them to chairs opposite.

"Yes, ma'am, and I do. I respected Stephen greatly, so I had to stop by." Fooks studied the woman in front of him. Something appeared out of kilter. Something wasn't right with the grieving-widow image she presented, a nervousness he couldn't put his finger on. "But that's not the sole reason I'm here."

"Oh?" Lucinda's eyes flicked from Fooks to Bennett and then back again.

It was Bennett who spoke.

"Mrs. Mercer, I realize this is difficult for you. Your husband's death may not be straightforward like I first thought. Mr. Crane has asked me to look again in more detail."

Lucinda swallowed hard. "W-why? You...you said he died in the fire. Those two men murdered him."

"Yes, and it's how it appeared at first glance. However..." Bennett glanced at Fooks. "Mr. Crane thinks there's maybe more to it."

Lucinda turned to Fooks. "Why would you think that?"

"Mrs. Mercer, your husband was extremely vocal about certain elements in society. Some influential men heard him and noted what he said, but by doing so, he made enemies. I've reason to believe someone other than Coleman and Murphy wanted to harm him." He paused, trying to gauge her reaction. "I fear they may have succeeded."

"Who?"

"I don't know. Yet."

"I don't understand," Lucinda said. "What gives you reason for suspicion? Stephen died at the hands of those two despicable men."

"I'm not at liberty to tell you. I can tell you the evidence we've found throws doubt on Coleman and Murphy being the ones responsible."

"With all due respect, Mr. Crane, Stephen was my husband. Surely, I have a right to know."

Fooks swallowed. "Yes, ma'am. And you will. Once I've gotten to the bottom of it."

"Mrs. Mercer, we came to inform you of our investigation as a courtesy," Bennett said.

"Can't I object? We laid Stephen to rest last week, and I would prefer if I..." She came to a shuddering halt. "I just want to get on with my life, Sheriff. Put this behind me."

"I appreciate that, ma'am, but Crane convinced me it warrants further investigation. Surely, you'd want us to find out the truth?"

Lucinda composed herself with difficulty. "Yes, of course," she murmured. She sniffed and touched a screwed-up handkerchief to her eyes. Fooks noticed her eyes were dry. He filed that piece of information away for reference. "You must do what you have to. I'm sorry this is hard to take in."

"Realize that, ma'am. We wanted to tell you Crane and me will be asking questions of several folks in town so it doesn't come as news and you wonder what is going in."

"Thank you, Sheriff. That's thoughtful of you."

"We'll leave you now."

Bennett and Fooks left and walked to the road. Bennett headed for town straight away, while Fooks remained at the gate, slapping his hand on the post.

"Something wrong, Crane?"

"Dunno yet," Fooks murmured. "Did you notice Mrs. Mercer's reaction when we told her we were looking at Stephen's death more closely?"

"No. What did you expect?"

Fooks pursed his lips. "Not that, exactly." He shook his head. "I don't know the woman, so it may be nothing." He peered back at the house, puzzled.

"Crane?"

Fooks started. "Where to now, Sheriff?"

Next, Bennett and Fooks tried Alan Long. The street where the realtor's office lay ran at right angles to Main Street. When they arrived, they found the office shut. Bennett said Alan lived above. They walked around to the back of the building and up the stairs to knock. No answer. They returned to the street, disappointed.

"Must be out somewhere. Catch him later, I expect," Bennett said.

"Hmmm," Fooks agreed. "Martha?"

Fooks and Bennett walked down the lane, which ran to the edge of town, until they reached the end property. A sizable garden sloped to the road, with the house perched on a bank at the top. Although early spring, the garden was colorful. As they walked up the brick-lined path, the aromatic scents made for a heady mixture. In full summer, the garden would be a riot of color and abuzz with insects.

Bennett rapped on the door.

"Beautiful garden," Fooks commented. They waited for the door to open. Gardening hadn't featured too heavily in his new domestic life. Mary's house had little land out back and was mainly grass.

"My wife comes and gets seeds from Martha to try out in our garden. She don't seem to have the same success. Ah!"

Bennett swept off his hat when the door opened. Fooks followed his example. The woman who stood before them was slight and in her early thirties. Her blonde hair had been swept into a severe bun, with tendrils escaping its confines.

"Good afternoon, Mark. What brings you to my door?" she asked in a soft voice.

"Hello, Martha. This is Joseph Crane. He's helping me investigate some suspicious occurrences surrounding Stephen Mercer's death. We've a few questions we'd like to ask you. May we come in for a spell?"

"Questions for me about Stephen?" she asked with a frown

"Crane wants to ask you about the dispute with Alan. The one Stephen acted for you."

"There's not much to tell, but very well. Please come in."

Martha stood aside and opened the door wider, allowing them to slip into a small hallway. This opened into a large, multi-purpose room cluttered with furniture, plants, ornaments, and decorations. Several cats dotted the room in their own personal spaces, licking paws or lounging. Martha shooed one black cat from the couch. It yowled in protest.

"Be off with you, Roger. You're a good boy, but our visitors would like to sit down."

Roger meowed his displeasure before stalking through the half-open back door. Martha shook her head and smiled fondly at him as he retreated.

"Roger maintains the couch is his. Please sit down, and I'll fetch some lemon cordial."

With nowhere else to sit, Fooks and Bennett found themselves crammed together on the small couch.

Although cluttered, the room was homey and not at all overbearing. A slight breeze filtered in through the door, making the room appear light and airy. Outside, wind chimes tinkled gently. Fooks could not discern the pleasing mixture of fragrances that filled the air. Despite his serious business, he relaxed. He glanced at Bennett, and they shared a brief smile.

"You have a lovely home here, ma'am," Fooks said when she returned to them.

"Thank you. I very much hope I can stay here. The thought of starting again somewhere else fills me with dread. Lemon cordial, gentlemen?"

Both reached for the drinks she offered. Fooks had never considered lemon cordial as a choice of tipple. Unsure, he took a tentative sip.

"Nice." He struggled to keep the surprise from his voice.

"Yes, Mr. Crane, I only ever serve nice cordial to my visitors," she said. She gave him a pleased smile.

Fooks had the overwhelming thought she was seeing deep into his soul. He should have been unnerved, but he wasn't. Usually, a man who coped well in any situation, the feeling threw him for a moment.

He smiled back.

"Could I have the recipe, please, ma'am? I'm sure my wife would welcome it."

Bennett sent Fooks a sharp look. Wife? He raised his eyebrows. Crane had a wife?

"Before you go." She unloaded a chair beside the table of its contents, swung it around expertly, and sat down. "Now, you want to ask me about Alan?"

Fooks considered his words before he spoke again. "How did your dispute with Alan over this property come about?"

"I've rented this house from Alan for some ten years. I always pay my rent on time, and he has no cause for complaint, yet now he wants to make what he calls improvements to the property, changes that aren't necessary and that I don't want. They would destroy part of my garden. He hasn't tried to make those changes, but he has increased the rent. I pay him what I usually do, but not the increase, so he is suing me."

"What was Stephen's advice?"

"Alan was harassing me, and Stephen advised me not to pay the increased rent. Stephen felt sure a judge would find in my favor."

"I see. Did Stephen talk to Alan about this?"

"Yes. Before Alan began his suit, they met here one evening. Their conversation became..."

"What, ma'am?" asked Fooks.

"Stephen suggested I leave things to him, so I went to my bedroom. I couldn't make out much of what they said. I only came out when their voices became rather fractious."

"What d'you mean by fractious?"

Martha swallowed. "This is a tranquil home. They were shouting. Shouting upsets me, so I asked them both to leave." She sighed. "Alan went immediately. Stephen became agitated, and I suggested he stay for a few minutes longer to let Alan get clear. I made Stephen some chamomile tea, and we talked for a brief time until he calmed. The next day, I received Alan's suit."

"Thank you."

"I don't understand. What does this have to do with Stephen's death? He died in the fire at the livery, didn't he?" She frowned at Bennett.

Bennett shifted uncomfortably. "That's what I thought at first. More evidence has come to light, throwing doubt on my assumption."

"We're not at liberty to discuss our suspicions further right now, ma'am. Thank you for seeing us," Fooks added. He smiled and held up his empty glass. "And for this."

"Oh, I promised you the recipe. One moment." Martha searched around for paper and pencil. Finding them, she wrote something on a slip of paper and handed it to Fooks with a smile. "I hope your wife likes it."

"I'm sure she will. Thank you, ma'am."

Martha showed them out and remained at the door while they walked down the path to the road.

"Oh, Sheriff?"

Fooks and Bennett turned back.

"There is perhaps one other thing I should mention." Martha wrung her hands.

"What is it, Martha?" Bennett asked once he and Fooks had made their way back to her.

"Well, I'm not sure I should say. Stephen told me in confidence." She trailed off, her face flustered.

"If it helps us find his killer, ma'am, then I don't think he'd mind," Fooks said.

"No, I suppose not." Martha hesitated. "Stephen told me after Alan left that night the reason the conversation between him and Alan had become heated. Stephen suspected Lucinda and Alan were having an affair. I don't think he had proof." She shrugged. "He didn't tell me anymore."

Fooks and Bennett swapped glances. That piece of information might turn out to be significant. Fooks decided to ask another question.

"Martha, was your relationship with Stephen...well, was it purely...?" he whispered, not wishing to be overheard.

"We weren't lovers, Mr. Crane, if that's what you were implying."

Fooks felt himself flush. He wasn't thinking in quite those terms, but it embarrassed him all the same. He mumbled an apology.

"I'm sorry we have to ask, Martha. The amount of time Stephen spent here caused some talk," Bennett said.

"I suppose so," Martha conceded. "Stephen lived for his work. We talked, and I encouraged him to do so. He had terrible headaches because he worked hard. I thought it might help if he unburdened himself a little."

"What did you talk about?" Fooks asked.

"Everything and anything. He came to confide in me. He didn't have many friends here in town."

"What about his wife?"

"We talked about her a lot. Sometime ago Stephen heard rumors about Lucinda and Preston Thompkins, and it hurt. He confronted Lucinda, but she wouldn't talk to him. She said the affair was over. Later, Preston told me his version in confidence. Stephen had forgiven her, but then came another rumor, this time about Lucinda and Alan. Stephen and Lucinda argued. She asked him, what did he expect? He was never home. He loved his work. He also loved his wife. He didn't know how to keep them both happy. Talking to me helped, but there was never anything physical between us."

"I see. Thank you again, ma'am." Fooks smiled and tipped his hat.

"If those men murdered him, then that's a tragedy. I liked Stephen, and I am so sad he couldn't work things out with Lucinda."

When Martha closed the door, Bennett and Fooks turned away.

"What now?" Bennett asked.

"If we can't see Alan, then we should go outta town. Who's nearest?"

"Celia Thorold."

Fooks nodded. "Celia, it is, then."

CHAPTER NINE

Back in town, Bennett and Fooks collected their horses. They rode to the Thorold horse-breeding ranch, about five miles outside of town. When they got there, Celia appeared to be either on the way out or coming back from somewhere.

She wore a yellow blouse and a black divided skirt. Like Lucinda, she was blonde. Unlike Lucinda, Celia had an immaculate coiffure, and she'd applied her makeup expertly. She gave the impression that entertaining a sheriff and his companion hadn't been high on her mind when she'd dressed that morning.

"We're sorry to be taking up your time, Mrs. Thorold. You ought to know we're looking more closely into Stephen Mercer's death," Bennett said.

"What do you mean, Sheriff? I thought Stephen died as the result of the livery fire." Celia saw the serious faces of the two men before her and added, "Didn't he?"

"We're not at liberty to discuss the intricacies of the case right now, Mrs. Thorold. I'm speaking to all parties in

Stephen's ongoing cases." Fooks smiled, seeking to put her at ease. "Not being from round these parts, I'm looking to understand the dynamics of each case."

"I see." Celia appeared mollified. "Please, sit down, gentlemen."

They sat, although Fooks perched on the edge of his seat. He weighed his next words.

"Now I understand, Mrs. Thorold, Stephen won your case against Tyler Callaghan."

"That is correct." As Celia smoothed her skirts, she seemed uncomfortable. "The odious man won't accept defeat and has appealed. Of course, he won't win."

Fooks raised his eyebrows. "What makes you think that?"

Celia spluttered. "Because Stephen said so, and I held him in the highest esteem."

"Hmmm," Fooks flashed a brief smile in her direction. "I'm afraid the law isn't quite that simple. Who will handle the case now? I'm presuming it will continue."

Celia took a deep breath. "It's up to Tyler Callaghan, isn't it?" Her eyes flashed, and she changed her tone. "I haven't decided who will represent me if the case goes ahead. I've no idea what Lucinda is planning to do with Stephen's business affairs." She swallowed hard.

Bennett said, "I'm not sure she knows yet. She's still distraught over what happened."

"Is she?" Celia raised an eyebrow. "I'm surprised."

Fooks narrowed his eyes, curious about her choice of words.

"Why do you say that, Mrs. Thorold?" he asked in a low voice. "Stephen's death was barely two weeks ago."

Celia shook herself. "Yes, of course. I was going on my own experience. When my husband died last year, I couldn't think clearly enough for months, let alone sort out his affairs."

She took a deep breath. "Lucinda is more world-wise than I was. That's all I meant. Nothing more."

Fooks glanced at Bennett. He seemed convinced, but Fooks wasn't. He would give Celia Thorold the benefit of the doubt, though, at least for now. He rose slowly, and Bennett rose with him, rubbing his chin.

"Well, thank you, Mrs. Thorold," Fooks said with a pleasant smile, holding out his hand.

Celia smiled politely as she shook his hand. "Not at all, Mr. Crane. I wish you well in your investigation."

They were on their way out when Fooks stopped. "Just one more thing, Mrs. Thorold."

"Yes?"

"The chest you gave to Stephen, do you have a spare key?"

Celia stared at him. The question seemed to flummox her, and Bennett appeared equally bemused.

"I don't understand what you mean."

Fooks grinned. "Idle curiosity, Mrs. Thorold. I noticed the chest when I was in the office yesterday. It is rather striking. Tubby said he doesn't know where the key to the padlock has gone. Wondered if you had a spare, is all. Not to worry." He turned away.

"But I don't understand what you're talking about. The chest didn't have a padlock when I gave it to Stephen."

Fooks masked his surprise. "Well, there's a big antique padlock on there now, and it's locked."

Celia sank into the chair. "I've really no idea, Mr. Crane. The chest only ever had a staple and a latch. If there is a padlock now, then Stephen must have put it there."

"Yes," Fooks agreed, turning back once more. "One other thing."

"Yes, Mr. Crane?" Celia said with barely concealed annoyance.

"Why did you give the chest to Stephen?"

Fooks detected a genuine smile from Celia for the first time.

"My late husband acquired it some years ago, but I never cared for it. Whenever Stephen visited, he always admired it. When he won the case for me, I gave the chest to him as a token of my appreciation. Serendipity, Mr. Crane, nothing more. Now, anything else?"

"No, ma'am." Fooks grinned. "Not for now," he added, sounding ominous.

Outside, they untied their horses, and Bennett hissed. "What's this about a chest? You said nothing about a chest to me."

Fooks mounted, chewing his lip. "Don't know, Sheriff. May be all or nothing." He sighed. "Another piece in this ever-expanding puzzle."

Bennett mounted his horse and glared at Fooks. "You've opened a can of worms here, Crane."

"Yep, sure looks that way. If it leads to the arrest of whoever murdered Stephen Mercer, it'll be worth it. Won't it?" He nudged his horse forward. "Where to now?"

Fooks and Bennett rode on to the Looped C Ranch to visit Tyler Callaghan. To allow Bennett to keep up on his elderly and slow plodder, Fooks held his horse on a tight rein. It wasn't happy, and it tossed its head and sidestepped. Recuperated from the long ride to Angelworth, it needed to stretch its legs.

As they rode along in silence, the creaking of their saddles seemed to Fooks to get louder and louder. Being alone in the sheriff's company made him wary, especially when he caught the sly glances Bennett slid his way. Was Bennett trying to suss him out?

Try making conversation, Fooks. "Is the Looped C a large spread?"

"Second biggest in the County. Gartland is bigger, but only by a smidge, I reckon."

"Uh-huh," Fooks said. "So, I guess Callaghan is a big shot round here."

"Ya could say."

"What's he like?"

Bennett adjusted his reins. "Like most ranchers. Businesslike, not much on chitchat. He's a busy man."

Despite further attempts at conversation, Bennett remained stubbornly taciturn.

It was a relief to reach the ranch and ask for Callaghan. Introductions were made, and the three men settled in the study. Fooks scanned what looked to be a typical cattle baron's retreat. Lots of buttoned leather furniture. Dark, chunky wood. Books on cattle management. Paintings of cows and cowboys. Mounted above the fireplace was an impressive set of Texas longhorns. Tyler Callaghan's home lived up to his stereotype, even if his person didn't.

Fooks hadn't known what to expect, exactly. Although he'd had dealings with powerful ranchers in the past, most were in their middle years. Tyler Callaghan appeared far too youthful. That shouldn't have surprised Fooks, though. As a contemporary of Tubby Wilson, the rancher would be in his late twenties, early thirties. Fooks made a mental note to ask Bennett later how Callaghan had come to own such an impressive ranch. For now, he smiled pleasantly at Callaghan's wife, who presented him with coffee.

After she left, Tyler Callaghan didn't waste time getting to business.

"So, ya think Stephen Mercer's death is something suspicious, do ya?"

"I do," said Fooks, "and Sheriff Bennett agrees with me." He stopped himself from adding "now" at the end.

"And you suspect me?"

Fooks flashed Callaghan a grin. "Stephen was working on a number of cases when he died. I'm speaking to all the parties involved. As background, y'understand. But I also understand you raised the alarm that the livery was on fire."

"Yeah, so?"

Fooks pressed his lips together into a thin line, clamping off his first impulsive thought. "Why were you in town so late?" he asked instead.

Tyler raised his chin in defiance. "What business is it of yours what I do in town at any time?"

"I'm not interested in your business." *So, that's the way of it, is it?* "I'll rephrase the question. Where were you coming from and going to?"

"Better answer the question now, Tyler. Crane won't let it go until ya do," Bennett said.

"You didn't ask me that question," Tyler said. He leveled an accusing glare at Bennett.

"I didn't because, at the time, I thought this a clear-cut case of murder by two wanted outlaws. Crane's investigations have shown me there's more to it than I first thought. The incidentals are irrelevant."

"Well, I suppose this is no secret, exactly." Tyler paused. "Once a month, a group of us get together. Take over the saloon's back room and play poker. The buy-in is five thousand dollars."

"That's a lot of money," Fooks said, impressed, though he'd frequented poker games where the buy-in could be a lot higher.

"The reason why none of us want gossip getting around is pots can pile up fast. Could be a source of easy money—"

"I get the picture, and I assure you this will go no further." Fooks turned to Bennett, who nodded.

Tyler seemed reassured. "So, that's where I was all evening. Broke up about one, one thirty, I suppose. As I walked down the street, past the livery, I saw flames shooting outta the back, so I roused the town."

"Given the lateness of the hour, I guess you planned to stay in town for the night. Where were you walking to? The hotel is in the opposite direction."

"I'd planned to stay with a friend."

"Ah! I see."

"No, you do not see. I have an arrangement with Tubby Wilson. I rent a room from his ma." He shrugged. "Gives them a little more income and me a place to stay when I'm in town. Works for all of us."

Fooks couldn't find anything suspicious. "Thank you, Mr. Callaghan. Now, about the case Stephen worked on. I understand he'd won for Celia Thorold but you appealed the decision."

"You're damn right I did! That piece of land belongs to me. Mentioned plain as day in the deeds."

"Mrs. Thorold said your father sold the land just before he died to Charlie Thorold. She has the signed receipt."

"I know about that. There's no entry in my books, and my bookkeeper knows nothing. Pa woulda told me if he sold land. And he didn't."

Fooks wasn't convinced, and he glanced at Bennett. The sheriff gave nothing away.

"So, you hoped to establish ownership by going to court. Couldn't you settle things privately?"

"Tried to, but the woman wouldn't see reason. She didn't want to play ball. Nothing else for it, so I sued her."

"The case went against you."

"Tell me about it. Damn fool judge reckoned my deeds are a forgery. I had to go file title to my own land, jus' in case some fool thinks they can come in here and throw me off."

"As I understand it—"

Tyler jumped to his feet. "Forgeries! It's that damn official land register that's forged. I'll show you forgeries."

He stalked to the alcove to the left of the fireplace and threw back the hinged painting. Behind it, a safe had been inserted in the wall. He twiddled furiously with the dial. Fooks respectfully lowered his eyes, but after the first number, he gave into curiosity. He couldn't make out the exact numbers of the combination. *Ha, that's never stopped me. Opening the safe wouldn't take long.*

Mentally, he shook himself. No, he wouldn't have to. He shouldn't even be thinking about it.

"Here. Those are the deeds. Do they look forged to you?"

Tyler tossed the documents into Fooks' lap.

Fooks began unfolding them. "Well, I'm no expert—"

"Jus' tell me what ya think," Tyler snapped.

"Okay." Fooks applied himself to reading.

"Paragraph six refers to the Northern Switchback Pasture. The land Celia claimed as Charlie's."

Fooks took his time. Contrary to what he'd said, he'd seen forged official documents before, and he knew the telltale signs. Finally, he pursed his lips and handed them back. Either this was an excellent forgery with nothing to spot, or it was genuine. Which begged the question, had someone tampered with the official land records instead?

"How did you find out Celia was laying claim to this piece of land?"

"During the fall round-up last year. The hands and me drove the herd from their summer pasture on Dupolo Mountain. We came across my land, all fenced over, Thorold ranch hands standing guard with rifles. My foreman reckoned we could drive the herd on through and take out their hands. My boys were willing. We've stopped there for years on the way up to the high country and down again. Nearest large water for miles. We were already late getting the herd, and I couldn't waste any more time disputin', and I do mean disputin'. I had thirsty cows to water, and I figured I'd go see Celia later. We drove 'em round and on to Indian Falls, 'nother ten miles. I lost sixty head of cattle 'cause we had to drive 'em on. Cows need water, and that is my water. I'm appealing 'cause I'm losing money."

"Did you speak to Celia about it?"

"Sure, I spoke to her. Even showed her my deeds. Celia said Charlie bought the land right before Pa died. Showed me the receipt, but I got nothing in my files." Tyler grunted and shook his head. "Celia seems determined to fight it out in court so I let her have her wish and I sued her. I reckon Mercer put her up to it."

"Why d'ya say that?" Bennett asked before Fooks could open his mouth.

"'Cause he was all cozy with her. Never had no trouble before. Ain't as though she's using the land for anything. If she'd come to me an' asked, I 'spect we coulda come to some arrangement. No, she just took it."

"Are you still going ahead with the appeal?" Fooks asked.

"Have to. I want my land back. I've been holding back for now outta respect, but I've already lined up a lawyer from Laramie who's prepared to take the case. He's waiting for me to give him the word."

"Give it another week," Bennett suggested. "Just until we've finished our investigations."

As Fooks and Bennett rode away, this time, Fooks was the one deep in thought.

"Didn't pick up nothing wrong there. Did you?"

Fooks pursed his lips. "That depends."

"On what?"

"Why the land is so important to him."

"He told ya. It's his land. Man has every right to protect his own property."

Fooks nodded. "Yep." He gathered the reins, preparing to move his horse faster. "If that's all there is to it." He kicked his horse into a gentle lope. "Gotta get back to town. Things to do."

CHAPTER TEN

Bennett couldn't spare any more time, so Fooks returned to Stephen's office alone, intent on studying the files again.

Instead, he stood regarding the chest, hands on hips, for at least five minutes. He could almost hear Tubby's nerves, so it came as no surprise when the young man spoke.

"Something wrong, Mr. Crane?"

"Nope. I'm wondering about this chest. I don't suppose the key has turned up yet?"

"No, I looked after you left yesterday, but no luck."

"Hmmm." Fooks leaned back against a desk, folded his arms, and contemplated the chest some more. "Mrs. Thorold says she doesn't have a spare key. She also said the chest didn't have a padlock when it left her. Well, there's one now." He waved a hand in the chest's direction.

"Yes, sir, but I remember distinctly the padlock being there on the chest at delivery."

"Who delivered the chest?"

"Alan Long."

Fooks frowned. "Alan Long? I don't understand. Why would he deliver it?"

Tubby shrugged. "I'm sorry, sir. I don't know."

Fooks smiled. "Hmmm, question for me to ask Mr. Long." *How am I gonna do that when I can't find him? One problem at a time, Fooks.* "You said at first there was no key, yet you found one on the doorstep sometime later."

"Yes, sir. I went out running errands, and I found it on the doorstep when I got back."

"Did you see Stephen use the key to open the chest?"

"No, sir, but I believe he did."

Fooks waited for a further explanation.

"I was leaving to go home when Mrs. Mercer came in. A friend caught me as I closed the door, so I didn't hear much of the conversation. Mr. Mercer showed her the chest. He seemed excited. I remember she said, 'Go on, Stephen, open it,' or something like that. My friend steered me away down the boardwalk at that point." Tubby paused. "I'm speculating Mr. Mercer opened the chest, sir. I'm not sure he did." His face creased with worry lines.

Fooks grinned. "It's all right, Tubby. It's the logical deduction."

He walked over to the chest, crouched, and rattled the padlock. Still locked, as he'd expected. He peered at the locking mechanism closely. Might take him a while to get in, and it was probably not the best idea to try in front of Tubby. He straightened, resolving to return later with Rev.

Before Fooks went back to the hotel, he tried Alan Long's office one more time. No luck. Still hadn't returned. From the corner of his eye, he saw the curtain twitch at the window of the apartment above. When he turned fully, the curtain was still.

Alan Long was becoming a mystery all to himself. Perhaps Rev would uncover some clues when Fooks met with him later.

Late that night, Fooks answered the knock at his door. Rev slipped in.

"What den of inequity have you brought me to, Fooks?" he asked when the door closed behind him.

"What d'you mean? What did you find out?"

Rev shuddered. "Plenty. Got any whiskey?"

Fooks went to the nightstand. He brought out a bottle and two glasses. Rev relieved him of the bottle before Fooks opened it. Fooks blinked in surprise and shook himself. Why was he surprised? He sat on the bed and waited until Rev drank his fill. To his disgust, that was about a third of the bottle.

"Spoke to the pastor first. Like ya told me. Whoo-ee! That man can talk when you get him going." He took another glug from the bottle.

Fooks motioned for him to hand the bottle over before all the contents disappeared. Rev looked surprised, and then he glanced at Fooks' empty glass before doing so. Once the glass was full, he immediately grabbed the bottle back.

"Did you know jus' 'bout every dang person in this town is having carnal knowledge?" Fooks raised his eyebrows. "With folks who ain't their lawful spouses," Rev whispered.

"I had a suspicion, but tell me what you found out."

"I steered the pastor round to the names on ya list. Now, what were they?" Rev raised his gaze to the ceiling. "That blacksmith fella who isn't. What's his name?

"Preston Thompkins?"

"Yeah, that's one. Him and Lucinda Mercer, for one. Take it that's the dead man's wife?"

"Yes." Fooks rolled his eyes. "Tubby already told me Stephen suspected his wife and Preston. Lucinda Mercer is a striking woman, but I've heard of someone else since then."

"Who?" Rev asked.

Fooks folded his arms and wrinkled his nose. "Martha Pickering told me Stephen suspected Alan Long was having an affair with his wife, not Preston Thompkins."

"Ah! Told ya, den of iniquity."

The two men laughed. Fooks paced, deep in thought. "All this is interesting, but what is this telling us?"

"Hold on, Fooks, there's more."

Fooks' eyes popped. "More?"

"Yeah. Stephen Mercer and Celia Thorold seem to have been more'n a little friendly."

"Hmmm, even more interesting," Fooks mused, arms folded.

"Why?"

Fooks shook his head. "Tyler Callaghan said something similar today."

"That's about it."

"I hope so." Fooks' eyes widened. "Oh, Rev, I thought there might be one sordid relationship here, but not an entire townful." He rubbed his forehead.

Rev grinned. "Complicated, ain't it?"

Fooks sat and puffed. "More'n I thought." He ran his hand through his hair. "But just 'cause there're rumors, it don't mean anything wrong is taking place. Sometimes the most innocent things get misconstrued."

"Y'know what they say. No smoke without fire."

"Not always true. How sure is the pastor about all this?"

"Sure as the Good Lord made little green apples."

"How does he know?" Fooks looked askance. "I mean, a man of God shouldn't go spreading rumors now." A sudden thought struck him, and he gasped in horror. "He didn't get these revelations in confidence, did he?"

"No. He was adamant. It's town gossip. I can hear anywhere if'n I kept my ears open. As for spreading rumors, nope, he shouldn't." Rev rolled his eyes and then tugged at his collar. "But when he has something in his tea, he's a regular chatterbox. Why, I could hardly shut him up."

"How did you leave him?"

Rev averted his gaze. "Well, see, he ain't exactly used to drinking more'n sacramental wine on Sundays, so he kinda passed out."

Fooks closed his eyes and shook his head.

"Now, don't go looking at me like that. I gotcha valuable information."

"Yeah, Rev. You sure did. Except, I dunno what I'm gonna do with it."

"Oh, I jus' remembered something else."

Fooks groaned. No more rumors about affairs, surely.

"Seems Preston Thompkins used to be real good friends with Emmett Woodward. Ain't he the cupboard man?"

"Yep."

Rev grunted. "Talk 'bout doing a job ya named for. Anyway, he and Preston fell out when Emmett heard Preston visited Martha Pickering regularly."

"Martha said she and Preston are just friends. I've no reason to believe otherwise."

Rev twitched his head. "Emmett's sweet on her, asked her to marry him, but she won't have him. Emmett and Preston had a serious falling out. Came to blows in the saloon 'bout two months ago."

"And straight afterward, Emmett sues Preston for damaging his property? Gotta be more'n a coincidence, don't it?"

Rev shrugged. "I'm telling ya, boy. I thought this a nice, quiet, respectable town." He let out a drunken laugh. "Scratch the surface, and ya discover all manner of goings-on. What d'you want me to do tomorrow?"

Fooks took a deep breath. "I want you to follow Alan Long. I tried to get to him today, twice. Both times, he wasn't around, but the second time, I know he was there."

"Perhaps out on business?"

"Possibly, but his name keeps coming up. Bennett tells me he does most of his work in town. He lives above his office. He must come back sometime." Fooks shook his head. "Not sure I fully understand what's behind his lawsuit against Martha."

"Okay, I'll see if I can get a look at him tomorrow."

Fooks shook his head, knowing it would take all his ingenuity to unravel the mystery. Rev had presented him with a whole load of suspects. He gave some thought to the problem, and an idea came to him. Playing everything out in his mind, he paced, as was his wont.

"Rev, all three cases I thought separate are, in fact, linked. Either directly or indirectly. The chest in Stephen's office is also bothering me. It's outta place, and y'know me." He flashed Rev a quick grin. "I need to get a closer look at it. Are you up for a spot of skulking around?"

When he glanced back, expecting a comment, Rev was snoring gently on the other bed. "Oh, great."

Fooks had let Rev sleep for a while before waking him. When he did, Rev appeared sober and alert enough to go with him on a spot of burglary. Now here they were, after midnight, at the back of Stephen Mercer's office.

"I'm worried about you, Boy," Rev whispered.

Fooks stopped fiddling with the window catch and looked back. "Me? Why?"

"'Cause you're making a meal of that. You're outta practice."

Fooks' brows furrowed in irritation. "I'm not outta practice. I run a hardware store. I'm called upon to let folks into their houses all the time. If you really wanna know, that's how I met my wife." He returned to the window.

"That's what I'm talkin' about. That's legal. This ain't. If you're caught, you're putting your freedom in jeopardy."

Fooks stopped what he was doing. "I know what I'm doing, Rev, but sometimes the means justify the end. And I won't get caught if you keep your voice down." He turned back to the lock. "'Sides, I'm not gonna steal anything."

"No, but we are breaking and entering."

"I may be entering, but I'm not breaking. I should get credit for one outta two." Fooks grunted. "There. Got it."

With a triumphant smirk at Rev, he pushed the casement up. "On tray, as they say in French."

As Rev climbed through the window, Fooks put away his tools. He took a last furtive scan round before following. He wouldn't be telling Mary about this when he got home.

Inside, they pulled the shade down and lit a low light.

"There's the chest." Fooks pointed to the corner.

"Striking piece of furniture."

"Yep. I guess that's why Stephen liked it. C'mon."

A few moments later, Fooks knelt in front of the chest. He took hold of the padlock.

"Ooh, this is a magnificent piece of workmanship," he crooned. With an eager, tight-lipped smile, he took out his tools. He was looking forward to picking the padlock. *I shouldn't be, but I am. This is a legitimate inquiry, though. Probably'll be okay, then.*

"Is this really necessary to get Brad and Sid off?" Rev asked.

"Maybe." Fooks sounded evasive.

"How?"

"I've a hunch something's not right with this chest. I can't explain. Now, leave me be. Poke around in Stephen's desk. That one there." Fooks pointed away from him.

Rev gave him an amused smile. Using Fooks' shoulder to lever himself up produced a squawk of protest. He went off to do as directed.

Fooks moved the lamp nearer to get a better view of the structure inside. "Hmmm." He selected a tool and set to work.

The padlock may be large, but it was not as complicated to pick as he'd first thought. He held the lock firmly in his left hand and teased the mechanism into the required order. He grinned with satisfaction at the click of release, but when the padlock sprang open, he yelled and dropped it.

Something had stabbed his left hand.

CHAPTER ELEVEN

"Sheesh! What was that?" Fooks opened his hand. He found a deep score in the leather of his glove across the top of his palm. A wetness spread around the edges. He tore off his glove, fearing he'd hurt his hand, and gasped in relief. Whatever had stabbed him hadn't penetrated his glove.

He pushed back his hat before removing the padlock. A quick peek inside confirmed the chest was empty. He turned his attention back to the padlock and flipped it over. What he saw made him stare open-mouthed. The back of the padlock concealed a sharp spike. This had sprung out into his hand when the mechanism had turned. Only the glove's thickness had saved him from a nasty stabbing.

"Rev, come and have a look at this." He beckoned without taking his eyes off the strange sight.

"What have ya got?" Rev leaned over.

"I'm not entirely sure." Fooks shook his head. "Seems this spike shot outta the padlock when it opened. I've never seen anything like this."

"Looks wet from this angle."

Fooks peered more closely. A thick gel glistened on the end of the spike. He swallowed hard and showed Rev his scored glove. His heart beat fast.

Rev stared. "What's it mean?"

"I don't know." Fooks swallowed again. "I really don't. This is just... I can't tell Bennett about this without... But he needs to know. This is important."

"How?"

"I don't know," Fooks said again. He wasn't used to his thoughts going around in circles. "But it is. It must be."

Fooks willed Rev to come up with an answer, knowing he wouldn't.

"Put it back. You'll find a way." Rev placed a reassuring hand on Fooks' shoulder.

"I'm not sure I should. This is dangerous, and I don't understand what this is." Fooks pointed at the substance on the end of the spike and swallowed hard.

"The key is missing. Right?"

"Yes."

"Then this ain't dangerous until it turns up."

"But—"

"Listen to me, boy. No one's gonna find the key anytime soon. Trust in the Lord, Fooks. If the padlock is as dangerous as you say, he don't want someone to find it."

"I wish I had your faith. But you're right. Until the key turns up, the padlock should be safe."

"Close it, and let's get outta here."

"Before I do, I'm gonna take a sample of this." Fooks waved his hand at the tip of the spike. "Whatever the heck this is. Scout around for something I can use."

"Such as?"

"I dunno." Fooks flicked Rev away and sat back on his heels, contemplating what he'd seen. He'd never come across anything like this, never even heard of anything like this.

Rev found a clean pen nib and inkbottle. "Will these do?"

"Perfect."

"Careful," Rev warned.

Fooks delicately transferred some of the mysterious substance to the pen nib. Then he deposited the nib in the inkbottle and screwed on the cap.

"I'll ask the doc if he can tell me what this stuff is," he said, putting the bottle in his pocket. He peered at his scored glove. "And this." He stuffed that in his pocket, too.

Fooks put the padlock back and closed the shackle. When he turned the padlock over, the spike had disappeared back into the body of the lock. A casual observer would be blissfully unaware.

"Did you find anything in Stephen's desk?" he asked, rising to his feet.

"Yes. Look at this."

An open ledger lay on top of the desk. Rev pointed at an entry.

"This is Stephen's work diary," Fooks said. "He has to record his time so he knows how much to charge his clients. What's this? Non-billable time MP. Sometimes during the day." He flicked through the pages. "Early evening, too." More turning of pages. "For weeks and weeks."

"Who or what is MP?"

"Only person I can think of is Martha Pickering. She's a client. See, he's put in some billable time for her here. Aw, might be a coincidence, I suppose. Yet her case shouldn't warrant a load of time spending on it."

"I thought it strange, which is why I mentioned it. Who would know?"

"Tubby, probably." Fooks shrugged. "I'll ask him tomorrow." And he would, straight after he'd seen Doc Sullivan.

Rev startled him out of his revelry. "Figure you owe me a drink now. Time for me to collect, I'd say."

Fooks gave him a tight-lipped smile. Rev should already had enough, but now it was Fooks who needed a drink.

The next morning, Fooks tripped along to Dr. Sullivan's office and into a waiting room full of people coughing, sneezing, and scratching. Hard pressed to squeeze through the door, he stood there, conscious of all the eyes focused on him.

"You're after me," a middle-aged woman said.

"Oh, I'm not here for treatment," Fooks informed her. "Official business," he added with a nod.

The woman gave him a disapproving sniff. Several other prospective patients talked amongst themselves, giving Fooks black looks. He hid behind other standing patients, but he couldn't escape them thinking him a potential line jumper. When Dr. Sullivan emerged from the back room, Fooks smiled with relief.

"Hi, Doc," he said, diverting Dr. Sullivan's attention away from the man who had risen for his turn.

Dr. Sullivan appeared doubtful. "Mr. Crane, what can I do for you this morning? As you can see, I have a full waiting room."

"This won't take a moment. I want to ask you one quick question. To do with my investigation."

"Very well." Dr. Sullivan nodded reassuringly to the man whose turn it was. Nevertheless, the man sat down with a growl before sneezing loudly into a handkerchief.

Fooks picked his way carefully across the room, half-expecting the waiting patients to trip him up at any moment. With relief, he made it to the consulting room without incident.

"Five minutes, Mr. Crane."

"Yes, of course." Fooks reached into his pocket for the scored glove. "Doc, where exactly was the cut on Stephen Mercer's hand?"

"Across the top of his palm. Diagonally under his first two fingers. Why?"

Fooks spread the glove palm up on the table. "About there?"

Dr. Sullivan studied the glove. "Yeah. Where did you get this?"

"Well, it's mine," Fooks said. "There's something else I'd like you to look at." He took out the bottle with a pen nib, but he hesitated before handing it over. "The tip of the nib has something on it. Be careful. I don't know what it is. Would you be able to tell me?"

"Scientifically, d'you mean?"

"Yes."

"I can run some tests. Would you mind telling me where you got this?"

Fooks licked his lips. "Rather not at this stage, Doc. Until I know what the stuff is, y'understand. When can you do your tests?"

Dr. Sullivan rolled his eyes toward the waiting room. "Won't be this morning. I'll try this afternoon. Unless, of course, an emergency comes up."

"Sure thing. Appreciate that. I'll come back this evening."

When Dr. Sullivan went to show Fooks out, Fooks touched his arm. "Is there a back way out? Might not make it out alive if I go that way."

With a chuckle, Dr. Sullivan showed him the back way. Next on the list was a pleasant ride out of town with Sheriff Bennett to see Preston Thompkins. Fooks scowled. *Not really. I can't think of anything worse, but needs must.*

In the event, Fooks left Bennett to deal with an incident in town and rode out to see Preston Thompkins alone. Bennett furnished Fooks with a detailed map, saying Thompkins Decorative Ironmongery was hard to find.

The morning was pleasant but cold; Fooks shivered in his suit, wishing he'd brought his red and green plaid coat. He trotted along at a fair clip, wanting to get quickly where he was going. He consulted the map once, and he soon saw the sign for his destination.

Riding down the ramp into the yard, a house stood out front. He came to a halt at the nearest hitching rail and dismounted. First, he settled his horse with water. Afterward he followed the trail around to the back of the house, where he found a series of work sheds and barns. The familiar clang of a blacksmith at work rang out from one of the sheds.

"Hallo?" he called, knowing there must be someone making the noise. He walked further into the shed and called again. Now he saw the back of a man at the furnace, who turned around at his call.

"Oh. Howdy."

The stubbled face of the dark-haired man was open and smiling. Most blacksmiths of Fooks' acquaintance were burly men with muscular arms. He tried to stay on the right side of them whenever possible. Experience had taught him they could be short-tempered fellas, likely 'cause of the constant heat from the furnace.

The slight man who came towards him now didn't fit the stereotype.

"Howdy. Preston Thompkins?"

"Here. What can I do for you?"

"Joseph Crane. Sheriff Bennett in Angelworth sent me."

"Sheriff Bennett?" Preston frowned.

Fooks pulled a face. "Well, that's probably not quite the way of it. We're making some inquiries about Stephen Mercer's death. I understand he was working on a case which involved you."

"Yeah." Preston's expression took on a cagey look. "But he's Emmett Woodward's lawyer, not mine."

"And who is yours?"

"Oh, I don't need one," Preston said, throwing his hands in the air. "Emmett's claim is pure hokum, and he knows it."

"Bit of a risk to take, though, isn't it? Representing yourself against a man of Stephen's reputation."

"I did not ruin Emmett's cupboard. The doors opened and closed fine when the cupboard left me. He musta done something to them after I gave it back to him. Stephen liked the quality of my work, so I reckon he knew Emmett's claim was wrong."

"Have you seen the cupboard since?"

"Yeah. It ain't my work."

"How long have you known Emmett?"

Preston dropped his hands to his hips, thinking. "Most of my life, I guess. We were boys together. Good friends until this." He let out a regretful sigh.

"What is the reason behind him making these allegations against you?"

Preston bit his lip. He could see Fooks wasn't going away empty-handed.

"Come into the office and have some coffee." He beckoned Fooks. Always up for coffee, Fooks smiled his tight-lipped smile and followed.

They moved to a separate area set aside as an office. This contained a desk, filing cabinet, and several mismatched chairs.

Fooks settled in a chair, nursing an enamel mug full of steaming black coffee. He surveyed his surroundings. The furnace stood at one end of the shed. From where he sat, the heat gave out a pleasant warmth. The enterprise appeared well set up and efficient. Examples of Preston's work, hinges, clasps, and locks, hung on the walls and pillars. They weren't ordinary items. Yes, they looked functional, but beyond that, they were ornate and aesthetically beautiful. Fooks appreciated the time and creativity that had gone into making them.

He sipped his coffee, deep in thought. Preston seemed like a man who obviously loved his profession and was proud of his skill. Why would a man like that sabotage someone else's property?

"You wanna know what's got Emmett's goat? Well, I'll tell you." Preston bounced into a chair. "He's got eyes for Martha Pickering. He doesn't like Martha and me, well, being friends."

"Just friends?" said Fooks, raising the mug to his lips.

"Yes, Mr. Crane, just friends." Preston shook his head adamantly, and Fooks believed him. "She is easy to talk to, and she is aware... Well, I have a few difficulties. She is a great comfort to me, and I can trust her to be discrete."

"So, how long has Emmett been interested in Martha?"

"We all went to school together, and I reckon Emmett has been sweet on her since then."

"A while ago, though?"

"Yes. Must be a slow burn," he said with a smile. "Thing is, it isn't what Martha wants. She's polite but firm. We've both told Emmett there is nothing between us other than friendship, but he ain't having it."

"So, he's jealous?"

"Yeah, I reckon."

Fooks rubbed his cheek in thought. "Perhaps Emmett thinks you're making a fool outta Martha."

"What exactly do you mean?" Preston demanded. He shot to his feet and stood in front of Fooks, clenching and unclenching his fists. "If you've something to say, then out with it."

Fooks sat still, determined not to flinch. He raised his head slowly.

"I heard a rumor about you and Lucinda Mercer a while back. Is there any truth to that, Mr. Thompkins?" he said, his voice low. Even without Swan there to back him, he wouldn't let Preston intimidate him.

Preston shifted uneasily and swallowed hard. He turned away.

"None of your business."

Fooks flashed a quick, smug grin and settled back in his chair.

"I'll take that as a yes."

"Look, it was last year and only lasted a matter of weeks."

"Why did things end?"

Preston shrugged. "These things do if they're not meant to be. Besides, Lucinda isn't my type."

"Married, d'you mean?"

"No."

Fooks stared at Preston hard, an uncomfortable idea forming in his mind. "What is your type?" he asked softly.

"You."

Preston wouldn't meet his eye and put his head down in embarrassment.

Fooks had come across unwanted male attention before. Usually, a suspicion alerted him before the subject came up. On this occasion, he'd had no clue. The suddenness of the admission uncharacteristically fazed him. If standing, he would have taken a step back. He knew he shouldn't, but he tried hard not to squirm in the chair.

"You oughta know I'm a married man with a baby on the way, likely in a matter of weeks," he gabbled quickly.

"Relax, Crane, I'm not gonna leap on you. I didn't mean you in particular," Preston snapped.

Fooks relaxed slightly. He pulled at his collar. "Well, if urm..." He cleared his throat. "If Lucinda Mercer is not your type, then why?"

"Lucinda is an attractive woman. She's fun to be with, but she's persistent. And well, it had been a while." Preston swallowed hard. "There are few opportunities for men who prefer my type."

Fooks nodded. "I understand. Thank you for being so candid with me." He stood. "I'll let you get on with your work now."

"I would appreciate—"

"Strictly between us. No one else needs to know."

Preston grinned with relief. "Thank you." After hearing his revelation, some men would be wary of him.

"I'll show you out through the house. Quicker than walking all the way round."

Fooks followed Preston through the house. As they passed the door to a small room, Fooks glanced in and pulled up short.

"Oh."

On the wall, facing the door hung several display boards containing a variety of locks.

Preston smiled.

"Hobby of mine. I collect 'em. Sometimes I use them for what I'm working on."

In awe, Fooks ventured in. The entire room contained locks of all descriptions. Big, small, old, new. Unique types. Some looked ancient. With a professional eye, he was already working out how he would tackle opening them. He grinned with delight.

"Amazing."

Preston grinned at his reaction. "Most people I show this room to say it's a little odd."

Fooks rolled his eyes. "If only you knew," he murmured, and when Preston frowned, he added. "It'll surprise you what folks collect. Some of these locks are unique. Can you tell me more about them?"

"Sure."

For the next half-hour, Preston explained the nuances of the more unusual locks. Fooks listened with fascination.

"Back in the medieval era, locks might not have been all they seemed, especially in parts of Italy. Sometimes a lock would have a hidden compartment filled with ink.

"Really?" Fooks' eyes popped. "How would that work, exactly?"

"There is a chamber in the back. When the key turns, a spike of metal shoots out, flicking ink over whoever is holding the lock. Ink would cover the culprit's hands for days. A sure sign of wrongdoing."

"Very interesting," Fooks murmured, his mind already whirling with possibilities. He blinked when Preston continued.

"It's all to do with how you hold the padlock when you unlock it. The usual way," Preston said as he took down an example, "is to hold it like this." His left hand held the body of the lock. "And you hold the key in the other. If you know about the ink, then the proper way to hold it is at the top and bottom. Still have to be careful of the spike, though."

The cut on Stephen's hand now swung into the forefront of Fooks' mind. He went cold and swallowed hard. His eyes widened even more at what Preston said next.

"It's a shame. I had one I coulda shown you until a few months ago."

"Why? What happened a few months ago?" Fooks asked, fearing the answer but not surprised when it came.

"I had a break-in. They took four of my more valuable and unusual locks." Preston shrugged. "I notified the sheriff at the time. Gave him a detailed description and a drawing of the missing items. I doubt if I'll ever get them back."

"No, probably not," Fooks agreed.

Fooks rode back to Angelworth, his mind overloaded with possibilities. His first port of call, the Sheriff's office, where he asked about Preston Thompkins' break in.

"Yeah, I remember," Bennett said when Fooks asked him about the Tompkins burglary. "Unusual things to take. Thieves are mostly after cash or jewelry. Preston didn't say they took anything like that."

"Almost as if the thief knew what he was after," Fooks said, rubbing his chin. "Did Preston give you descriptions of the missing items?"

"Yeah. He drew me some pictures as well. Should have 'em somewhere."

Bennett went to the filing cupboard and rummaged around. Like usual, every time Fooks was in the sheriff's office, his eyes strayed to the notice board. There he was, in big black capitals. He shuddered. *Gonna have to do something about that.*

After a few minutes, Bennett brought out several sheets and presented them to Fooks. Then he went back to his desk, leaving Fooks to pore through them.

A drawing labeled "Italian Lock" brought Fooks up short. He went to the description sheet. Sure enough, an "Italian Lock" mentioned a secret compartment.

"Sheriff."

Bennett glanced up, and Fooks turned the drawing around.

"Yeah?"

"This is the padlock that's now on the chest in Stephen's office."

"What are you saying, Crane?" said Bennett. "What is it about this chest? I ain't even seen this chest."

"It's in Stephen's office. You can go see anytime," Fooks said. Flippancy had sprung out of him before he could stop himself. He'd better watch it. He didn't want Bennett getting even more suspicious than he already was.

"Too many question marks over it."

"Such as?" Bennett demanded.

"Such as I've found out a few things I haven't told you." Fooks shifted his weight guiltily.

"Alan Long delivered the chest to Stephen's office. Why Alan Long? Why did Celia Thorold deny the presence of a padlock? Tubby told me the chest had one when Alan delivered the chest. He also told me the key to the padlock miraculously appeared a few hours after Alan delivered the chest. Why does the padlock on the chest now look like the selfsame one Preston Thompkins claims was stolen from his place three months ago?"

The two men glared at each other.

"Okay, what's ya point?" Bennett said.

"Before I get to that, there's something else." Fooks hadn't wanted to admit this to the sheriff before he had all the answers. Now seemed like the right time to bring it into the open.

"What?"

"You're not going to like this." Fooks pulled at his collar. Why was it suddenly too tight? He was unaccustomed to confessing to a sheriff.

"I don't like a lot of what you say. Hasn't stopped ya so far."

"Well, I had a closer inspection of the chest last night. At the padlock in particular." Fooks swallowed hard at Bennett's intense stare. "As I opened the padlock..." That should have generated a question or two, but Bennett only took a deep breath. "...a metal spike dug into my glove. If I hadn't been wearing gloves, it would have pierced my skin." Fooks puffed, conscious of Bennett's stern gaze on him. "I noticed a substance covering the top of the spike."

"What was it?"

"Dunno." Fooks hunched his shoulders. "Could be something innocent, such as lubrication for the locking mechanism." He let his shoulders relax. "Or might be something more suspicious."

"Like what?"

"Well, I'm not sure. I took a sample, and the doc's analyzing it now."

Bennett rubbed his forehead. "Crane..." He shook his head. "This was a nice, simple, tidy murder until you came along."

Fooks chewed his lips. "It was never that. Someone just made it look like it," he said softly.

"Yeah, I'm beginning to believe you," Bennett conceded. "So, Preston Thompkins...known the man for near on fifteen years—"

"He's not your murderer."

"Then who is?" Bennett barked. "If someone is running round out—"

Fooks shook his head. "Stephen was the target. The only target. Preston Thompkins didn't have a reason to kill him."

"What about the court case? Preston planned to defend himself against Stephen. Man wouldn't stand a chance against him in court."

Fooks rubbed his chin. "Preston said Emmett's claim against him was false. And Stephen knew."

"Then why did Stephen take the case? Not like him. He was always fair."

"He heard the rumor about Preston and Lucinda having an affair."

"Oh, that was months ago." Bennett waved a hand in dismissal. "Lots of malicious tongues in this town. They soon stopped when there was no longer anything to yak about."

"I doubt Stephen appreciated the gossip about his wife, especially when he suspected Lucinda and yet another man more recently," Fooks said. "Martha told us this."

"Ya mean Alan?" Bennett asked.

"Yes," Fooks said. "Martha said Stephen believed it."

"Alan? Nah. Never even seen 'em together, let alone...well, y'know."

"Curious, though, isn't it? Two out of the three cases Stephen worked on involved men who are the opposition allegedly having affairs with Lucinda Mercer. The way it looks, Stephen believed those rumors."

"Ya don't know for sure. Ya can't."

"You're right. I don't know for sure. And that's why I need more information. Like what is on the metal spike, for starters. Doc Sullivan said to come back late this afternoon for the results."

Bennett glanced at the clock and scraped back his chair. "Well, let's go see if he has any answers now."

CHAPTER TWELVE

"Glad you're here, Sheriff. I wanted you here when I told Crane the results of my test," Sullivan said when Fooks and Bennett arrived.

"What d'ya find out?" Bennett asked.

"Well, it's aconite." When Bennett and Fooks regarded Sullivan with blank expressions, he added. "It's the sap from a plant, *Aconitum napellus*. The common name is Wolfsbane."

"So, is the sap poisonous?" Fooks asked.

"Yes, and it's a potent poison, especially if absorbed through the skin."

Fooks drew himself up and exhaled slowly. He swallowed hard.

"So, if just touching it is dangerous..." He glanced at Bennett, whose mouth fell open. "What would happen to a person if, say, they had a cut on their hand and the poison got into the cut?" His mouth had gone dry, and he was having difficulty getting his words to form coherent thoughts.

Sullivan blinked. "Sap coming into contact with any mucous membrane always has consequences. It can lead to cardiac and respiratory failure." Seeing Fooks was about to ask another question, he went on. "Symptoms are almost immediate. Even with prompt medical treatment, I'm afraid death is the usual outcome."

Fooks chewed his lips and glanced at Bennett. He never thought he would feel sorry for a sheriff. On this occasion, he did. The revelation was way outside what a small-town sheriff usually dealt with.

"You say mucous membrane?" Fooks ran his hands through his hair. "What d'you mean, exactly?"

"Any part of the body that is moist. Lips, nose, eyes. More intimate parts."

"So, er..." Fooks groped for the chair behind him as a wave of dizziness swept over him. "If you, er, had a cut to your hand, the natural reaction would be to put it to your mouth."

"I reckon."

"Sheesh!" Fooks put his head in his hands, resting his elbows on his knees.

"You're thinking of the cut on Stephen Mercer's hand," Sullivan said.

The sheriff snapped from his torpor. "How much would it take?" he asked, and Fooks looked up. "To kill?"

"Hard to say for sure. I'm no expert. The sample you gave me contained something else, but not enough for me to determine what." Sullivan shook his head. "Wolfsbane is a very poisonous plant. I doubt if it would take much."

"What are the symptoms?" Fooks asked. A sudden weariness had overtaken him.

"There might be a tingling sensation extending up the arm to the shoulder. There might be a general feeling of being unwell. A shortness of breath." Sullivan swallowed. "Then it would affect the heart. Cardiac arrest and finally death."

Fooks rubbed his forehead. "How long?"

Sullivan pursed his lips. "Again, hard to say precisely. Depends on the quantity of the poison, the patient's health, physique." He shrugged. "It might happen quickly. A matter of minutes." He shrugged again. "Might take a few hours. Too many variables for me to say."

"Was Stephen a well man?" Bennett asked.

"A patient's health is confidential." Sullivan's eyes moved from Bennett to Crane. "Under the circumstances, Stephen was well enough for a man his age and relatively sedentary lifestyle. But he suffered from debilitating headaches. I advised him to cut back his workload, stop the late-night working by lamplight. Relax a little."

"Did you prescribe anything?"

"Nothing I gave him worked."

"Apart from you, Doc, who else in town would know about Wolfsbane?" Fooks asked.

"It's used in various medical treatments. Ralph Lingwood, the pharmacist, would. His wife, possibly. She helps him in the shop sometimes." Sullivan thought some more. "Oh, and Martha Pickering, I suppose, but I'm not sure how good her medical training is."

"Why Martha Pickering?"

Both Sullivan and Bennett regarded Fooks with surprise. Fooks glowered. Both seemed far too smug at his expense.

"'Cause she's an herbalist," Bennett said. "You saw her garden. You remarked on it."

Fooks nodded. Yes, he had. He licked his lips and tentatively asked his next question.

"Stephen has only been dead a few weeks. How do we go about exhuming the body?"

Bennett puffed. "Lotta paperwork."

"You're suggesting an autopsy, Mr. Crane?"

"Yeah, I guess I am."

Doc Sullivan shook his head. "Wouldn't do no good. Aconite only stays in the body for about twenty-four hours. I couldn't determine now if it had been present or not."

Both Fooks and Bennett let out sighs of relief. An autopsy would be controversial in this closely knit conservative town.

"We need to go have another talk with Martha," Bennett said.

"Yeah, I think so, too. Before we do, I want to speak to Tubby."

"Why?" Bennett asked with curiosity.

"'Cause Tubby knows everyone involved," Fooks said, setting off toward Stephen's office.

Bennett stomped after him.

Bennett and Fooks caught Tubby locking Mercer's former office for the evening. He sighed heavily at the delay they were causing him and begrudgingly invited them into the privacy of the office.

Fooks said, "Tubby, you told me you went to school with most of the people in the cases Stephen was working on."

"Yes, sir."

"Who was friends with who?"

"Hmmm, let's see. Angelworth was a smaller town in those days. Weren't many kids, so we were all kinda close friends."

"Anyone form any particular friendships? Say, that continued into adulthood."

"I guess Tyler and Alan. Mebbe Preston and Emmett before they fell out over the cupboard. Charlie Thorold hung out with all of 'em."

"What about Martha? Did she have any female friends?"

Tubby wrinkled his nose. "Not particularly. There were two other girls at school, but they moved away long ago. Nope, Martha always kept apart from everyone. Kinda different. Quiet. Kept herself to herself. Ma called her fey." He laughed. "I remember Emmett pulling her pigtails in class and hiding spiders in her desk." He became pensive. "She hated it."

"Speaking of Emmett and Martha, I heard he proposed to her but she turned him down."

Tubby's eyes widened. "Really? Dunno why he thought she'd accept him after the way he treated her as kids. Looking back now, Emmett was a bully. 'Course, as kids, we accepted it as normal behavior."

"Just one more thing. Did Mr. Mercer hurt his hand the day he died?"

Tubby shook his head. "No, sir, not that I recall."

"Thanks, Tubby, we won't keep you any longer." Fooks gave him a tight-lipped smile.

Outside, Bennett and Fooks ambled back towards the jail, leaving Tubby to lock up.

"What now?"

"We should talk to Martha." Fooks shook his head. "I need to do some thinking first. There's a lot to take in, and I need to make some sense of it all." He saw Bennett's skeptical look. "Martha isn't going anywhere, Sheriff. I'll see you in the morning."

As he walked back towards the hotel, Fooks thought he would try Alan Long one more time. He came away disappointed again. Perhaps Rev would have some news on the man's whereabouts when they met later.

When Rev arrived to give his nightly update, he found Fooks sitting at the writing desk.

"What are ya doing?" he asked, craning his neck to catch sight of Fooks' scribblings.

"Trying to make sense of all this. See the links between the various suspects."

"Ah, so you have suspects?"

"Too many. The trick is to narrow 'em down to one." Fooks rested his hands on the chair back. "Any luck with Alan today? Did the mystery man put in an appearance?"

"Sure did."

Rev went to the nightstand cupboard and took out the bottle of whiskey he found. Fooks blinked. He hadn't even asked. "And?"

"Sat and watched his place after breakfast for 'bout an hour afore he came outta his hidey-hole. He went to his office, and I sat and kept a lookout for 'bout 'nother hour. He came out and went to the bank. Far as I can tell, he made a withdrawal. Nothing unusual. He went to the café for lunch. They do a good steak pie, Fooks. Ya outta try it."

Rev heaved himself onto the bed and put his feet up. He took a long glug of whiskey.

"And after lunch?" Fooks prompted.

"He went back to his office for a short while. Then he got a horse and rode outta town."

"Where did he go?"

"Not far. The Thorold horse-breeding ranch."

Fooks' eyes widened. "Why did he go there?"

"I dunno the nature of his business. Too many folks in the yard. Weren't about to ask any of 'em why he was there, and I couldn't sneak around now, could I? Was there about two hours, I'd say. He looked pretty pleased with himself when he came out." Rev laughed salaciously.

Fooks' eyes widened further. "When you spoke to the pastor the other day, did he mention anything about Alan and Celia Thorold?"

"Nope. Afterward he rode back into town." Rev pursed his lips thoughtfully. "He passed by the Mercer place. Kinda gave it a funny look as he passed."

"How d'you mean?"

"Well, I didn't see his face clearly on account of me being behind him. He sorta smiled as he passed."

"What did he do after he got back into town?"

"He went back into the office for a few minutes and then came right out and went upstairs. I gave it 'nother couple of hours and figured he must be turning in for the night."

"So, apart from Celia Thorold, who else did he speak to?"

Rev pursed his lips. "No one relevant to our investigation, I reckon. And you're only assuming he went to visit Celia Thorold."

"Well, who else would he go to visit out there?"

Rev shrugged.

"This is getting far too complicated." Fooks turned back to the writing desk. "Rev, when you're out and about tomorrow, will you buy some large sheets of plain paper?"

"Sure. Why?"

"Also, some colored pencils, thumbtacks, and a ball of string."

Rev let out a rare laugh. "Fooks, being law-abiding hasn't changed ya."

"What d'you mean?"

"Still as mysterious as ever, boy."

Fooks flashed a quick grin. "That's me." He sobered quickly. "Talking of mysteries, Bennett and me are gonna see Martha Pickering in the morning. Think she may hold the key to this."

CHAPTER THIRTEEN

The next morning, Fooks and Bennett walked to Martha Pickering's house on the edge of town.

"Ma'am, I didn't realize last time we were here that you are an herbalist," Fooks said. Once again, he and Bennett found themselves crammed onto the couch. "I understand now folks often seek your advice on medical matters."

"That is correct."

"And you sell pills and potions of your own devising?"

"You make me out to be some quack preying on the vulnerable, Mr. Crane. I can assure you I am nothing of the sort. My treatments work." Martha's eyes flashed with a fire Fooks hadn't thought possible for such a gentlewoman. The black cat, Roger, leaped onto her lap, and she stroked him. To reassure him or her? Fooks wasn't sure.

"I'm sorry, ma'am. I didn't mean to be insulting," he said, not liking the way the cat glowered at him. "Dr. Sullivan said—"

"Dr. Sullivan and I don't always agree," Martha interrupted. "But we do often discuss patient symptoms, anonymously, of course. Their causes and treatment. Including what works and what does not."

Fooks glanced at Bennett and nodded for him to ask the next question.

"Martha, were you treating Stephen Mercer?"

Martha hesitated before answering. "Yes."

Bennett leaned forward. "For what?"

"Are you accusing me of something?"

"No, ma'am, but it would help our inquiries if you would answer the question."

"Very well. This wasn't common knowledge, but poor Stephen suffered awful, unbearable headaches. I mentioned this the last time you came."

"Yes, you did," both men said together.

Martha continued. "They would come on suddenly and had the effect of curtailing his work. That he might suffer an attack in court or another inopportune time scared him. Nothing Dr. Sullivan prescribed seemed to work. Stephen came to me as a last resort. He was desperate."

"What did you give him?"

"I made up a preparation for him."

Fooks and Bennett swapped glances.

"What was in the preparation?" Bennett asked.

"Predominantly aconite. This can be bitter, so it requires sweetening. At first, I used licorice, but Stephen preferred ginger."

"And what exactly is aconite?" Bennett glanced at Fooks. They'd agreed before calling that, if the subject came up, Martha should explain in her own words.

"It is an extract I make from the Wolfsbane plant." Her eyes flickered from one man to the other. "Gentleman, you're looking at me as if I have done something wrong. It is unnerving."

Fooks stood and walked to the window. "Is aconite something you use often?" he asked without turning.

"Yes. In many of my preparations."

Now Fooks turned. "So, the preparation you gave to Stephen wasn't the first time you used aconite?"

"No. I've used it for years. It's useful in lots of ways."

"Such as?"

"As a cream to treat skin diseases. As a rub for joint pain and gout. Watered down, it's useful as a disinfectant and to clean wounds."

"Do you ever use it for preparations taken orally?"

"Yes, for colds and influenza, laryngitis, asthma. Why are you asking me all these questions about aconite?"

Fooks swallowed hard. He didn't want to reveal his hand yet. There was still more he wanted to know from Martha before he did so.

"Did you make Stephen an oral preparation?"

"Yes."

"How long had he been taking it?"

Martha considered. "Two months. Maybe ten weeks."

"Was he to take the preparation only when he felt a headache coming on?"

"Each person is unique. In Stephen's case, aconite worked better for him as a preventative. I recommended he take a little each morning and evening. That frequency appeared to work well for him. His headaches came less often and reduced in their intensity."

Fooks glanced at Bennett. The answer to his next question would be the most telling.

"Ms. Pickering, are you aware of how toxic aconite is?"

"Of course," she said. "You are obviously leading up to something. What is it?"

"Would the aconite you gave Stephen kill him?"

Martha sat up straight and blinked in surprise. She stared at Fooks, open-mouthed.

"Answer the question, please, Martha," Bennett said firmly.

Martha blinked again. "No, Sheriff. The amount I advised, no, it wasn't enough to kill him." She glanced from one to the other. "What makes you ask that?"

Fooks put his head down and walked to the window again. He shook his head. He had difficulty reconciling the woman in front of him with a murderer.

"Dr. Sullivan told us all parts of the Wolfsbane plant are dangerous. Is that true?" Bennett asked with one eye on Fooks' back.

"Yes. What does this mean?" she cried. "Are you saying I killed Stephen accidentally?"

"Now, Martha." Bennett reached for her.

Martha gasped. "Stephen had strict instructions on dosage," she burst out. "I gave him enough for one or two days at a time. He came to see me regularly for more." She took a deep breath.

When Fooks turned, she collected herself. "Like most herbal medicines, aconite works when taken a little but frequently. I told him how dangerous aconite was, and I didn't want him to overdose accidentally. He assured me he would not take too much at any one time. However, I still declined to give him a larger quantity." Martha wrinkled her brow and bit her lip.

"Does this plant grow in your garden?" Fooks asked.

"Yes."

"Would you show us, ma'am?"

"Yes, of course."

Martha shrugged into a jacket and wrapped a scarf around her neck. She led them outside via the back door. Here the bank on which the house sat widened out. To the left were various allotments of vegetables and fruit. Some plants, Fooks recognized as herbs. All looked carefully tended, with little markers identifying what grew where. To the right, the garden sloped towards the road.

Martha led them along the top of the bank until a spot where trees overshadowed the garden.

"Here." She indicated a patch of earth where shoots appeared. "I keep it here, out of the way because, as you say, all parts of the plant are dangerous. Even brushing against the plant is hazardous. The skin easily absorbs aconite. I am aware gardeners have died because they handled the plant without wearing gloves. I would hate to hurt a casual admirer of my garden by accident."

Fooks stood with hands on hips, regarding the patch. Then he took in where the patch lay precisely relative to the house and the road. In the dark, a person accessing the plant could go about their business unobserved.

"Have you known any tampering with your plants, ma'am?"

Martha shook her head. "No, not to my knowledge."

Fooks rubbed his cheek. "Well, if someone wanted to..." He broke off, not sure where he was going. "Do you show folks around your garden often?"

Martha smiled. "Yes. People come to me all the time. For seeds, ideas about what to plant where, what plants do well next to others. Why, Mrs. Bennett was here only last week."

Bennett grimaced. "Yeah, I know, Martha. I had to do the digging."

Fooks smiled at Bennett, whose face descended into a scowl.

"Do you ever let anyone buy this plant?"

Martha shook her head. "It has pretty, bluebell-like flowers and is particularly attractive in June and July. I can understand why I'm asked. Most people accept the reason I refuse once I've explained the dangers to them."

"You said most people. Did anyone disagree?"

"Not that I recall."

"Anyone particularly interested in this plant?" Bennett asked, hoping Martha wouldn't say Mrs. Bennett.

"No..." She broke off suddenly.

"Martha?"

"Last year, last summer. When Alan first talked to me about the house, we walked in the garden. I explained to him how his plans would affect me. My plants are my livelihood." She glanced at the house before turning back. "He wanted to dig a drainage ditch along here, which would go straight through this patch of Wolfsbane. But there really isn't anywhere else suitable in the garden for it to grow. It likes the shade from the trees and is out of the way here."

"Did Alan ask questions about Wolfsbane?" Bennett asked.

"Did you tell him how toxic it was?" Fooks asked before Martha answered.

"Martha, this is extremely important. Did Alan Long ask you about this plant?" Bennett asked.

Martha wrung her hands. "Not exactly," she breathed. "I explained the root was the most dangerous. I only ever use small quantities. To dig up the whole plant would be difficult to do safely, and even with the utmost care, I did not wish to do so. I explained about the sap and how careful I have to be when I use the plant in my preparations."

"Apart from the root, what other parts do you use, ma'am?"

"The whole plant is useful, but I mainly use the leaves and the flowers. I soak them for a full day and boil them for several hours. This reduces the toxicity, yet the therapeutic properties remain. I've done this for years and never had any problems."

"We're not accusing you." Bennett raised an eyebrow at Fooks, who shook his head. "Crane and me should go now. We've a lot to discuss."

"You've given us a lot to chew over, ma'am. We appreciate your time."

Down at the bottom of the slope, Fooks stopped and twitched his nose. Bennett also stopped and waited. By now, he recognized Fooks' thought process.

"I can't believe she done it," Bennett said, breaking the silence.

"No, I don't think she did, either." Fooks studied the house again. "On the face of it, there are several suspects in this case, Martha being one of them."

"Yeah, so?"

"There's too many. Someone is covering their tracks. Throwing suspicion elsewhere rather than at them."

"Who?"

Fooks shook his head. "What we need to do is find the link." He twitched his nose. "Sheriff, I've gotta an idea, but I dunno how you'd feel about it." He hitched his pants and stood with hands on hips.

"Try me."

"Something has to happen. Something to draw out the real murderer. Make 'em careless."

"How do we do that?"

Fooks glanced at the house again. "By arresting Martha."

"Now, just a minute. You can't put her through that."

Fooks shook his head. "But we can make it look like it. Will she co-operate?"

"I don't like it," Bennett said, shaking his head as he considered the idea. "No, I can't have it."

Fooks looked disappointed at first but then rallied. "No, I guess not. Let's keep it in reserve, huh, Sheriff?" He drew himself up. "We need to handle this carefully. There's a lot here. I'll ponder on it."

"I've gotta get on back. Dare say you can do with some of my good coffee while ya ponder on it."

Bennett walked away, leaving Fooks grinning.

Fooks shook his head. *Am I making a friendship here?* He groaned. Long way to go.

Fooks followed Bennett to his office and availed himself of the sheriff's good coffee, which was a matter of taste. It helped with his thinking, though. He absently paced the room before an exasperated Bennett tossed him the cell keys.

"Here."

Fooks, even in surprise, caught them expertly.

"What are these for?" Was Bennett expecting him to lock himself up?

"Go and do that in there," Bennett ordered and waved a hand at the cellblock door.

Fooks grinned. His pacing got on most folks' nerves. With the keys in his possession, he was in no danger of suffering a lock-in by accident.

"Sure thing," he said, giving a salute.

Fooks flopped onto a bunk and stared at the ceiling, turning over in his mind everything he'd learned so far. He idly played with the key ring while lying on his stomach. Four keys. Four cells. Hmmm, a fifth key. He frowned and raised his head, studying it more closely. He ran his forefinger over the bit, feeling the notches. Different and smaller than the others. Ha, of course, for the front door. He held it in front of his face and grinned. *Not exactly the height of security, Sheriff.* He detached the key from the ring. *What are you doing, Fooks? Ah, but it might come in handy. I'll replace it later.*

The door to the cellblock stood ajar. When the outside door of the sheriff's office opened, Fooks clearly heard the footsteps of a man entering. At first, the conversation was of no interest to him.

"I want to make a complaint."

"Howdy, Alan. What can I do for you?"

Now Fooks' ears pricked up. Could this Alan be the elusive Alan Long?

"What sorta complaint?" Fooks heard Bennett reach for a sheet of paper.

"Well, I can't be sure, but someone followed me yesterday."

Fooks rolled his eyes. He'd asked Rev to be careful.

"Who was it?"

"Dunno. Suspicious-looking fella dressed all in black."

"What makes you think he was following you?"

"I first saw him in the bank. Didn't pay him too much heed at first. He came in right after me. I went up to the teller. He went to the writing desk. Looked to be filling out a form or something. Anyway, I'd finished my business at the teller, leaving it free for him, but he followed me outside almost straight away."

Fooks glared at the ceiling. Great.

"Maybe he changed his mind?"

"That's what I thought at first. Till he followed me into the café shortly after I went in. Ate lunch, same as I did. Still didn't think too much of it until I went to visit Celia Thorold in the afternoon. Didn't notice him on the way out." Alan paused. "Yet he was there when I made my way back into town, like he'd been waiting for me to finish my business with Celia. I got back to the office, and he's sitting on the hotel porch. Oh, he made out he was reading a book of some sort, but I could tell he was watching my property. I don't mind telling ya, Sheriff, the man gave me the creeps."

"Okay, I'll try getting a look at him today. Can ya describe him any better?"

Fooks rubbed his forehead. *No need. I know who you're gonna describe.*

"Well, like I said, he was dressed all in black. Wore one of those wide-brimmed hats those preaching fellas wear. Y'know the kinda fella I mean."

Fooks nodded. *Yeah, I do.*

"Yeah, I know the kinda fella y'mean," Bennett said.

"Rough looking, too. I didn't wanna tangle with him."

"No, and you shouldn't. You plan on going outta town today?"

"No. Figure I'll stay in town until you've got it sorted."

"Leave it with me. I'll find out what I can."

Fooks raised his head when Bennett came into the cellblock after Alan left.

"Alan Long, I take it?"

"Yep."

Fooks dropped his head back on the pillow.

"Ah, so he does exist."

"Did ya hear? He was making a complaint. Says someone followed him yesterday. Now, what do you know about it?"

"What makes you think I know anything?" Fooks held his hands out, protesting his innocence. "I was with you most of the day, Sheriff." He gave Bennett a dazzling grin.

"Yeah, ya were," Bennett said begrudgingly.

"So, Alan is in town now." Fooks rolled up to sit on the edge of the bunk. "Wonder why he didn't come see you first thing."

Bennett shrugged. "Mebbe, he had other business earlier."

"Mebbe." Fooks wasn't convinced. "Best go see if he can talk to us now. Fit us into his busy day."

As Fooks stood, Bennett blocked the cell's doorway and didn't move until Fooks stepped forward. Bennett slowly moved out of his way.

"Something wrong?" Fooks asked, his eyes following Bennett's to the bunk where he had lain.

Bennett's tongue washed round his mouth, and he grunted. "No." He followed Fooks out of the cellblock. "Listen, I'm gonna head off for some lunch. You ask if Alan will see us later."

Fooks nodded, unsettled by Bennett's change of mood. "Okay, Sheriff." He took down his hat and was heading for the door when Bennett tapped the desk.

"Keys, Crane."

Fooks feigned surprise at the cellblock keys still in his hand. "Oops, nearly forgot." He'd done no such thing. Caught, he had no option but to hand them over, minus the one key he'd palmed.

Fooks flashed a quick grin, put on his hat, and headed out. On the boardwalk, his face fell. Bennett might be beginning to suspect him. He'd better watch his step from now on.

CHAPTER FOURTEEN

Over at the realtor's office, Fooks found Alan behind his desk. To his surprise, Lucinda Mercer was also there. *Ah, perhaps this was the business preventing Alan from seeing the sheriff earlier.*

"Mrs. Mercer, I didn't expect to find you here," Fooks said when he walked in. He'd heard them discussing the sale of her property.

"I have a lot to consider now, Mr. Crane. I'm merely asking Mr. Long his opinion on my property." Lucinda shifted in her seat.

Whatever the reason for her discomfort, Fooks couldn't immediately determine. However, being caught in Alan's office, discussing the disposal of the marital home so soon after becoming a widow, was high on his list.

"Mr. Long, Joseph Crane. Tried to catch you on several occasions. Is now a good time?"

Alan glanced at Lucinda. "No, Mr. Crane. My client, Mrs. Mercer, is here. We haven't finished our discussion."

"Hmmm, can I make an appointment? When it is convenient."

Alan harrumphed and flicked through several pages in his diary. Fooks couldn't see much penciled in, but he wasn't surprised when Alan said, "A week on Thursday? How does two o'clock suit you?"

Fooks stepped forward, the fingers of his right hand casually hooked under his belt. With his left hand, he flicked back the pages of the diary until he reached the present day. Alan threw him a black look.

"How about four o'clock *today*, Mr. Long?" He tapped the page. "I see you have nothing pressing, and my business with you is urgent." Fooks' voice was low and deliberate.

"Very well. Four o'clock today." Alan reached for a pencil and made a note.

Fooks gave them a tight-lipped smile. He walked away, and as he opened the door, he grinned back.

"Oh! I forgot to say, Sheriff Bennett will join us." He closed the door, smiling faintly at the indignant protests from inside.

"Never thought I'd be breaking into a sheriff's office," Rev murmured.

He stood with his back to the door, keeping watch on the street. Under his arm, he held rolled-up papers. Behind him, Fooks bent over the lock.

"You're not, and neither am I." Fooks finagled the lock open. "I have a key."

He pushed open the door and grinned. 'Course, Bennett doesn't know. Stretching the truth was a deeply ingrained habit. Caution around Bennett had taken second place. He needed to solve this murder quickly so he could get back to Mary. Burglary wasn't his forte, and he briefly considered whether he was being too careless in his haste.

They quickly closed the door behind them. The shades were down, but they didn't bother lighting a lamp. Enough daylight filtered through so they could see. Fooks scrabbled around in Bennett's desk for the cell keys and quickly returned the door key to the large ring.

"Couldn't this have waited until he was back?" Rev asked, handing the rolled-up papers to Fooks.

"No. I can't pin these up in the hotel 'cause I don't trust the staff. Don't want any unauthorized eyes on this, and I wanna do some figuring before Bennett sees it as well. This wall here is perfect."

Fooks pointed to the back wall, blank except for a map of the county. Fooks handed the roll back to Rev and stepped forward to take down the framed map. He propped it at the foot of the wall.

"While I'm here." Fooks moved to the noticeboard. A moment later, a poster for Pete "Deadeye" Dingus overlaid his and Swan's.

"Which order do you want these in?"

"Doesn't matter. Start pinning them up."

Rev raised an eyebrow at Fooks. "Hope ya right 'bout this, Fooks. Sheriff ain't gonna be too pleased with little holes all over his wall."

"Aw, he won't mind if it means we crack this case." Fooks waved a hand, dismissing the possibility of any objections.

The wood paneling provided an ideal notice board. On a separate sheet, Fooks had written the names of the six people with different colored pencils. Fooks and Rev pinned each in a clock face formation. At the center of the clock, Fooks added two more sheets, one each for Stephen and Lucinda.

Fooks stepped back to get a better view, leaned against the desk, and rubbed his bottom lip.

"What's the string for?" Rev asked.

"Hmmm? Oh, now we add the links. Let's start with Celia." Fooks took the ball of string and cut it to length. "Stephen worked on her land dispute with Tyler." Taking the cut length, he thumbtacked one end to her sheet. The other end, he tacked onto the sheet for Stephen. "We also reckon maybe more than a professional relationship between them." A similar length of string was cut and tacked next to the first length. "You think something is going on between Celia and Alan Long."

"Now, I didn't say that," Rev cautioned.

"You followed him to her place, and you implied it. I'm inclined to agree until we find out more." Fooks inspected his handiwork. "Well, we're sure there is a link between Celia and Tyler Callaghan 'cause of the court case. Not sure what I feel about him. He seemed stressed." Fooks connected them with a line of string. "Mebbe just down to running a large ranch. Who knows?"

He stood back to admire his handiwork. "Can you think of any more links for Tyler?"

Rev shook his head.

"Okay, let's go back to Stephen."

Fooks strung lines between Stephen and his two remaining clients, and also between the clients.

"Emmett had a falling out with Preston. Preston is friends with Martha Pickering, the herbalist. Martha is being wooed by Emmett." Rev cut the correct length of string, and Fooks pinned it up.

"That's a nice, neat triangle," Fooks declared, standing back. "Now, what else? Preston admitted to me he'd had a brief dalliance with Lucinda Mercer, yet Martha told me Stephen thought something was going on between Lucinda and Alan Long."

"So, where does this leave us?" Rev asked after Fooks reviewed his tableau for some minutes.

"Confused," Fooks murmured. His eyes flicked up when the door opened.

"What the...? Crane, what the heck are ya doing in my office?"

"Afternoon, Sheriff." Fooks greeted Bennett with a brilliant smile.

"How did ya get in here? I know I locked the door."

Fooks blinked in confusion. He had the key, so how did...? Ah, of course, Bennett must have had a duplicate with his personal keys. Made sense. Couldn't carry around that big ol' bunch all the time, could he?

Fooks shrugged. "What can I tell you, Sheriff? I turned the handle, and the door opened."

Fooks was a picture of innocence.

Bennett gave him a doubtful look and turned his attention to Rev.

"Who are you?"

"Allow me to make the introductions. Mark, this is Reverend Josiah Wedgwood. Rev, meet Sheriff Mark Bennett." Fooks paused before adding, "He's the man following Alan Long."

"Josiah Wedgewood? I thought ya made pots," Bennett muttered, then shook himself, as if nothing more could surprise him. "He's working with you?"

"I never work alone."

"I thought ya weren't here in your official capacity," Bennett said.

Fooks shrugged nonchalantly. "I told you I'm not."

"Didn't realize you were on vacation," Rev said with devilment.

Bennett moved to study his wall. "What's all this?"

"Our case. Represented graphically." Fooks went to stand at his side. He folded his arms. "Good, huh?" he said with a wide grin. Seeing the sheriff wasn't convinced, he explained, "See, I've got all the suspects and the links between 'em. It's the latest thing in crime-busting, Mark."

Bennett scowled. "Since when did we get on first-name terms?"

"Awh, Sheriff, I don't mind if you call me Joe." Fooks paused. "Can't I call you Mark?" he asked in all innocence.

"Only on special occasions."

"What kinda special occasions?"

"Not now."

Fooks smacked his lips and smiled ruefully, but he quickly sobered. "I made an appointment to see Alan earlier, like you asked. Reckon you oughta come with me."

"I reckon, too."

Fooks glanced at the clock. "Right about now."

"Now see here. Where do you...?" Bennett broke off when he saw arguing was futile. "Aw, Crane, I suppose the sooner we can clear this case up, the sooner I can get rid of you."

Fooks frowned in umbrage. "There's no call for talk like that. Where would ya be without me?"

"A darn sight happier." Bennett waved a hand at the wall. "You leaving that there?"

"Yeah, might have to add to it shortly."

"I'd better lock up. Again. You." He pointed at Rev. "Out."

Bennett and Fooks walked over to Alan's office. Fooks directed Rev to sit on the hotel porch and surreptitiously nodded for him to keep an eye out. If he was right, this should be interesting.

Exchanging pleasantries gave Fooks time to scan the office and the sparse furnishings, one uncluttered desk, an office chair, and two rigid-backed visitors' chairs. The office gave off a faint smell of disuse mingled with furniture polish. Not a place to linger in. Might explain why Alan Long was hard to find here.

"A few things I don't understand, Mr. Long," Fooks said.

"Go on."

"First, why are you so intent on making improvements to the house Martha Pickering rents from you?"

"I like to keep my properties well maintained and up to date. Putting in a mains water supply and drainage is a worthwhile expense in my book. It's what a lot of my clients are now demanding."

"As far as I'm aware, Martha Pickering has no plans to move out. In fact, she told me your plans would devastate her garden. It's her livelihood, and your destruction would seriously impinge on her ability to pay her rent at all, let alone the increase you are asking."

Alan shrugged. "Her problem. If she wants to continue to live there, she needs to pay the going rate."

"One plant in the garden is important to Martha's remedies and needs specific growing conditions. There is nowhere else in the garden suitable for it to grow. Your plans would decimate that part of the garden. She told us she made you aware of this. If you're restricting Martha's ability to make a living, how can you expect her to pay her rent?"

Alan shrugged again. "I've given her fair notice to make alternative arrangements for her plants."

Fooks sighed. That line of questioning was getting him nowhere. "Okay, let's leave it for now. Before Stephen Mercer died, Celia Thorold presented him with a wooden chest. You delivered it to his office on the day he died. Why did *you* deliver it?"

Alan laughed. "I was at Celia's ranch when she mentioned she had the chest to deliver. I was coming back into town, so I saved her a trip. Nothing more."

"Why were you with Celia Thorold?"

"Celia's an old friend. I went to school with her late husband, and I've known her since their marriage. I took it upon myself to look out for her when Charlie died."

"Mrs. Thorold says the chest didn't have a padlock, yet Tubby Wilson says, when you delivered it, the big antique padlock on there now was present. How do you explain that?"

"I can't. The chest had a padlock. Exactly what I delivered."

"The key went missing for a while. Turned up on the doorstep hours later. Anything you can tell me?"

"Nope. I didn't see any key."

"Wasn't in your pocket when you delivered the chest, and you forgot to give the key to Stephen at the time?"

"Nope, that's not right."

Fooks frowned. Another dead end.

"Mr. Long, I understand you tipped the sheriff here off about Coleman and Murphy being in town. How did you know they were Coleman and Murphy?"

"I didn't. Emmett Woodward pointed 'em out to me when they rode into town."

Fooks considered this. "Why did you tell the sheriff and not Emmett?"

"Emmett needed to get home. I live in town; I said I'd do it."

Hmmm, convenient how you're always in town when something needs doing. Took me ages to track you down when I wanted you.

With nothing more to ask, Fooks and Bennett took their leave.

"Thoughts, Crane?" Bennett asked as they walked back to the jail.

Fooks didn't answer immediately. They walked in silence, and when they reached the door of the jail, he squared up to Bennett.

"Think I'm gonna need more string."

He turned to open the door, leaving Bennett muttering under his breath, only to turn back when he found the door locked.

They had been in the jail only a few moments when Rev joined them.

"Long have anything useful to say?" Rev asked, shutting the door.

"Yeah. He's processing it now," Bennett said, waving a hand at Fooks' back. Fooks gnawed his thumbnail, contemplating the wall. Bennett smirked and sat.

"Best not disturb him," Rev whispered and leaned on the sheriff's desk. "Here's something. Lucinda overheard your meeting with Long."

Bennett frowned. "What d'ya mean?"

Rev nodded towards Fooks, who showed no sign that anyone else was in the room. "She was upstairs. Mighta been listening. After you left, Long went up."

Bennett shrugged.

"You say anything to upset her, Sheriff? She came tearing down a bit after, all outta sorts."

Bennett pursed his lips. "We asked him about the chest he delivered to Stephen Mercer from Celia Thorold."

Rev stood back and grinned. "Guess that mighta done it. She looked real mad."

"Ah, well, thanks for letting us know. I'll tell him when he's back with us," Bennett said with a nod to Fooks.

Rev's grin widened. "Might be a while, Sheriff. Known him to stand like that for hours."

"I can hear you, y'know," Fooks said.

Bennett and Rev swapped grins as Fooks flopped wearily into a chair.

"It's there. I know it is," Fooks said sadly. "I just can't see it."

Fooks turned back to the wall. "One person I haven't spoken to yet. Emmett. He seemed to recognize Coleman and Murphy. Wonder how he knows them? Any ideas?"

Bennett shook his head. "I'm not the town's keeper. I'm just here to keep it law-abiding."

"How are you fixed for tomorrow?"

"We can ride out there in the morning," Bennett said, giving Fooks the first genuine smile since he'd arrived.

Fooks recognized it for what it was and smiled back. "Thanks, Sheriff."

CHAPTER FIFTEEN

The next morning, Fooks and Bennett rode over to visit Emmett Woodward. Fooks had mulled over Bennett's manner yesterday, and on impulse, he'd strapped on his gun belt as a precaution. He'd dressed today in range gear, as wearing a gun with his suit would appear out of place.

He glanced at his riding companion, who appeared deep in thought. "Something wrong, Sheriff?" he asked, breaking the uncomfortable silence.

"Nope. Never seen ya in anything other than that brown suit of yours. Ya look kinda different. Familiar."

Fooks barked a laugh. "You're used to me now. Why, we're almost old friends."

"Ya haven't made my Christmas card list yet."

Fooks smiled, and Bennett mirrored it and the unease between them disappeared.

They met Emmett in front of his house, painting the picket fence.

"Yeah, I remember selling Charlie Thorold a wooden chest. Years ago," he said in response to Fooks' initial question.

"Mr. Woodward, can you remember if the chest had a padlock on it?"

Emmett rubbed his chin, thinking, oblivious to the white streak of paint he'd smeared across his face. "No, I can't recall exactly, but if Charlie asked me 'bout a padlock, I'da sent him to see Preston Thompkins. He keeps antique ironmongery. Bound to find something suitable."

"Talking of Preston Thompkins, will you tell me about the dispute between you?"

"Aw! Don't wanna talk about it."

Emmett stalked away to the end of the fence, where he slapped paint wildly on the uprights.

Fooks followed. "Mr. Woodward, if you're friends with Preston—"

"Who said we're friends?" Emmett spun around abruptly, brandishing the loaded paintbrush. The paint drips brought Fooks up short. *Can't afford a splattering. Don't have a clean shirt right now.*

"Tubby Wilson told me about your schooldays. About it being a small school and all the kids were friends."

"So? We all knew each other. Had to. No hiding place."

"Anyone you were close to, Mr. Woodward?"

Emmett idly dipped the paintbrush again as he thought. "Charlie, I guess. What is this? I thought you wanted to ask me questions about Stephen Mercer."

"Well, yeah, I do," Fooks said. "I'm getting there."

"Crane likes to circle the wagons first," Bennett said.

Fooks flashed him a warning: Not helping. He folded his arms and said to Emmett, "Preston takes great pride in his workmanship. Hard to believe he would deliberately sabotage a piece of furniture."

"Well, he did." Emmett dunked the paintbrush.

"He says he didn't."

Emmett bent to apply paint with more care. "Why I'm taking him to court. Let them decide who's right and who's wrong."

"Hmmm, seems to me that course of action has several drawbacks, doesn't it?"

"Not if I get compensation."

Fooks glanced at Bennett.

"Did Stephen think you'd win the case?"

Emmett didn't answer.

"Stephen was an excellent lawyer. What I don't understand is why he would take a case knowing he would lose. Can you offer me any explanation?"

"I don't have to answer. The reasons are between me and Stephen. Attorney-client privilege, he said it were." He walked into the garden and shut the gate firmly.

Bennett smacked his lips and undid the latch.

"Emmett, attorney-client privilege stopped when Stephen died." Emmett turned to face him. Bennett entered the garden, letting the gate shut on Fooks. "We're investigating his murder. Anything you can tell us about this case may be useful to our investigation." Bennett took a moment before going on. "Withholding information is an arrestable offense, Emmett. You could be in serious trouble yourself."

Fooks wasn't sure that was true in this situation, but he'd go along with it. He rubbed his thigh where the gate had hit him. *Vicious spring.*

Emmett groaned and rubbed his forehead. He sank onto the bench by the side of the front door and put his head in his hands.

"Preston is sparking my gal."

"Your gal?" Fooks asked from Bennett's side.

"Martha Pickering."

"Well, not the way I heard it," Bennett said. "Didn't she turn ya down?"

Emmett shifted uncomfortably. "Yeah, but she was coming around, and she woulda done if he hadn't continued on. I warned him to stop seeing her."

Fooks pressed his lips together and glanced at Bennett to continue.

"You're prepared to damage a man's professional reputation because he is friends with a gal you have designs on. A gal who has turned you down. Is that it?" Bennett asked.

"You're making it sound childish."

"Well, isn't it?"

"I didn't want Martha hurt, especially when I heard about Preston carrying on with Lucinda Mercer."

Fooks considered this. "Mr. Woodward, whose idea was it to sue Preston Thompkins?" When Emmett didn't answer, he said, "Mr. Woodward, you and Preston had a set-to in the saloon one night, didn't you?"

"Yeah."

"And a short while afterward, you opened proceedings against Preston, right?"

"Yeah."

"So, whose idea was it, Emmett?"

"Stephen's," Emmett mumbled, keeping his head down.

Bennett and Fooks swapped glances.

"Did Stephen say why he wanted to go along with such a case? After all, he knew he would lose."

"Don't think losing mattered to him," Emmett said with a deep sigh. "Ya right. I suppose it don't matter none now. Stephen wanted Preston's reputation to suffer. Even if Preston won, there would always be a doubt in some folks' minds that he did the damage to my cupboard. They would wonder why I felt compelled to sue him if it wasn't true. We were real good friends. Until he started seeing Martha."

Fooks crouched in front of Emmett, and his voice took on a more kindly tone.

"I hate to tell you this, but nothing is going on between Martha and Preston. They're friends, is all."

"He's always at her place."

Fooks made a tight-lipped smile. "Preston is trying to work through a few issues. She's easy to talk to, that's all. You've no reason to be jealous."

Emmett raised his eyebrows eagerly. "Then maybe she will come around?"

"Possibly. Or perhaps she's the kinda woman who enjoys being on her own."

Fooks straightened.

"Mr. Woodward, on a different subject. Alan Long says he was with you when you spotted Coleman and Murphy riding into town. How d'you know Coleman and Murphy?"

Emmett laughed. "Oh, that's easy. My sister lives over at Burton Wells. Y'know, the town nearest to Guardian Wall?"

"Yes, I know Burton Wells." Fooks swallowed hard. He resisted the temptation to look at Bennett, fully aware his eyes were on him.

"Then ya know it's the town frequented by the Guardian Wall Gang. It's where they go for their supplies, their drinking, and their whoring. Why, most folks in town know who they all are. I visited once when they all came riding into town. My sister pointed out who was who. She knew 'em all. Why, she told me she even had a right friendly conversation with Florian Fooks hisself once."

Fooks let out a humorless laugh. "Really? Wow." He blinked and shook his head, swallowing hard. "So, I guess you have no doubt in your mind who they were?"

"No siree. I knew straight off, and I told Alan we'd better tell the sheriff. I was in a hurry to get home. I figured Bennett would ask me questions and hold me up. Alan said he'd go tell him."

There was nothing further to add.

Fooks and Bennett rode back to town, the former in silence, mulling over what he'd learned. Bennett didn't seem surprised when Fooks pulled up as they reached a fork in the road.

"I'd like to pay Preston Thompkins another visit, Mark," Fooks said, turning his horse's head away from town.

"Want me to come with ya?"

Fooks pursed his lips and shook his head. "Not if you can't spare the time. I wanna ask him some more about the padlock. How it works. That kinda thing."

"Guess ya don't need me for that. Be seeing ya."

The two men parted, Bennett to town, Fooks to Thompkins Decorative Ironmongery. On the way, the weather took a turn for the worse. Fooks turned his collar up against the driving rain and pressed on.

At the forge, Fooks settled in Preston's office with a cup of coffee, grateful for the warm greeting. He appreciated how Preston made his coffee: strong, just how he liked it. He'd decided not to mention the padlock. Presumably, the one stolen from Preston had reappeared.

"Preston, did you show anyone your missing padlocks, especially the one with the secret compartment? The one you described to Sheriff Bennett as an Italian Lock?"

"Yes."

"Who did you show?"

"About anyone who ever visited here. Most of my friends. Emmett. Tyler. Tubby. Alan." He shrugged.

"Quite a list there."

"It's special, and I was rather proud of it."

"Did you show Martha Pickering?"

Preston laughed. "No. Why would I?"

"She's your friend."

Preston laughed. "Yes, I value her friendship, but she's a gentle person. I doubt she is interested in padlocks with a secret."

Fooks smiled in agreement.

"The chamber inside the Italian lock, how does it work, exactly?"

"A small key unlocks an inside chamber. The keyhole disguises itself as part of the lock construction. When it's unlocked, the chamber pulls out. Like a shotgun cartridge. Fills easily, and once ya pop it back in and lock back up, ya wouldn't suspect it was there at all."

"You said they used dye in the chamber. Anyone tampering with the lock would get covered. Could it contain anything else?"

"Like what?"

Fooks paced, considering how to proceed. "Poison, perhaps?" He turned, and Preston stiffened. Did he know something? "You said yourself there were some unscrupulous people in those times," Fooks added quickly.

"Yeah." Preston sniffed. "I suppose. What are you getting at?"

Fooks shook his head. "I'm thinking that when the key turns in the lock, the spike shoots out, scratching the unwary. Injury would be so slight the victim thinks nothing of it." He stood, hands on hips, staring at the forge. It had been at working temperature when he'd arrived, but now it emitted nothing more than a cozy glow. "I'm just thinking that if there was poison on the spike, the victim could die from the cut almost immediately. Or it might take several hours, depending on the virulence of the poison, of course."

Preston puffed and scratched his head. "Nothing I've ever heard of, but I suppose that's a possibility."

Fooks stared at him hard, trying to detect any sign of subterfuge. "Did you have the key for the chamber?" he asked in a low, hard voice.

"Yeah, on a chain looped through the top of the primary key." Preston blinked in alarm. "Have you found it? Was it used for something?"

Fooks grinned. Preston's reaction had satisfied him for now. "I'm curious how it worked, that's all."

"Long way to come asking for just idle curiosity." Preston narrowed his eyes.

"Let's just say you've finally met a person as enthusiastic about locks as you are," Fooks said with a laugh.

Preston chuckled.

Fooks drained his coffee and held out his hand. "Thank you for your time again. Oh, one more question. When you showed off the padlock, did you demonstrate how the chamber worked?"

"Yes. It's unusual, and I was proud of it."

Fooks nodded. "I can understand that." With a smile and a cheery wave, he left. He had a lot to think about on the way back to town.

Rev found Fooks slumped in a chair on the hotel porch. He'd changed back into his suit for dinner and was gnawing at his thumbnail as he contemplated the information he'd gleaned during the day.

"You need a rest." Rev put a hand on Fooks' shoulder. "What say you and me take ourselves over to the saloon for a drink or two? Get ourselves a bite to eat and unwind a little. Play some poker?"

"No poker." Fooks shook his head. "Yeah, you're right. I need to take my mind off this."

As they walked to the saloon, Fooks glanced into the sheriff's office. Bennett was still there.

In the saloon, after a few shots of whiskey, and most of the bottle in Rev's case, Fooks relaxed. The cabaret act was in full swing. Scantily clad girls kicked their legs up on the stage to the thump of the out-of-key piano. Comfortable being a married man, he had no interest in them, whereas, once upon a time, he would have been at the forefront of the applause and whistles. Instead, he gazed longingly at the poker tables and knew that direction held no distraction, either. He could sit at any table and clean up. But no, he had to keep to his self-imposed embargo. Playing poker was not the act of a responsible husband and family man. He turned his back to the noisy room. Not good. He could still see the play in the bar mirror.

"'Bout time for some food. Table over there?" Fooks pointed to a quiet table in the corner, away from the main proceedings.

"Sure."

Rev picked up what remained of his bottle. Fooks deliberately sat with his back to the barroom, knowing Rev would sit where he could view the room.

"Tell me 'bout your wife, boy. Sid says she's real purty."

Fooks smiled. "Yes, she sure is. I miss her. I'm trying not to think about her and the baby, 'cause, if I do, I'll be on m'horse and riding outta town."

"Don't do that. You're making progress in this case."

"I dunno, Rev. It's not what I should worry about right now. The longer this drags on... I might not get back in time, Rev. I want to be there for Mary."

Fooks reached for the bottle, sloshed a generous measure into his glass, and downed it in one gulp.

"You'll get back to her. An' even if ya don't make it in time, you'll make it up to her and the babe. You'll be a great father, Fooks. I know ya will." Rev saluted him with his own drink.

"I'm not so sure, Rev."

"No one knows how to be a father until ya are one. And you've already had some practice."

"Huh?"

Rev leaned in and dropped his voice. "Leading Guardian Wall was no picnic. Some of the younger boys looked up to you and Swan. Like ya were their fathers."

"Hardly the same thing, Rev."

When his dinner arrived, Fooks sat back. The smell of the juicy steak reminded him he hadn't eaten since breakfast. He was about to tuck in eagerly when the clearing of a throat made him look up. On the table between him and Rev lay a dog-eared Bible. Rev patted it meaningfully. Fooks rolled his eyes and put down his knife and fork, respectfully allowing Rev to say a brief grace.

"Gotta keep up standards, boy. Otherwise, anarchy will ensue," Rev said, tucking the Bible away.

"Thought anymore 'bout going back to ministering?" Fooks asked casually.

"Always thinking 'bout it. Jus' waiting for the right time."

"And when's that?"

"When I cen make enough money outta it."

"Doesn't that put you at odds with the message?"

"Yep." Rev nodded. "That's why it's not the right time. Yet." He waved his fork. "They'll come a time. Ya jus' gotta have faith. The Good Lord will provide."

Fooks smiled and kept his thoughts to himself. Tomorrow would be a decisive day; he could feel it. First, he had to get through the rest of the evening without giving in to temptation.

After a convivial evening in the saloon, Fooks and Rev made their way back to the hotel. Evening morphed into night. The moon lit up the town, from a bright white dazzle in the middle of the street to an inky blackness in the deep shadows. A bizarre piano key pattern of black and white painted the boardwalk on which they walked.

Fooks had drunk more than he'd intended, and he stumbled along at Rev's side. Rev, the more sober man, offered a hand to Fooks now and then as he swayed along.

The crack of a rifle rang out, followed by the heavy thud of a bullet hitting the woodwork behind them. Rev pushed an already unbalanced Fooks to the ground.

"Wha'?" Fooks gasped.

Rev shuffled them both behind the relative safety provided by a water trough.

"What was that?" Fooks' eyes widened. He wasn't at all sure why he lay sprawled on the ground.

"Ya all right, boy?"

"Yeah. I think so," Fooks confirmed, shocked.

"Someone jus' took a shot at us, I reckon."

"You don't say?" Fooks scowled and rallied his businesslike persona. "D'you see from where?"

"Not exactly." Rev shook his head. "We ain't safe here, boy. We've gotta move."

The single shot hadn't been enough to alert the town. The noise from the saloon had covered the sound. Now that it was winding down for the evening, customers would likely spill out in about ten minutes or so. Right then, though, not a single other person was on the street. No safety in numbers.

They scanned around, assessing their options.

"Are you armed, Rev?" The stumble, the sudden heavy tackle to the ground, and the danger, all these things helped revive Fooks' alcohol-dazed wits.

"Nope. You?"

"Nope."

"Sounded like a rifle to me."

Rev cautiously peered around the side of the trough. "Yeah, way I figured it, too."

"Anyone out there?"

"Can't make out any movement." Rev ducked back and lay on his back next to Fooks. "What d'ya wanna do?"

Fooks gulped. "Not get shot."

"Took that as a given, boy."

Fooks blinked. "Well, we can't stay here. That's for sure."

"No, it's not exactly a comfortable spot."

"Is he still out there?"

"Don't think he was out on the street." Rev chewed his bottom lip. "The shot came from higher up. First-floor window, I'd say."

Fooks nodded. "Then he's well hid and comfortable. He can wait us out."

"Yep. That is, a'course, it was a he."

Fooks turned his head slowly to glare at Rev. "I was being generic." He took a deep breath. "We're gonna have to make a move."

"Yep. Well, if he's that way." Rev thumbed behind him and to the left. "We oughta go this way." He pointed across his body and to the right.

Fooks considered. "Can we make it to the alley?"

Rev glanced at the moon. "Damn light ain't gonna go away anytime soon. Your white shirt is gonna shine so bright."

"What d'you want me to do? I can't take it off. My henley underneath is white, too," Fooks hissed.

Rev gathered the hem of his long tunic. "Only one thing we can do. I'll shield ya best as I can, seeing as how I'm wearing the more practical color of garb."

Fooks bit off the retort forming in his mind. Enough dust clung to his brown suit to make it light. Now was not the time to snipe.

"You prepared to do that?" he asked.

"Well, figure I still owe you for saving my life down in Addison," Rev said, referring to a time after a heist when the pursuing posse had shot his horse from underneath him. Fooks had ridden back, hauled him up behind him, and then made off under gunfire.

"Aw, you repaid me more'n twice over already."

"Maybe, but I figure the man, whoever he is, was shooting at you, not me."

CHAPTER SIXTEEN

Fooks lay still. He'd already come to the same conclusion. An uncomfortable thought. Even more uncomfortable was knowing he daren't risk the chance they were both wrong. He didn't want Rev hurt or killed by accident. He glanced around, considering his options.

"Is that my hat there?" His homburg had flown off when Rev had hit him and now sat in the middle of the street. In the full moonlight.

"Yeah." Rev looked at Fooks in surprise. "Ya head cold?"

"No, but I've got an idea."

Fooks unfastened his belt and slid it from the loops of his pants. He folded the frame back and pulled the stiff prong so it stuck out. Rev watched, curious. Fooks looped the strap back through the frame. He pushed it flat, leaving the prong sticking out.

"How are you at fishing, Rev?" Fooks asked, holding out the Fooks-styled hook.

"What d'ya want me to do?"

"See if you can hook the prong in the crown and drag my hat over. I'll watch for any movement back there."

Rev shuffled onto his side and gathered the belt to throw into the street. Fooks moved into his customary crouch, keeping his head low.

"Ready?"

"Yes."

As Rev threw the belt, Fooks peered around the edge of the water trough. Nothing happened. No movement. No rifle crack. Only the sound of a hat scuffing along in the dirt.

"D'ya think he's gone?"

"No. He's smart enough not to give away his location for a self-propelling hat." Fooks gave the retrieved article a slap against his thigh.

"Now what?"

"Now we'll find out if he's still there."

Rev blinked in surprise when Fooks tugged off his left boot. He sniffed as he balanced his hat on the toe of the boot. Gingerly he raised the boot-hat combo above his head and the edge of the water trough.

Rev guessed Fooks plan. "Ain't gonna fool anyone."

"Alternative is to use your hat," Fooks said with a nonchalant shrug. "With your head still in it." He gave Rev a smug grin.

Rev grunted, disgruntled, and Fooks carried on with his plan.

When nothing immediately happened, Fooks moved the hat towards the edge of the trough, making it appear someone was creeping along, preparing to make a dash for the nearby alley. Fooks almost gave up when two shots rang out. The bullets struck close enough. Splinters of wood and water from the trough showered over the skulking pair.

"Sheesh!"

This time the shots roused the town. Lamps flickered into life. Nightwear-clad occupants of homes and businesses emerged. The saloon emptied out its remaining customers. Everyone was asking each other what was going on. Fooks and Rev swapped glances. With people milling about, it was probably safe to get up.

No sooner were they on their feet than Bennett appeared, pulling his vest with the badge on over his henley.

"You two! What have you been doing now?" he demanded.

"Trying not to get shot." Fooks irritably stomped into his boot and clapped his hat on his head.

"What d'ya mean? Who was doing the shooting?"

"Dunno who, but someone took a shot at us as we made our way back from the saloon. Here."

Fooks pointed at the wall behind him, now resplendently embellished with a bullet.

"We ducked behind this here water—" Rev said.

"Yeah, and when we moved to somewhere more secure, he took two more shots at us. If we look round here, we'll find the bullets," Fooks said, was ushering bodies out of the way with a flap of his hat.

"Did ya get a look at who it was? Where did the shots come from?" Bennett asked.

"Dunno who, but yeah..." Rev broke off, conscious they had now attracted a crowd. Lowering his voice, he said, "I saw where the shots came from, but we'd better discuss this in private, Sheriff."

Bennett pursed his lips as he considered the implications. Finally, he nodded. "Let's talk 'bout this in my office. Bring him." He inclined his head to where Fooks was searching for the other bullets.

"Joseph?"

Fooks' head jerked up. He brushed back his hair where it had fallen forward as he'd scoured the ground.

"Sheriff wants a word."

Fooks stepped onto the boardwalk and stopped.

"What's he doing now?" Bennett asked, watching Fooks as he lifted his right leg and reached into his boot.

Fooks took out a thin blade and began digging the bullet from the wall.

"Evidence."

Fooks and Rev joined Bennett in his office. To Fooks' surprise, two men followed them in.

"I told you my regular deputy's away right now. I have two part-time deputies I can call on in case of emergencies. Reckon this is an emergency. Meet Patterson and Stoner."

The two men nodded an acknowledgment. Neither appeared deputy material, but more used to dealing with small, inconsequential disputes rather than major crime.

"So ya got shot at," Bennett said, getting Fooks' attention. Fooks held up the bullet he'd dug from the building. "What's that?"

"The first. Missed me by a fraction." Fooks slammed it on the desk. "I don't enjoy being shot at."

Bennett studied the bullet. "No, I don't suppose *you* do," he murmured.

Fooks narrowed his eyes. *Why did you emphasize the word* you, *Sheriff? Is now going to be the standoff?*

Bennett turned to Rev. "You thought ya knew where the shots came from. Care to let me in?"

Rev glanced at Fooks. "Waal, it looked to me like it was coming from the direction of Alan Long's place. From upstairs."

"Does Alan own a rifle, Sheriff?" Fooks asked before Bennett could dwell too long on the implications.

"Yeah, I expect. Most folks do round these parts. Are you saying Alan tried to kill you?" Bennett asked.

"What my friend here is saying is the shots came from the direction of Alan's office. But don't take his word for it.

You and your deputies oughta head off down the street and ask some questions. Someone else might have seen something."

Bennett locked eyes with Fooks, who had no intention of backing down. Bennett glanced away first, albeit reluctantly.

"All right. Patterson, work ya way down this side of the street. Ask some questions. Stoner, you're with me." He turned back and shook his finger at Fooks and Rev. "And you two go back to the hotel and stay there. If I catch either of you out on the street, I'll lock you up. Understand?"

Fooks and Rev didn't have long to wait for an answer. They had been in Fooks' hotel room for about ten minutes when Bennett knocked.

"Sorry, Crane, no one saw anything."

"What about Alan Long? Did you arrest him?"

Bennett pursed his lips. "Nope. All dark and quiet."

"Did you knock?" Fooks stood, hands on hips.

Rev bit his lip and shifted. *Don't like this. Fooks needs to calm down.*

"'Course I knocked."

"He musta heard all the ruckus going on. Rev's sure that's where the shots came from." Fooks paced away before turning on his heel and walking back to face Bennett. "He coulda been hiding. You shoulda broke down the door."

Bennett held a finger in front of Fooks' face.

"No, Crane, I couldn't." Bennett was firm and controlled.

"Why the heck not?"

Rev stood, poised to step in. Fooks had a way of pushing a man past endurance.

"I need more to go on. He wasn't there, I'm telling ya."

Fooks ran a hand through his hair and rubbed his neck. "Okay. We'll talk in the morning."

"Yeah, I'll look forward to it," Bennett said and left Fooks to pace.

Rev poured a glass of whiskey and settled on the bed with the rest of the bottle. He watched Fooks for a while before growing tired of his perambulating friend.

"Don't ya think you're a little too angry," he said finally. *Here's hoping Fooks will stop.* For a moment, it looked like it would work.

"I've a right to be angry. I dislike getting shot at." Fooks glared at Rev before stalking up and down some more.

"Fooks—"

"I told you, Rev, my wife is having a baby any day now. My daughter very nearly didn't get to meet her father."

"Fooks—"

"And another thing. Where is murdering me gonna get him? Huh? Except finding himself in a whole lot more trouble."

"Now, ya don't know it was Alan Long—"

"'Course it was him."

"But ya don't know for sure."

Rev watched Fooks pace angrily. *Gotta do something here. Afore, he appears. Not sure I cen manage him without Swan here. Perhaps appealing to his calm, rational side will do it. Hmmm, that side might be on a break right now.*

Rev pulled himself up. Well, here goes. This'll get him. "Florian!"

At the mention of his hated given name, Fooks' head snapped around at Rev. "What?"

Rev went to him. "Ya getting all worked up, an' that ain't good. Take a deep breath an' look at this thing calmly." Rev took Fooks by the upper arms and held his eyes. "Remember. Who. You. Are," he said slowly and deliberately.

Fooks slumped onto the bed.

"I'm not that man anymore," Fooks said. He shook his head sadly. "I own a hardware store in a small town in Wyoming, and I'm making a nice, honest living. It's my life now, and I'm happy."

"Yet all the same, ya're here, trying to solve this mystery." Rev hesitated. "Because you need to, Fooks."

"I dunno, Rev. I thought my days of getting shot at were over. This is turning into a nightmare." Fooks rasped out a sigh and threw up his hands weakly. "I'm not sure I wanna carry on," he added, shaking his head despondently.

"An' let Brad an' Sid down?"

Fooks shook his head again. "I'm sure Bennett can figure out the rest."

"Now, listen to me, Fooks. The Good Lord brought you inta this mess for a reason. He won't give you anything ya can't handle." Rev sat on the bed next to Fooks. "Y'know Bennett's outta his depth with this. He needs your help." He considered his words. "Remember the positives, not the negatives. You didn't get shot. Not even a little bit."

"I came this close to dying, Rev." Fooks specified an inch with his fingers. His voice broke, and he nervously finger-combed his hair back. "What would happen to Mary and our baby if I had?" Fooks was wide-eyed. "I can't take the risk it could happen."

Rev pulled a face. "All that says to me is the Good Lord is looking out for ya."

"Twice now," Fooks said as if Rev hadn't spoken. "Damn chest mighta poisoned me." He rubbed his eyes. "Oh, Rev, I'm so tired."

"Ya oughta get some sleep—"

"Oh, I can't sleep. I'm too wound up." He threw himself up and walked away, keeping his back to Rev.

"Here." Rev held out the glass of whiskey he'd poured earlier.

Fooks looked back and shook his head. "No, I don't need it. Why don't you go back to your room? Take the bottle with you."

"And leave you like this?"

"I'll be all right." Fooks gave Rev a slight smile. "Not as though I've never been shot at before, is it?"

Rev smiled. "Ya said your babe's not born yet?"

Fooks rolled his eyes. "No, not yet. Any day."

Rev grinned, showing tobacco-stained teeth. "Then what makes ya think you're getting a girl?"

Fooks' dimples slowly appeared as he smiled. "'Cause Mary is convinced, and well, I think I believe her." He fidgeted, embarrassed. "Be kinda nice to have a daughter."

Rev snatched the bottle. "You think 'bout meeting her and telling her how her Pa saved two innocent men from the hangman. She'll be proud of ya when she's old enough to understand."

He hesitated for a moment before getting up. "I'll leave ya to think on it."

Fooks didn't sleep well that night. He lay in bed, turning things over repeatedly in his mind. Finally, he climbed out of bed and took Mary's photograph from his wallet.

"Love you," he whispered. "I'm sorry. I can't leave just yet. Things mighta come to a head tonight. I want a word with Mr. Alan Long tomorrow, but I must be careful. I can't just blunder in, or Bennett will arrest me, and I won't get home to you. Ever, if he finds out who I really am."

CHAPTER SEVENTEEN

The next morning found Fooks crouched once again in front of the chest in Stephen's office, examining the padlock. Carefully, now he knew what it contained. Turning it over in his gloved hand, he identified the secret lock. A casual observer would surmise the tiny hole was part of the padlock housing. He admired the lock maker's art and ingenuity and he shook his head.

"Beautiful," he murmured.

He stood, hands on hips, and stared at the chest.

"You seem very interested in the chest," Tubby said.

Fooks stepped over to Tubby. "It's intriguing." He smiled pleasantly and then wrinkled his nose. "Take it the key hasn't reappeared?"

As expected, the answer was a no.

Fooks walked along the boardwalk, puzzling over what he'd learned in the last few days. He was on his way to the jail. There he planned to string a few more connections onto his already crowded map.

His brown suit had taken some punishment the previous night, so he had left it to the tender mercies of the hotel laundry. The laundress had expressed doubt, telling him it might be beyond her skills. He'd told her to try her best. He was aware he was taking a risk, appearing again in range gear and his battered, dark gray hat in front of Bennett. No choice. The brown suit had become a mite too whiffy, even for a man used to whiffs.

When he walked into the sheriff's office, Alan Long was there.

"Morning, Sheriff. Mr. Long," Fooks said, closing the door. He kept his face impassive. Alan Long was the last person he'd expected to see, given his suspicions from last night. Just as well, he'd rehung the county map, hiding his string artwork from prying eyes. Alan's presence in the office wrong-footed him for a moment, and he turned to pour himself a cup of coffee. He grimaced. Could be hotter.

Bennett explained Alan's presence. "Alan's asking me whether I found out anything about the man who followed him the other day. I told him he's an associate of yours, Crane."

Fooks flashed a brief grin when Alan stared at him, expecting an explanation.

"You are a tough man to reach, Mr. Long. My investigation was stalling until I spoke to you."

"Is that a fact?" Alan asked. "I don't like being followed."

"I don't like being shot at," Fooks snapped back. "So, I guess we're just about even," he added, settling on the edge of a desk.

"What's that supposed to mean?" Alan demanded, pushing to his feet.

"Now, Alan." Bennett jumped to intervene between the two men. "Crane."

Fooks held up his hand in surrender. "My apologies. Haven't you heard what happened in town last night?"

"No." Alan's denial was cautious, and he glanced at Bennett.

Bennett strongly suggested Alan should retake his seat.

"Someone took several shots at Crane and his friend last night. Crane's associate, Wedgwood reckoned they came from near your place. We knocked on your door, Alan. Where were you?"

"That's my business. All you need to know is I wasn't home. I knew nothing about this shooting until now."

Bennett glanced at Fooks, looking for a sign that the explanation had satisfied him.

Fooks let out an ambiguous grunt. *He's lying. Why?*

"Well, whoever it was sure put the willies up me. Been jumpy all day." He smiled pleasantly. "But I'm glad you're here, Mr. Long," he said, seeing Alan rising to his feet again. "I have a few more questions about my investigation into Stephen's murder."

Alan gave him a murderous look and sat back. "Go on, then. Ask ya questions," he snapped.

"When you delivered the chest, was Stephen in the office?"

"No, not at first. He came in as Tubby and me set the chest down."

"So, Tubby helped you?"

"Only to get it off the springboard. It's heavy. Awkward to move about on your own."

"Did you and Stephen argue?"

"He weren't happy 'bout me being in his office, that's for sure. Soon as Tubby gave me the tarp, I left."

"Tarp?" Fooks narrowed his eyes.

"Yeah, Celia had the chest wrapped in a tarp. Keep the dust off, she said."

"So, you didn't actually see the chest at Celia's?"

"No," Alan said and glanced at Bennett. "I jus' delivered the thing."

Fooks paced, deep in thought, with one hand on his hip and the other squeezing his bottom lip. "Yet you said the other day you noticed the chest had a padlock," he said, turning to face Alan.

"After Tubby gave me the tarp, I eyed the thing, and I mighta said something to Stephen 'bout I hoped he enjoyed it. Y'know, kinda sarcastic."

Fooks nodded and returned to pacing. Bennett and Alan watched him. Abruptly, Fooks turned.

"So, why did you shoot at me last night?" he asked.

Alan's eyes widened in surprise. "How...?"

"Crane," Bennett protested. He leaped from his chair, ready to intervene.

Fooks waved him down.

"You own the livery stable, don't you?"

Alan nodded slowly. "Yeah."

Bennett also appeared puzzled.

"Do you have the keys?"

Alan's looked up in alarm. "What?"

Fooks moved to stand in front of him. "You own the property. Do you have a set of keys for the livery?" he asked, shrugging. "Simple enough question."

Alan shifted uncomfortably. "What is this? I came in here to ask about the man who followed me the other day."

"And we've answered that. Now I want some questions answered." Fooks gazed at him, now in full outlaw mode. "I repeat, do you have a set of keys for the livery stable?"

Alan swallowed hard. "Yeah, I might. Somewhere." He shook his head. "Jerome's rented it from me for so long now—"

"Shall we go see?"

CHAPTER EIGHTEEN

Alan appealed to Bennett. "Is this really necessary?"

Bennett glanced at Fooks and considered.

"Yeah, Alan, it is."

Alan growled.

Fooks nodded, silently acknowledging Bennett's trust in him.

Alan led them upstairs to his apartment. Bennett and Fooks swapped glances of surprise.

"You don't keep the keys to your properties in the office?" Fooks queried.

"No," Alan said. "I'm not there much, and it's the first place a thief would go."

Fooks twitched his head, accepting the explanation, and continued to climb the stairs. At the top was a small landing, with a door leading into the apartment proper. This comprised a sizable room, with a bedroom leading off. A kitchen area made up one of the room's corners. Alan crossed the room to a large wall cupboard, which he unlocked. He threw open the door to show a vast collection of keys hanging on hooks.

"Should be here somewhere," he said, rolling his eyes. "Not all 'em have labels."

"You have a lot of properties, Mr. Long," Fooks said, hands on hips, as he studied the cupboard.

"That's why I dunno if I still have any keys for the livery. Help yourself." Alan stepped aside to allow Bennett and Fooks access. Bennett started at the top, Fooks at the bottom, and they worked their way along each row, reading the labels when present. When a label was devoid of identification, they asked Alan.

Fooks had an idea what to check for, and he narrowed his eyes when he found it. Yet the label for the set of keys said, "Marjoram Homestead Inn." A quick flick of his eyes over the other keys told him this label appeared newer than the rest. A sly glance at Alan told him the man was watching him intently.

Fooks laughed inwardly. He recognized a guilty conscience when he saw one. With a smile, he moved on to the next set of keys.

Before long, Bennett and Fooks finished checking the keys.

"Doesn't look as though ya still have them, Alan," Bennett declared.

"No, I wasn't sure," agreed Alan. "Satisfied, Mr. Crane?" He placed his hand on the cupboard door, ready to close it.

"No." Like lightning, Fooks' hand shot out. His fingers closed around the keys for the Marjoram Homestead Inn. "Tell me about these," he said, holding them up and then throwing them onto the table.

The three men regarded them, each with a different expression: Bennett with a frown, Fooks in expectation, and Alan blanching and licking his lips.

"Marjoram Homestead Inn," Bennett mused. "I thought I saw those keys up here." Bennett inspected the top row. Fooks kept his face impassive, while Alan sucked air through his teeth in irritation. "Yeah, here we are."

Bennett placed another set on the table, this one very different, not even a duplicate.

"Hmmm," mused Fooks.

"The Marjoram Homestead Inn?" Bennett said. "Didn't that burn down a few years ago?"

"Yeah. I had to rebuild." Alan grinned. "That's it. These must be the old keys." He pointed at the set Bennett found. "And these the new ones. See new label."

With his thumbs tucked into his gun belt, Fooks continued to inspect the keys.

"Hmmm. Nope." He raised his head. Bennett, with his usual slight frown, looked on. Alan licked his lips nervously. "These are all new." Fooks pointed at the set Bennett had found. "You can tell by the design of the bow and the bit is machine-cut. They're all pretty much uniform." He spread the keys out on the table so they could see more clearly what he was saying. "These..." He pointed at the other set. "...are older. Blacksmith-made, I would guess. They're all different, but the clincher..." He gave Alan a tight-lipped smile and a wink. "Well, they look more like industrial keys to me rather than the sorta key you'd find in a modern hotel."

Alan looked sullen.

Fooks went on regardless, his voice dropping. "If I was a betting man, I'd say this one..." A slim index finger poked the smallest key away from the rest. "...likely opens the side door at the livery."

"Don't be ridiculous," Alan snapped, snatching the set of keys. "These belong to the Marjoram Homestead Inn. Says so clear on the label here."

"Yeah," Fooks agreed. "I can see what it says," he said pointedly.

"Well, there's one way to settle this. Let's ride out there!" Alan yelled.

"Alan, calm down. I'm sure there is a simple explanation," Bennett said.

"You bet there is."

"We don't need to ride anywhere. Walk down to the livery will tell us." Fooks held his left hand out. "The keys, please, Mr. Long."

Fooks met Alan's eyes and held them fast, well aware his face revealed his determination to get at the truth. He also projected just enough menace, he hoped, to unsettle the other man.

Alan glanced down. Fooks' right hand, the thumb still tucked in his gun belt, shifted slightly to the right, nearer to his gun. Alan took in every detail, especially the well-worn holster.

"You wear ya gun tied down, Crane. D'ya know how to use it?" he asked slowly.

"I'm no gunfighter, Mr. Long, but yeah, I know how to use it." Fooks lowered his voice. "If I have need." He didn't take his eyes from Alan's face.

Alan swallowed hard before holding out the keys. He hesitated and then dropped them into the waiting hand. With a disgusted snarl, he shook his head slightly.

"Thank you."

Bennett let out a deep breath as the tension in the room dissipated.

Fooks glanced at Bennett, aware that the sheriff thought him a pain in the neck, with his cavalier attitude to rules and his lighthearted manner. Fooks figured Bennett now thought this deceptive and that he was a much more ominous figure. Like a notorious outlaw, perhaps? *Watch your step, Fooks. Don't give him any more reasons to speculate.*

Bennett glanced at Alan. Not usually a man easily cowed, Alan shook his head, cross more with himself than Crane.

"Close up, and we'll get along to the livery," Fooks whispered, weary all of a sudden.

He moved to the window and looked out. Nice view all the way down Main Street. He hadn't enjoyed facing down Long. Not on his own. Usually, Swan was there to back him up. Alan didn't wear a gun, so he had to be content with the knowledge *he* did.

Bennett supervised Alan as he put the other sets of keys back and locking the cupboard. When ready, both waited for Fooks. He continued to stare out of the window until he felt their eyes upon him. He looked around and stood up.

"Pleasant view you have from up here," he said with a bright grin. "Can see a long way." He pinched his bottom lip and stole a sly glance back. "Do you have a rifle, Mr. Long?"

Alan glared at Fooks as he moved away from the window.

"I told ya before, Crane. I did not shoot at you last night."

"Ha!" Fooks tossed his head and grinned. "Interesting."

Alan was about to speak, but Fooks continued. "Y'see, when the sheriff told you earlier about the attempted murder, 'cause that's what we're talking about, after all, of my friend and me, I don't recall him saying the weapon used." Fooks smiled. "You've assumed me asking if you have a rifle is because of last night's incident." He flashed a wide, smug grin. "Kinda interesting, don't you think?"

"Alan, I've seen ya with a rifle a time or two," Bennett said. Tension crackled again between the Fooks and Alan. Bennet's fingers closed around the butt of his gun in case of trouble.

Alan glanced at Bennett before turning his gaze back to Fooks. "Yeah, I have a rifle, Crane. What of it?"

"May I see it?"

Alan glanced at Bennett.

"Better do as he says, Alan."

Alan stared icily at Fooks before tossing his head. "In the cupboard by the stairs."

Fooks dropped to the chair between the window and table and waited.

"What? Ya want me to wait on ya as well?" Alan snapped. When Fooks replied with a tight-lipped smile, Alan tutted and stomped out onto the landing.

"Ya're pushing it a little, ain't ya?" Bennett asked in a low growl.

"Maybe," Fooks admitted. "Seems to be working," he added with a sniff before turning his attention to the keys in his hand. *So much for not giving Bennett any further cause to look more closely at me. When would he learn?*

Fooks' gamble paid off. Alan brought back a rifle, but Fooks knew at first glance it wasn't the one used to shoot at him. Alan unbuckled the leather scabbard and removed a Sharps single-shot rifle. Two of the shots the previous evening had come in quick succession. No one could reload that fast. No, this was definitely not the rifle used.

Alan made a grand show of presenting it to Fooks, palms up. He even nodded his head in deference.

Fooks took it and went through the motions of inspecting it. He broke the rifle and peered down the chambers. Empty, as he expected. No sign the rifle had fired recently.

"Very nice. Thank you," he said with a smile. He put the rifle on the table but left his hand on it. Alan went to pick it up, but Fooks' hand tightened. "Now, show me the one in the back of the cupboard," he said, weary of playing games.

Fooks studied Alan's face. He blinked in surprise.

"W-what d'ya mean? This..."

Behind Alan, Bennett stepped out onto the landing. They heard rummaging, and then he reappeared, holding another rifle, this time a Winchester repeating rifle.

Ah, that's more like it. Fooks fought the smug smile forming on his lips as he kept his eyes locked on Alan.

"That's not mine," Alan said quickly. "You asked me specifically if I had a rifle." He gestured at the rifle on the table.

"Must we trouble ourselves with splitting hairs, Mr. Long?" Fooks accepted the rifle Bennett handed him. "Makes so much mess."

Alan had a sour face, as if he were chewing a lemon, and he glanced at Bennett, who shrugged.

This time when Fooks broke the rifle and found it empty, he lifted the breech to his nose and sniffed. He turned the rifle around and peered down the barrel. He turned the rifle back, ran his forefinger across the end, and rubbed his thumb over his finger before sniffing it. He slowly looked at Alan.

"This rifle has been fired recently." Alan took a step backward. "Sheriff Bennett, please arrest Mr. Long for the attempted murder of me and my friend last night." Fooks was casual in his request.

"Oh, now, wait a minute, Crane," Alan said, backing away. Bennett moved towards him. "I had nothing to do with that. I told you I wasn't here."

"Then where were you? Can someone provide you with an alibi?"

"Ya'd better answer the question, Alan," Bennett advised.

"You're not serious about taking the word of this...this..." Alan spluttered.

"I'm sure we can straighten it all out. Where were ya, Alan?" Bennett persisted.

"Er, well, I...was with a friend. Someone I don't want dragging into this." Alan swallowed hard.

"Who?"

"I'm sure we can straighten this all out, Sheriff." Fooks pushed to his feet slowly. "Down at the jail," he added, his hand creeping closer to his gun.

Alan's eyes flicked from one to the other as he considered his options.

"Arrest him, Sheriff. Until he can give us the name of someone who can corroborate his story."

Bennett hesitated, and Fooks held up the recently fired rifle.

A while later, with Alan Long protesting about his treatment and threatening to sue the pants off everyone in sight, Bennett closed the cellblock door. He slid the bolt across and turned to Fooks.

"Let him cool his heels there for a while, and mebbe he'll be more forthcoming with some answers." Bennett regarded Fooks. "How did ya know there was another rifle?"

"I didn't," Fooks replied. "Push a man hard enough, sometimes they tell you what you want to know all by themselves."

"Crane, I don't like your methods."

"Neither do I, Sheriff," Fooks said, shaking his head, hands on hips. "But I sense the veil is lifting. Suggest you keep him there while we check out his alibi. If he has one."

Fooks took a deep breath. "In the meantime, I'm gonna try these keys in the livery, and then there are a few more questions I want to ask Tubby."

CHAPTER NINETEEN

Fooks walked from the alley by the side of the livery with a smug smile. As he suspected, the smaller key on the set opened the side door. He tucked the keys away in the inside pocket of his red and green plaid coat. Next stop, Tubby.

"Tubby, tell me about the day Alan delivered the chest." Fooks settled on the edge of a desk.

"What d'you want to know, exactly?"

Fooks wasn't sure. "Take me through the sequence of events," he said with a splutter. "Alan turns up with the chest from Celia. Does he manage alone?" Fooks sat on the edge of the desk.

"No, sir. I went out and helped him."

"Was there a tarp?"

"Tarp?"

"Yeah. Back up a bit. Start from the beginning." Fooks narrowed his eyes at Tubby.

A moment later, the penny having dropped, the younger man's face lit up. "Alan came into the office, saying he had a chest to deliver for Mr. Mercer from Mrs. Thorold. He asked me to give him a hand, as it's heavy. When I went outside, the chest was under a tarp. We hauled the chest in, and it hasn't moved since." Tubby pointed to the chest in the corner.

Fooks considered the chest, swinging his leg.

"Who ended up with the folded tarp?"

"I don't understand."

"Did you and Alan fold the tarp together?"

"Yes, sir."

"Which of you two ended up with it?"

Tubby thought back. Finally, he shrugged. "Me, I think." He frowned.

"And what did you do with it?"

Tubby thought harder. In the end, he plumped for, "Well, I gave it back to Alan, of course."

"Did this happen outside? Before you brought the chest in?"

"I don't recall exactly, sir. Left on, the tarp would get in the way."

Fooks smacked his lips. "Thank you, Tubby. Now I want to ask you something else. You said, the day Stephen died, Mrs. Mercer came into the office as you were leaving."

"Yes, sir."

"Can you remember what time this was?"

"Yes, sir. I always leave promptly at six. You and Sheriff Bennett caught me the other evening just as I was leaving." Tubby cleared his throat. "On the day Mr. Mercer died, I was about to leave when Mrs. Mercer arrived. I held the door open for her."

Fooks nodded, taking in what Tubby said.

"You also said you thought you heard Mrs. Mercer encourage Stephen to open the chest?"

"Yes, sir."

"Someone came up to you and steered you away from the door. Who was that?"

"Tyler Callaghan."

"Tyler Callaghan?" Fooks raised an eyebrow. He'd expected another name. "What did he want?"

Tubby blinked. "We're good friends. I hadn't seen him for a while."

You didn't say this before," Fooks said sharply, "when I asked you about school friends."

Tubby reddened. "I'm sorry. I thought you meant people involved in the cases. The ones Mr. Mercer represented."

Fooks had, so he accepted his oversight.

"You are still friends? Even though your boss represented a client Tyler was pursuing via the court?"

Tubby showed surprise. "Well, yes, sir. Nothing to do with me personally. Tyler and me, we've been friends for years. Since school."

"I thought you had problems with kids at school. Calling you names and such."

"Yes, sir, but Tyler was never one of 'em. He always stuck up for me."

Fooks tried a different tack. "Okay, he came up to you, and the two of you walked away from the office door here."

"Yes, sir."

"How long did you talk for?"

"Oh, a few minutes. Tyler had to see someone."

"Who?"

"He didn't say."

"Okay. Did you notice Mrs. Mercer leave the office?"

"Yes."

"How long afterward?"

Tubby thought for a moment. "Hmmm. About five minutes, I suppose. After I said goodbye to Tyler, I crossed the street, and as I did so, I looked back and saw Mrs. Mercer leave."

"How did she seem?"

"I was behind her, and she walked away from me quickly."

"Where did she go?"

"Up the street aways, but I really wasn't paying her any attention, sir."

"All right, Tubby. Thank you." Fooks pursed his lips. "Did you see where Tyler went?"

"No, sir. I'm sorry, sir. I was anxious to get home. Ma is not well, and..."

Fooks smiled. "All right, Tubby. You're not in any trouble. In fact, you've been very helpful."

"I have?"

"Yes."

On the way back to the jail from Stephen's office, Fooks walked past the hotel. Rev was sitting on the porch, nose in his Bible. Fooks silently slid into the chair by Rev's side. He leaned back and tilted his hat low over his eyes.

"Did the sheriff arrest Alan Long?" Rev asked casually.

"Yep. Suspect in the incident last night. Can't prove anything yet. There's enough to hold him until someone gives him an alibi."

Rev nodded, not surprised. "Want me to do anything?"

"Yes. Ask around the stores opposite and around Stephen's office. The day Stephen died, Alan Long delivered a chest covered by a tarp. Tubby helped haul it inside, but I need to be sure if they removed the tarp beforehand. The tarp may still be there when they hauled it inside. One of them is lying, and I need to find out who."

"Why is that important?"

"Because Celia says, when the chest left her, there was no padlock. If she's telling us the truth, someone must have put it there before getting to Stephen's office."

"Long seems the most likely, boy."

"Yes, and he's saying it wasn't there. What better place to hide a padlock than under a tarp? We also need to rule out the other possibility. Someone put the padlock on *in* Stephen's office."

"So, you want me to ask if anyone noticed a padlock on the chest during delivery."

Fooks twitched his head. "Would only stand a chance of spotting it if they took the tarp off outside. You can try, but I'm not sure if anyone would remember that amount of detail."

"I'll give it a go. Ya never know."

"Here's something else. Tubby says Lucinda visited the office as he left for the day, about six. He also said Tyler Callaghan stopped him. Tyler went somewhere after speaking to Tubby. Where?" Fooks smacked his lips. "I've an awful feeling, Rev."

He shook his head and jiggled the livery keys in his hand. "Another thing. These are the keys to the livery stables. And guess what?" He grinned and held up the smaller key. "This is the key to the side door. The one not used but with the recently oiled lock."

Rev took the keys from Fooks and studied the appropriate one.

"What are you thinking, boy?" he asked, handing them back.

"I'm thinking Stephen died in his office but someone moved his body into the livery. Tried to disguise his death by setting fire to the livery. Nearly worked, too." Fooks bit his lip thoughtfully. "I've narrowed the suspects, and top of my list is Mr. Alan Long. He won't say where he was last night, and the shooting at us can't be a coincidence. Now, that's not the action of an honest man, is it?"

Rev shrugged. "Dunno." He paused, tongue in cheek. "Long time since I met one."

Fooks rolled his eyes.

Fooks sat pondering his artwork on the sheriff's wall. The amount of string crisscrossing his graphical representation made it resemble a spider's web. He paced, moved strings about, and added more. He paced again. He poured coffee for himself. Bennett sat at his desk, trying to deal with paperwork. Rev sat at the absent deputy's desk, nose in his Bible.

"I must be missing something," Fooks said suddenly. Bennett and Rev both jumped. Rev knocked over the reading lamp and scrambled to stand it up quickly before the oil leaked out. "Any thoughts, gentlemen?"

"Strange how all the female suspects in this case are blonde," Rev said.

"Is that significant?" Bennett asked.

Fooks was about ready to consider anything, however remote. Finally, he shook his head. "I doubt it is, but if so, it's a helluva clue we're overlooking."

He studied the wall critically. "There are too many possibilities. We need to start eliminatin'" He stood, hands on hips. "Gentlemen. I need your attention."

"Sure thing," said Rev, sitting up straight, ready to begin.

"Why not? This paperwork is good at doing itself. Don't need me," agreed Bennett, throwing down his pencil.

"The murderer has to be someone in this group. I haven't come across anyone else it might be." He waited for the others to nod their agreement. "Let's start with Emmett. He has no means, no motive, and no opportunity to kill Stephen. Agreed?"

Rev and Bennett grunted in confirmation. Fooks unpinned the strings connecting Emmett to the rest.

"Next I'm gonna eliminate Martha. She has the knowledge, but she had no reason to kill Stephen."

He unstrung Martha from the board.

"Now Preston." Fooks leaned back against the desk and folded his arms. "I don't think it's him, but we only have his word he lost his padlock three months ago. He might have kept it for later use. He stays for now. That leaves us with Celia, Tyler, Alan, and Lucinda Mercer. Apart from Stephen, what are the links?"

"Lucinda's been pretty free with her extramarital affections," Rev offered.

"Yeah, Preston and Alan. She's not the only one, though. We believe Celia dallied with Alan as well, and we're not sure if there's anything between her and Stephen."

"Tyler and Alan are friends," said Bennett.

"Really?" Fooks frowned.

"Yeah, Tubby said so. Remember?" Bennett grinned ruefully when he saw Fooks' disgusted face.

"Yeah, I remember now."

Rev cut a length of string and dangled it out to Fooks. He applied the string to the diagram and took a step back.

"Curious how Alan's name keeps coming up." Fooks waved a hand at the wall. "He has links to everyone because they're all friends. Since school." He walked over to the diagram. "They were all there together. Preston, Tyler, Alan, Celia's late husband, Charlie." He waved a hand at each person's sheet before turning to the ones he'd already eliminated. "Emmett, Martha, and..."

Suddenly he swallowed hard and blanched.

"Are ya alright?" Bennett asked.

"Yes," Fooks said. "They were all at school...with...Tubby. He's not...here." His eyes widened in realization. "Oh, sheesh! I never considered."

Bennett stared, open-mouthed, and then his face spread into a grin. "Oh, now, Crane—"

Fooks regarded Bennett with wide eyes. "We shouldn't dismiss him outta hand. Rev, find me a fresh sheet of paper for Tubby. Then we've got some more stringing to do."

With a revised diagram to study, Fooks stepped back and contemplated it. Bennett returned to his paperwork. Rev excused himself, saying they had missed lunch. He came back sometime later with three sandwiches wrapped in wax paper. One went to Bennett, who seemed surprised, but he nodded his thanks. Rev leaned against the desk next to Fooks, unwrapped one sandwich, and nudged Fooks' arm.

Fooks glanced around and shook his head. Rev insisted.

"Gotta keep ya strength up, boy. Ya can't solve a murder on an empty stomach. Eat."

Fooks huffed, accepted the offered sandwich, and took a bite. "Hmmm, needed this," he murmured. His eyes hadn't left the diagram.

Bennett watched him for a while. "What reason would Tubby have for murdering Stephen? He had a good job—"

"Yes." Fooks settled on the edge of the desk. "Lucinda Mercer said Tubby merged into the background. Folks didn't always realize he was there. Imagine what it must be like, day in, day out. Doing all the work. Not getting any recognition. Someone else...Stephen taking all the credit. Earning the big bucks. Top legislators fawning over him."

"Tubby is..." Bennett trailed off with a pained expression. "One of the first things ya said to me," he conceded quietly, "a motive doesn't always have to make sense."

"Exactly."

"I can't believe it. Not Tubby."

"But everything fits." Fooks straightened his shoulders. "How's this? Preston showed him the padlock with the secret compartment, and this gets him thinking. He steals it and waits for the right time. Tubby said, every time Stephen went to the Thorold place, he always admired the chest. When Celia sent the chest to Stephen as a thank you, Tubby was here when the chest came. Musta seemed like the perfect opportunity. He coulda slipped the padlock on while Alan and Stephen talked. When Tubby hands Alan the tarp, Alan looks back at the chest, and the padlock is on. So, Alan and Celia are both right."

"A mite far-fetched," Rev said.

Fooks pulled a face. "I know. Too many unanswered questions, and I'm not sure..." He took another bite from his sandwich. Rev patiently waited as Fooks chewed. "Not sure who can answer them."

"You oughta make a list," Rev suggested.

Fooks shook his head doubtfully. "Gonna be a lengthy list."

Rev tapped a fresh sheet of paper. When Fooks didn't move, he held out a pencil. Fooks took it and sat behind the desk. He scribbled immediately, sandwich forgotten.

It was some time before he sat up and held his list at arm's length.

"This is what I've come up with. No particular order." Making sure Bennett and Rev were listening, he read, "Who put the aconite in the padlock?"

He waited for a reaction. Other than pulling faces and shrugs, none. He offered his own explanation.

"Preston told me he showed everyone how the padlock worked. Tubby would know what to do."

"Where did he get the aconite from?" Bennett asked. "Apart from the doc, Martha seems to be the only one who knows how to use it, an' ya've already dismissed her."

Fooks winced and added the question to his list.

"Who stole the padlocks? Was it Tubby? Or someone else?" More face pulling and shrugs.

"Still not convinced it's Tubby," Bennett said, shaking his head.

"I don't want it to be, either." Fooks twitched a brief smile in sympathy. "I've outlined how Tubby mighta done it, and I'm trying real hard to be objective about this. Let's see where this list takes us, huh?"

Bennett directed Fooks to continue with his list.

"Was there something between Celia and Alan?"

"Hearsay, I reckon," Bennett said, turning to Rev for confirmation.

"More 'n' likely, but like ya say, nothing to prove it," Rev agreed.

"Okay." Fooks returned to his list. "How did Tyler Callaghan get his ranch?"

"Ah, now, that I know," Bennett said and grinned. "He inherited from his pa 'bout three years ago. Why is it important?"

"He seemed kinda young. Most cattle barons I've met are in their middling years at least. Does he have any problems? I mean, apart from with Celia."

"Well, his pa didn't leave things too tidy, and he had a tough time at first. Seems to have turned things around lately. I reckon he's doing alright now."

"Hmmm." Fooks flattened his lips. "Was it sudden? His change of fortune."

Bennett pulled a face. "I'm just a small-town sheriff. I don't know the intricacies behind the finances of cattle ranching."

"Okay. What time did Alan tell you Coleman and Murphy were in town?"

Bennett considered the question. "Kinda late. I was locking up. 'Bout ten, I reckon."

"Hmmm, wonder what took him so long before he came to you. I got the impression Emmett was in town with him a lot earlier."

Bennett shrugged.

Fooks continued with his list.

"Was there something between Celia and Stephen?"

"Reckon only Celia can answer that one," Rev said.

"You volunteering to ask her?" Fooks asked.

Rev laughed. "Oh, not me, boy."

Fooks flashed a quick grin. *Yep, thought that'd be the case.* He returned to his list.

"Why is Alan trying to drive Martha from her house?"

"He says he's not," Bennett said.

Fooks gnawed at his thumbnail. "Yeah, he sounded plausible, but I can't help feeling...I dunno. The next question is the biggie. If Stephen died in his office, how did he end up in the livery?"

Bennett and Rev had no answers, either. He hesitated before suggesting his theory.

"Stephen cut his hand on the padlock. It made him ill, and he died. Someone moved his body into the livery and set the fire, hoping to cover up his murder. What I can't get at yet is who." He rolled his eyes. "I sure hope it's not Tubby."

"Frustrating. Sounds like ya nearly got it, boy."

"Yeah, I reckon so, too. There's one more question. The answer might unlock the whole mystery. Who shot at me and Rev? You're holding Alan, but he hasn't admitted it." Fooks glanced at the cellblock door behind him. "Perhaps this friend who owns the rifle is the same one with Alan last night."

"You mean he's protecting the real shooter?" Bennett suggested.

"Yes." Fooks laid his list down carefully. "Makes sense." He pushed up. "We're not gonna learn anymore tonight. I'll tackle Alan again tomorrow. Time for a drink, Rev."

CHAPTER TWENTY

The next day found Fooks once again in Bennett's office.

"How's your prisoner?" he asked after pleasantries had been exchanged.

"Quiet."

"Is he talking?"

"Nope. 'Less ya count threatening to sue for wrongful arrest. I had to send a telegram to his lawyer in Laramie. Reckon he'll be here later."

Fooks nodded. "We'll need more evidence to hold him."

"Yep, an' unless we get it, we're in a heap of trouble. I went along with arresting him yesterday because I agreed with your suspicions. When his lawyer gets involved—"

"Yeah, I understand." Fooks handed Bennett his gun. He sniffed and hitched up his pants. "Okay, let me in there, and I'll see what I can do."

The look on the sheriff's face told Fooks that Bennett didn't fancy his chances. Bennett went to slide the catch open, but Fooks stopped him.

Fooks did it instead, putting a finger across his lips to indicate silence. He opened the door a crack and peeped into the cellblock. Alan had his back to the door and didn't react to the door opening.

Bennett's face morphed into his usual frown at Fooks' actions. He watched as Fooks sneaked in.

Fooks licked his lips with devilment. He came to a silent halt by the side of Alan's cell.

"Morning," he sang brightly. His lips twitched into a smile when Alan jumped.

Alan scowled at him. "What d'you want?"

"Wondering how you were this morning. Has a night in jail loosened your tongue?"

"It's cold in here. And the bunk is hard and lumpy."

"I'll tell Bennett to improve his prisoner hospitality skills."

"My lawyer will be here later."

"Yes, and no doubt, he will advise you to name the person who can give you an alibi."

Alan turned away.

"Making yourself veerry guilty." Fooks rolled his eyes and his r's.

Alan took a deep breath.

"Whoever this person is, they must be a good friend for you to withhold their name from the law like this."

Alan didn't answer.

Fooks folded his arms.

"This is a small town, Alan. A lot of tongues wag on things that are none of their business. I suspect, if Rev asks around enough, he can find out where you were that night."

Alan turned his head slightly, a gesture not lost on Fooks. Must be getting through.

"Co-operation might get you outta here quicker."

Alan took another deep breath.

Fooks took a different tack. "Of course, if you name this person, you'd have to have some trust in 'em."

"I trust her," Alan snapped. Then he realized what he'd said and tapped his forehead, annoyed with himself.

"Ah! You've made up," Fooks said before he could stop himself. At the same time, he hoped he'd assumed correctly. *Would be embarrassing if I'm wrong.*

Alan's shoulders slumped in defeat.
"All right!" He licked his lips. "I was with Lucinda Mercer," he said finally.
"Thank you."
Fooks walked away.

Bennett sent a deputy to find Lucinda Mercer.
"Took a closer look at the rifle last night. Found this." Bennett held out the rifle to Fooks, stock forward. "On the end."
Fooks found a stamp. "LF?" He frowned. "Must be the initials of the friend it belongs to."
"Possibly. Y'know..." Bennett paused, chewing his bottom lip thoughtfully. "Lucinda Mercer is a crack shot."
Fooks' head flew up. "What?" he asked, wide-eyed.
"Yeah, surprising, ain't it? She's won two rifle-shooting contests here, once when the Mercers first came to Angelworth and another last year. She wiped the floor with the rest of the competitors. Organizers asked her not to enter no more to give other folks a chance. Haven't seen her with a rifle since, but I don't suppose it's something ya forget how to do so quickly."
An image of a half-covered poster sprang into Fooks' mind. He'd seen it on the day he'd arrived in Angelworth. The winner's initials had been LM. *That was it. M for Mercer.* "No, I don't suppose it is," Fooks murmured. He paled at the significance and swallowed hard. "Another question to ask Mrs. Mercer."
While they waited, their discussion covered other things, laughing at family life and swapping stories of employee relations. Fooks was careful not to be too specific about his recollections.
Rev's arrival interrupted their conversation.

"Hi, Rev," Fooks said with a grin.

"Morning," Rev said, tipping his hat to both.

"Help yaself to some coffee," Bennett said, and at Rev's gape of surprise, he added, "Crane said ya'd be along."

"Don't mind if I do."

Fooks and Bennett waited for Rev to settle in the absent deputy's chair and deposit his wide-brimmed hat on the desk.

"Spoke to the storekeepers opposite. Messenger boy from the telegraph office remembers the chest delivery. Then only 'cause he nearly ran into them as he went 'bout his business."

Fooks sat up. "Well?"

"He says Tubby and Alan Long struggled to turn the thing around so they could get through the office door. Boy got curious about what it was, all wrapped up in a tarp, so he asked. Long told him to mind his nose and get outta the way."

Fooks looked disappointed. "So, Tubby was lying. He said they removed the tarp before bringing the chest into the office. His exact words were, 'The tarp would've gotten in the way if we'd left it on.'"

Fooks rose, planning to go ask Tubby right then. He stopped when Lucinda Mercer arrived. Fooks nodded at Rev to go, and Rev slipped out discretely.

"There better be a good reason for dragging me away like this, Mark," she huffed in greeting.

"Yes, ma'am. Please take a seat," Bennett said politely, offering her a chair.

Fooks filled his coffee cup, keeping his back to them on purpose. Best if Bennett asked the salient point. He would jump in later.

"Ma'am, would you tell me where you were night before last?" Bennett asked when she'd flounced into the offered chair.

"At home, of course. Where else would I be?" She pulled off her gloves.

"Were you alone?"

Lucinda looked sharply at Bennett. "What are you implying?"

Fooks looked round, surprised at her hostility. He met Bennett's eyes and rolled his own.

"I'm not implying anything, ma'am. You'll have heard about the shooting that night," Bennett said matter-of-factly.

"Of course." Lucinda gave the sheriff a weak smile. "I hope you weren't hurt, Mr. Crane," she said graciously.

"No, ma'am. My friend and I survived unscathed. My suit, on the other hand, may never recover." He smiled.

"I'm holding a suspect right now," Bennett said.

"Oh, that's good," Lucinda said. The smile didn't reach her eyes.

"It's Alan Long."

Lucinda audibly sucked in a breath, and she stared at Bennett, open-mouthed. Then she let out a short laugh. "Alan? Oh, that's ridiculous. He wouldn't do such a thing."

"He says, ma'am, he was with you that night. That true?"

Lucinda went still. She opened her mouth several times before the words would come. "I-I hardly know him. How dare he?" She struggled into her gloves and prepared to stand.

"What time did he arrive?" Fooks asked and casually took a sip of coffee.

Lucinda stared at him. "I don't—"

"No matter, but seeing as you're here, would you answer some questions about your husband?"

Fooks settled on the desk, communicating the foregone conclusion she would stay.

"Our investigation into his murder has reached a crucial point, y'see."

Lucinda swallowed and, with resigned dignity, retook her seat. "Very well," she said begrudgingly.

"Thank you. Did you see your husband the day he died?"

"Of course. We ate breakfast together as usual before he left for the office."

"Did you see him later in the day?"

Lucinda paused before answering. Fooks studied her. Under his intense gaze, she shifted uncomfortably.

"Yes," she admitted. The answer appeared to have been wrung out of her.

"When was this?"

Lucinda considered this. Trying to appear casual, she said, "Ooh, I suppose it must have been in the afternoon sometime."

"Hmmm, a little vague. Can you be more specific?"

"No. I...I really can't. I'm not in the habit of logging my movements to the minute."

Fooks tried a different tack. "Early or late afternoon? After lunch or nearer suppertime?"

Lucinda shrugged. "I don't remember, Mr. Crane."

"Was Tubby in the office when you got there?"

Lucinda appeared to give this some thought before finally shaking her head. "No, I don't believe so."

Fooks widened his eyes. "You don't recall whether your husband's clerk was present?"

Lucinda shook her head in confusion. "No, why would I?" Realizing that what she'd said demanded more explanation, she added, "He...he merges into the background. I don't always realize he's around."

"Hmmm. You don't remember him holding the door for you?"

"Why should I? The door was open, and I walked through. If he held the door, I didn't notice him." She shrugged. "But he's a polite young man. I suppose it wouldn't be unusual."

"Yes, he is. I'm surprised you think this," Fooks said rather curtly, "given you barely notice him."

"What do you mean?" she demanded.

Fooks touched the tip of his tongue to his top lip. "Mrs. Mercer, I am talking about the day of your husband's murder. Someone you lived with. Someone you loved. I can tell you from personal experience, every single moment of that day is ingrained in our memory."

Fooks put more fire into the comment than he'd intended. He and Lucinda locked eyes in a battle of wills.

"Well, not mine, Mr. Crane. It's a day I'm trying to forget."

Lucinda won the battle. Fooks put down his head, a muscle in his cheek twitching, ashamed at how easily his personal feelings had intruded.

"Now, is there anything else? I have a lot to do." She rose to her feet.

Fooks snapped his head up. "Yes, Mrs. Mercer, there is. Sit down!"

Bennett shifted, growling a warning. Fooks acknowledged the rebuke.

Up until now, Fooks had affected the appearance of a mild-mannered gentleman with an easygoing countenance. Did Lucinda recognize the command and menace in his voice just now? Was he frightening her?

He received his answer when she retook her seat.

"What else do you wish to know?" Her voice shuddered, and she smoothed her hair, a comforting gesture.

"Did Stephen show you the chest Celia Thorold gave him?"

"Oh, that silly chest! He'd talked of little else for weeks," she blurted out before collecting herself. "Yes, he showed me."

"Did he...?" Now that he'd come to it, Fooks struggled to ask the question. He didn't want to hear the answer. "While you were with Stephen, did you encourage him to open the padlock?"

It was a while before Lucinda answered, and when she did, it was in a small voice. "Yes," she admitted, "but he didn't need any encouragement. He'd coveted the chest for months. Heaven knows why."

Fooks sought Bennett's approval to continue. They'd agreed Fooks would take the lead in the questioning. Bennett gave him a reassuring nod.

After a swallow, Fooks opened his mouth, hesitating. "Did anything happen, Mrs. Mercer, when Stephen opened the padlock?"

Lucinda shuddered and closed her eyes. "Like what?" she asked.

Fooks ran a hand over his mouth, considering what to say.

"Did something unexpected happen, Mrs. Mercer?" Bennett said.

She nodded slowly.

"What was it?"

"He..." Lucinda waved her hand casually. "The padlock was old, and the edges are sharp. He cut his hand."

"What happened next?" Fooks asked.

"As you might expect, he jumped back in surprise."

"Did you see the cut?"

"Yes."

"Was it deep?"

"I'm not a doctor," Lucinda said. "It was bloody." She swallowed hard. "Stephen put it to his mouth, and I suggested he use a bandage, but he said it was fine."

Bennett and Fooks swapped glances again.

"Then what happened?" Fooks asked slowly.

"He said he would work late and not to expect him for supper. I left him to it."

"How did he seem when you left?"

"Fine." She swallowed. "He was fine," she breathed. "Can I go now, Mark? Please."

Bennett was sympathetic and about to say yes when Fooks held up his hand.

"I have one more question, Mrs. Mercer, and then you can go." His tone was now more kindly.

Bennett smiled at Lucinda and gave Fooks the go-ahead to continue.

"When you left the office, did anyone go in?"

Lucinda stared at Fooks. Her face, already drained of color, paled even more. Her breath shuddered. "I...I...don't know. Maybe..." She swallowed hard.

"So, there mighta been someone. Who d'you think it might have been?" Fooks asked gently.

Lucinda gasped. "You...said." She sniffed. "Only one more question." On the verge of tears, she struggled to control herself.

"I did, but this is a question I need to ask, ma'am." Fooks took a seat at her side. "I think it's a question you want me to ask," he added quietly. He gazed at her. "Isn't it?"

"Yes." Lucinda sniffed. She gasped for breath. "I saw..." She swallowed hard and licked her lips. "They didn't mean to kill him," she cried. "That was never the plan."

CHAPTER TWENTY-ONE

A sob escaped from Lucinda, a sudden dam burst. Trembling, she covered her face with her hands and rocked back and forth.

The two men looked on helplessly, neither comfortable with feminine tears. Lucinda's distress was heart-wrenching, not attention-seeking. Fooks, being nearest, rested a hand on her shoulder.

"I'm sorry, ma'am, I have to ask, who you are talking about?" At that moment, he knew the answer wasn't worth the pain he'd inflicted.

Bennett frantically searched his desk for anything remotely like a handkerchief. Coming up empty, he had to resort to collecting the towel from by the stove to act as a substitute. This, he thrust at Fooks, who gave him a look of disbelief. Bennett responded with an "I couldn't find anything else" expression.

"I'll get some water," Bennett said, and he moved away in a hurry to do so.

Lucinda sobbed uncontrollably. Both men saw her trying to hold the tears back, trying to maintain some control over her emotions. Both saw her losing the battle.

"I loved him so much." Lucinda snatched the towel from Fooks' grasp, and he blinked in surprise. It didn't look clean. She dabbed at her eyes, but the gesture did nothing to stem the tide of tears and mascara streaming down her cheeks. "I just wanted him to spend more time with me," she wailed before folding over again, her shoulders shaking with her grief.

Fooks met Bennett's eyes and swallowed hard. Bennett appeared as shocked as Fooks felt. Neither had expected this.

"Here," Bennett whispered, holding out the glass of water.

Fooks placed it near Lucinda. With no sign of her crying stopping, Fooks glanced at Bennett again, helpless. Bennett inclined his head and gave Fooks a reassuring smile. Fooks rolled his eyes in reply and laid a hand on Lucinda's arm.

"Ma'am?"

With another glance at Bennett for moral support, Fooks fixed a smile to his face, which he didn't feel.

"Ma'am, let it all out. It may not seem it right now, but what you're doing is the best thing. Shows you cared deeply for Stephen."

Lucinda gave a loud sniff, and her head came up. She wiped her face, sat up, and sniffed some more. A shaking hand reached for the glass. Fooks handed it to her and steadied her as she took several gulps. She wiped her eyes again and examined the black stains on the towel without interest.

"Oh, I must look a complete fright," she gasped. "I'm sorry."

Fooks smiled at her as he took back the glass. "Feeling better?"

Lucinda sniffed. "Yes. A little." She shook her head at Fooks and then at Bennett. "I did nothing, Sheriff," she choked. "That was the problem. I didn't...*do* anything. I should have stopped it. Oh, God! Poor Stephen."

Fresh tears flowed, and she dabbed at them. "I didn't want any of this to happen. I just wanted..." She sniffed. "...Stephen to show me some attention."

She sniffed again and reached for the glass. With a tight-lipped smile, Fooks handed it to her. He watched her drink.

"I know this is hard, ma'am. I need to know what happened. Will you tell me?" he asked gently.

Lucinda took a deep breath. "Yes. I will. A moment, please."

"Take ya time, Mrs. Mercer," Bennett said, drawing up a chair.

Lucinda scrubbed roughly at her eyes, sniffed, and gave Fooks a weak smile. He returned a genuine smile of sympathy overlain with relief at her recovery, albeit slight.

"Stephen worked hard. I appreciated how important his work was to him, always had been. Even before our marriage, I knew he was a man determined to make a name for himself. He liked causes. Particularly if..." She sniffed "...his work involved an underdog. Or..." She glanced at Fooks. "Or a matter of public importance deserving justice."

Fooks shifted uncomfortably. *Does she know who I am?* He shook himself. *You're getting paranoid, Fooks. Stop it.*

Lucinda dabbed her eyes before continuing.

"He found a few such cases here recently. He was so busy. I hardly saw him." She gasped. "I was so lonely."

She took her time. When she continued, her voice shuddered with her unhappiness and relief at finally being able to tell her story.

"When...certain other men showed me attention, I hoped Stephen would realize he was driving me away. Then we could talk. Put it behind us." She swallowed hard, her fingers tearing at Bennett's towel. "On reflection, that wasn't the way to do things. It only seemed to drive him further away from me."

Fresh tears flowed, and she scrubbed at them. Sniffing, she took hold of herself. "He began seeing Celia Thorold, and then..." She raised her eyes to the ceiling. "...Martha Pickering. That's when I knew I'd lost him. If he preferred someone like that to me." She shook her head in despair.

Fooks and Bennett's eyes met. Was now the time to reveal the true reason for Stephen's visits with Martha? Surely, Lucinda must know about his headaches? Fooks decided he had to ask. He took a moment to consider how to broach the subject.

"Martha helped Stephen with his headaches, ma'am."

"H-headaches?" Lucinda blinked rapidly. She shook herself. "Yes. Yes, of course. You mean, he went to her...for a cure?"

"Yes, ma'am." Fooks scanned Lucinda as she sobbed again.

"Oh, no!" she wailed. "He didn't tell me. I thought..." Lucinda doubled over, wracked with sobs.

Fooks blinked, finding his own eyes wet. Bennett, equally affected, closed his eyes and shook his head. Both men realized that a couple's inability to communicate with one another had led to a deadly conclusion.

"Ma'am, will you tell us what happened?" Fooks asked.

Lucinda gasped and sat up, her face streaked with tears and mascara, beyond caring. She took a few deep breaths.

"You said there was a plan but they didn't mean to kill him. Who are 'they'?" Bennett pushed, receiving a glare from Fooks.

"Yes, we had a plan." Lucinda swallowed. "Tyler Callaghan and Alan thought it up."

"Was Tubby involved?"

"Tubby? No, of course not. Why do you think it involved him?"

Fooks shrugged and pulled a face.

"Never mind. Carry on, ma'am."

"I didn't..." She shook her head and swallowed hard. "...want to hear the details." She swallowed again. "It involved the chest. Alan..." She pushed back her hair. "Alan had a padlock which..." She took a deep breath before continuing. "...had a secret compartment he would fill with...he didn't say with what...something to make Stephen listen. He wanted Stephen to stop defending Celia."

Fooks chewed his lips. "Why did this concern Alan? It didn't affect him."

Lucinda shook her head. "I don't know." Seeing Fooks' doubtful expression, she added, "Really, I don't."

Fooks accepted her word.

"Was Stephen using Emmett to get back at Preston for having an affair with you?" Fooks asked.

Lucinda nodded. "Why couldn't he...talk to me? We could have worked it out. I know we could have." Lucinda wiped her nose on the dirty towel.

"So, the plan involved Tyler. How?"

"He went into Stephen's office when I left."

"Was this part of the plan?"

"Yes." She sniffed. "We counted on Stephen wanting to show me the chest. He would open the padlock...and he did. We expected it to make him ill. Tyler and Alan would slip in and persuade him to drop the case. I went along with the plan because I thought if Stephen became ill, he'd have to spend more time at home. With me." She swallowed hard. "Stupid, stupid idea." She shook her head. "Something went wrong. I don't know what happened, exactly. I wasn't there."

"We understand, ma'am. Do you know any more about what happened?" Fooks pressed.

Lucinda shook her head. "I went home and waited. They said they'd bring him home, but...they never did." She sniffed. "He never came home again." She wiped her eyes and looked at Bennett. "You told me the next morning they found Stephen in the livery. D-Dead."

"What did Alan say happened?" Fooks asked.

"He didn't understand, either. He said..." Lucinda shook her head. "I didn't want to know the details. You must ask him yourself."

"Yes, we'll be doing that."

Bennett inclined his head for Fooks to come with him to the corner of the office. With a glance at Lucinda, Bennett said in a hushed voice. "I'm gonna need to arrest her."

"Yes," Fooks agreed.

"I don't have the facilities to keep a woman here. 'Sides, looks like I'll be keeping Long regardless of what his clever lawyer says when he gets here. What d'ya suggest I do with her?"

Now, here was something, Bennett willingly asking him for advice. Fooks resisted the impulse to grin. "Well, way I see it, you have two options. You put her in a cell." Fooks pulled a face and shook his head. "Or you take a room at the hotel, keep the door locked, and set one of your deputies outside."

"Yeah, I like your idea. Good thinking. I'll take her over now."

Fooks caught his arm. "Before you do."

Bennett frowned. "What now?"

Fooks walked back to Lucinda and sat by her. She was tearing at the towel again, but she was dry-eyed and more composed.

"How are you feeling, ma'am?"

"Better. W-what happens now?"

"The sheriff will take you to the hotel and get you settled in a room."

"The hotel?" Lucinda blinked. "I thought..." She pointed behind her at the cellblock door.

Fooks shook his head. "No, you'll be more comfortable in the hotel. There'll be a deputy right outside."

Lucinda took a deep breath. "I see." She squared her shoulders and turned to Bennett. "Are you charging me with Stephen's murder?"

"No, ma'am."

Lucinda slumped back in the chair.

"I have to arrest ya for conspiracy. Judge'll have to decide what the exact charge is later, and...well, Crane and me haven't got to the bottom of it all yet."

Lucinda nodded. "I understand. Thank you."

"Before the sheriff takes you over, I have one more question."

"Yes," she said, tiredness taking effect.

"What was your last name before your marriage?"

"My last name? What possible reason can you have for asking?" she said with a laugh.

"Please answer the question," Bennett said curtly.

"Very well. It was Francis."

Fooks glanced at Bennett before asking his next question.

"Do you own a rifle?"

She widened her eyes in surprise. "A rifle?"

Bennett fetched the rifle they had taken from Alan.

"Is this yours, ma'am?"

"I've no idea. All guns are the same to me," she said with the first smile in a while.

"Now, Lucinda, that's not exactly true, is it?" Fooks said, studying her face carefully.

"W-what do you mean?"

"Did ya think I would forget? How you beat some of the best riflemen in the county? First, just after you and Stephen came to Angelworth and again last year?"

Lucinda swallowed hard. It was plain on her face that this was exactly what she'd hoped. "I-I haven't held a rifle for some time," she offered.

Fooks frowned. Odd choice of words. "Except, perhaps, until the other night? When you shot at me?" He stared at her hard.

Lucinda groaned. She put a hand to her face and shook her head. "I'm sorry. I'm sorry. He asked me to do it, but I made sure I didn't hit you. I was careful."

Fooks put a reassuring hand on her arm. "Who asked you, Lucinda?"

Lucinda glanced from him to Bennett. "Alan. He wanted me to frighten you off."

"Where did you shoot from?"

"From Alan's apartment. There's a view all the way down Main Street."

"Yeah, Rev figured the shots came from there. After the shooting, Sheriff Bennett and his deputies asked around town, hoping someone had seen something. They knocked on Alan's door. There was no answer. Where were you?"

"After the shots alerted the town, we left the rifle in Alan's apartment and went to my house." Lucinda hesitated. "Where...Alan stayed the night."

"Thank you, ma'am." Fooks put a reassuring hand on her shoulder and smiled at her.

This morning hadn't gone the way he'd thought. Lucinda had revealed far more than he'd expected. She'd filled in a lot of gaps, but there was still more to find out. He hoped his nerves were up to it.

After Bennett and Lucinda had gone, Rev entered the office. He found Fooks sitting with his hands over his eyes. Fooks rallied when he saw who it was.

"Sure hope you've got some good news for me," he said bitterly.

"Not exactly. Tubby wasn't in the office. All closed up."

"Strange."

"'Tis lunchtime," Rev reminded Fooks.

"Oh, is it? Hadn't noticed."

Rev sat on the edge of the desk where Fooks was sitting. "What happened with Mrs. Mercer?"

Fooks groaned loudly and stood up stiffly. He arched his back and stretched. Pacing would help. "Things are a lot clearer now." He gave a weary sigh before proceeding to tell Rev what happened.

When he finished, Rev glanced at the wall. "Filled in a lot of those gaps," he murmured.

"Yeah. It makes me feel sick." Fooks shook his head. "How could they have even contemplated doing what they did? I dunno, Rev, I've come across some hard and ruthless men in my time, but nothing compares to this."

"Man's inhumanity to man. Sometimes it doesn't take much for someone to flip. Sounds to me, from what ya told me, Lucinda was kinda desperate, an' those two men took advantage of her."

"Yeah. Tell you what, Rev. I can't wait to get back to Mary and my nice, quiet life. Who'da thought hardware was the height of excitement for me these days?" Fooks sat down heavily.

"Think ya're nearly there, Fooks. Can't be long now."

"I sure hope so."

Silence descended before Rev broke it. "Here's something. I asked around the storekeepers opposite Stephen's office, like ya asked me to."

Fooks sat up, interested. Any distraction was welcome to take his mind off Lucinda's confession.

"Two of 'em confirmed Lucinda left Stephen's office. Closing up time, see? Lot of folks about. Both said Callaghan went in after she left."

"Okay, they can confirm Lucinda's story," Fooks said. "She wasn't there. Glad 'bout that." He smiled. "But Tyler was."

Rev shook Fooks' shoulder. "She didn't kill him, boy. Perhaps the court will go easy with her."

"Mebbe."

"Where does this leave us?"

Fooks rubbed his forehead. "Lucinda said the plan didn't involve Tubby, but I can't get it outta my head that he's not telling me the truth. This business with the tarp is bugging me."

"Could be he don't remember," Rev said gently. "It was three weeks ago, and it's an inconsequential thing."

"Yeah." Fooks rested his arms on the desk. "I still need to ask him again. You say he's not in the office?"

"No."

"Okay, when Bennett comes back, we'll ask him where Tubby lives. He might be more forthcoming at home."

CHAPTER TWENTY-TWO

Sometime later, furnished with directions to Tubby Wilson's house, Fooks and Rev set off.

Tubby opened the door when Fooks knocked, and Fooks explained why they were there. Tubby seemed reluctant, but he invited them in.

Rev patted Fooks' arm as they passed a room on the left. When Fooks glanced back, Rev pointed at the padlock on the door.

"Is this one of the missing padlocks? Didn't ya say there was more'n one?"

"I did." Fooks inspected the padlock. "Have to check, but I'm pretty sure this is one of 'em. Looks old enough."

Fooks and Rev swapped glances and continued their way into the sitting room, where they found another surprise.

Martha Pickering was tending to Mrs. Wilson's rheumatism. Mrs. Wilson wasn't as elderly or infirm as Fooks had imagined her to be. Instead, an attractive woman sat in a high-backed chair. Her auburn hair shone luxuriously, and her bright blue eyes were striking. Martha was wrapping one of Mrs. Wilson's ankles in bandages. Her other ankle was similarly wrapped.

"Better, Ma?" Tubby asked, standing by her side.

"Yes. My legs always feel better after Martha has seen to them. Whatever is in the rub, my gal sure does the trick."

Martha smiled. "There, all done." She stood and acknowledged the arrivals. "Excuse me, gentlemen. I must wash my hands."

She disappeared with Tubby, leaving Fooks and Rev to introduce themselves to Mrs. Wilson.

"Joseph Crane, ma'am," Fooks said, reaching over to shake hands. "I'm investigating Stephen Mercer's murder."

"Josiah Wedgwood," Rev said.

Mrs. Wilson regarded Rev with open admiration. "Well now, you look like one of those preaching fellas, all dressed in black."

"Yes, ma'am, I am that."

"You sit right down here next to me and tell me something the Good Lord said."

Rev found his arm grabbed, and he was pulled into a chair next to her. He widened his eyes at Fooks.

Fooks tried not to laugh at Rev's predicament, and a moment later, he was genuinely not laughing. He glanced at the detritus Martha had left after treating Mrs. Wilson. Spotting the label on a bottle of liniment, he bent and picked it up for a closer view. He gulped. The label said, "Rub," and below that, "Aconite."

He angled the bottle around so Rev could see and then closed his hand around it.

"I cen do better'n that, ma'am." Rev took the hint Fooks wanted him to distract Mrs. Wilson. "I have here an entire book of his word." Rev reached for his battered

Bible. "Now, what's your favorite scripture? Tell me, an' I'll read it to ya."

Fooks saw Rev would occupy Mrs. Wilson, so he went off in search of Tubby and Martha. He found them in the kitchen, where Martha was scrubbing her hands with soap and warm water.

"Sorry, Mr. Crane. Just finding out how Ma is," Tubby said. "Won't be long."

"There's nothing more I can tell you, Tubby. Her rheumatism won't get better. All I can do is apply the rub every few days. It seems to make a difference to her," Martha said gently.

Tubby appeared disappointed for a second, and he smiled, nodding. "Yes, she is brighter after you've been. Some days she can walk around the house on her own. Other days are more difficult for her."

"I'm afraid that's the nature of the illness, Tubby. Make sure she's warm and not in any draughts. I know you're concerned, but don't baby her. She should try doing things for herself as far as she is able. She'll soon tell you if she can't do something."

"I know. She hates depending on me, but I don't enjoy seeing her struggle so."

"You're a wonderful son. I know she appreciates all you do for her."

Tubby smiled.

Fooks had not wanted to intrude on the conversation. Now that there was a break, he summoned Tubby over.

"Sorry, Mr. Crane. You wanted to ask me a question?"

Fooks glared at him hard. "Yes, Tubby, I do, and it now appears I have more questions than I thought." He inclined his head to the hall. Tubby moved, and Fooks put a hand on his arm, stopping him. "One moment."

Fooks walked over to Martha as she finished washing her hands. He handed her a towel and gave her a tight-lipped smile.

"I heard someone shot at you the other night, Mr. Crane? Are you well?"

"Yes, thank you quite well. Don't disappear, Ms. Pickering. I would like a word with you as well."

His smile disappeared, and he opened his hand, showing her the bottle. He raised his eyebrows knowingly at her, and she nodded.

Fooks re-joined Tubby in the hall.

"You're being mysterious, Mr. Crane. Have I done something wrong?"

"Well now, it all depends," Fooks said, drawing himself up. "Tell me again about the tarp covering the chest?"

"The tarp?" Tubby frowned. "Why is it so important?"

"Tell me, Tubby," Fooks said firmly in a low, menacing voice.

Tubby shook his head in confusion. "Alan delivered the chest. He asked me to help him carry in the chest. We folded the tarp, which covered it for the journey, and brought the chest inside. I don't—"

"You still insist you took the tarp off outside the office?"

Tubby swallowed. "I can't remember, but it would make sense."

"Do you remember the telegraph messenger boy running up as you and Alan brought the chest in?"

"Yes."

"Well, if you remember that, then why can't you remember if the tarp was on or not?" Fooks snapped.

"Why? What difference does it make?"

Fooks fixed Tubby with a stony expression. "'Cause either you or Alan is lying to me. Right now, my money is on you! The boy says whatever you and Alan were bringing in had a tarp covering it. He asked Alan what was underneath."

Tubby swallowed hard.

"And Alan tells me you folded the tarp and handed it back to him in the office."

"If Alan says that, I guess I did." Tubby shrugged and chewed his bottom lip.

Fooks stomped away in frustration.

"I don't know what else to tell you. I really don't remember."

"All right." Fooks mastered his frustration with difficulty. "Tell me about this." He tapped the padlock behind Tubby's head. "Where did you get it?"

Tubby shook his head. "It's not mine. Tyler rents this room from Ma."

"Doesn't he trust you?"

"Of course."

"Then why padlock the room?"

"He doesn't want Ma to clean in there."

"Your mother can hardly walk!"

"Sh-she can. On occasion, she's quite sprightly," Tubby said defensively.

"Tubby, what are you trying to hide?"

"I have nothing to hide."

"Why are you looking guilty?"

Tubby bit his lip and failed to meet Fooks' eye. "Mr. Crane, if you persist, I-I must ask you to leave. You'll upset Ma."

Fooks glanced into the lounge. Mrs. Wilson didn't seem upset as she laughed with Rev. In fact, they appeared to be rather cozy.

"Can you let me in there?" Fooks asked, tapping the door.

"No, sir. Tyler has the only key."

Fooks backed off. Continuing to press wouldn't accomplish anything further.

"Okay, Tubby. Thank you."

Tubby walked into the lounge, leaving Fooks standing in the hall, undecided. Martha saved him from his indecision.

"You wanted to ask me something, Mr. Crane?"

"Yes." Fooks reached into his pocket and brought out the bottle. "Tell me about this."

"It's the bottle of liniment I used on Mrs. Wilson's ankles."

"Yes. It contains aconite."

"I told you I use aconite in a lot of my preparations."

"Yes, you did." Fooks carefully took the stopper from the bottle and sniffed. "What is this mixed with?"

"Glycerin and a little alcohol."

"Can you tell me how you make this?"

"I grind the root into a powder—"

"I thought you said you didn't use the root." The accusation in his voice testified to his exasperation. He ran a hand through his hair.

"No, I didn't say that, Mr. Crane. I said I mainly use the leaves and flowers, but I do use small quantities of the root. It is easier to grind into a powder." She stared at Fooks hard until he nodded in contrition. "I add alcohol and distill for twenty-four hours before adding glycerin. This helps prevent evaporation when applied. Then I bandage the affected part of the body. This keeps the liniment close to the skin. It also prevents accidental contact with any other body part."

"You also said the skin absorbs aconite easily. Yet you tended to Mrs. Wilson without wearing gloves."

"Yes, but I applied a barrier cream first, and I washed my hands thoroughly afterward." Martha tilted her head. "Mr. Crane, you're troubled. You'll benefit from some chamomile tea. I'm sure Tubby won't mind if I prepare—"

"No. No, thank you, Ms. Pickering." Fooks said, trying not to sound irritated. Chamomile tea? Calming down was the last thing he wanted. "When you've finished here, would you come with me to Dr. Sullivan's office, please?"

Martha nodded. "I suppose so. Why?"

Fooks ran a trembling hand through his hair again. "I have a theory...a medical theory I would like to run by you both together. I'd prefer to do so somewhere private."

"Very well. Let me get my things."

Fooks waited until she went into the sitting room before studying the padlock again. It was old and ornate. He turned it over, revealing that this one didn't contain a hidden chamber. He flipped it back and inspected the locking mechanism. His hand strayed to his inside pocket, where he kept his tools. The sound of giggling intruded into his consciousness. He stopped and grinned.

Rev's laugh, a rare and distinctive thing, overlaid uncontrolled feminine spluttering. Fooks chuckled. It seemed Mrs. Wilson and Rev were getting along rather well. This was confirmed by a red-faced Tubby joining him in the hall a moment later.

"Your ma is enjoying herself," Fooks said, amused.

"Yes." Tubby gulped hard. "A little too well for my delicate ears, but it's nice to hear her laugh. Is she in safe hands?"

"Yes," Fooks said. "She'll be fine. Rev is an honorable man."

"Good, 'cause I need to get back to the office."

Martha escaped from the room, a flush rising up her neck. She clutched her bag tightly and swallowed hard.

"They say laughter is the best medicine." She rolled her eyes. "I hope they're right."

Doc Sullivan was finishing his lunch when Fooks and Martha entered. The smell of roast beef and mustard hung in the air. Martha's nose wrinkled in disgust.

"What can I do for you two? I take it you're together?"

"I want to ask you both something. Makes sense to get you together." Fooks gave the doc a tight-lipped smile.

Sullivan indicated two chairs in front of his desk. He wiped his mouth with a napkin and pushed the remains of his lunch aside. Fooks waited until Martha sat before taking his own chair.

"How can I help?" Sullivan asked, his hands clasped together on the desk.

Fooks dug into his pocket, brought out the liniment bottle, and set it down.

"This. I'd like you to check if what's in here is the same as the sample I gave you the other day."

Sullivan turned the bottle around to view the label. "Is this yours?" he asked Martha.

"Yes. It's a rub I make for patients with rheumatism."

"Hmmm."

"It works, Lester."

"Oh, I'm not saying it doesn't," Sullivan said with a quick laugh. "Has Mr. Crane told you his suspicions about aconite?"

Martha looked askance at Fooks. "Yes, I'm well aware of Mr. Crane's theories."

Fooks took a deep breath. "What I haven't told either of you is why I think what I do."

Fooks described the padlock and Stephen's injury when he opened it. He left out any mention of Lucinda's, Alan's, and Tyler's involvement, only describing the movement of the body in the vaguest terms.

"Incredible," Sullivan said when Fooks had finished.

"I'm not at liberty to say more, you understand, but Sheriff Bennett and me agree how it happened." When they both nodded, he continued. "Doc, when you analyzed the sample I gave you before, you said two things. First, you weren't able to tell what the other substance was. Second, you didn't think it contained enough aconite to kill Stephen."

"Correct, but it was a tiny sample, Mr. Crane."

"Could the other substance be glycerin? That's what Martha says is in this."

"Gloopy enough," Sullivan said with a smug smile. "Technical term." He sobered when no reaction came from his audience. "What are the parts, Martha?"

"One of aconite distilled in alcohol to three of glycerin."

"Martha treated Stephen with aconite for his headaches," Fooks said quietly.

"Ah!"

"I'm not responsible for Stephen's death, Lester," Martha said with a worried frown.

Sullivan smiled at her reassuringly.

"No one is suggesting you are, Martha. Honestly." Fooks leaned closer. "You said Stephen took your preparation morning and evening?"

Martha drew herself up. "That's what I recommended."

"It was about six when Stephen opened the padlock—"

"How do you know the time?" Martha asked.

Fooks held up his hand. "I can't tell you. You must take my word for it. Now, the way I figure, Stephen took his evening dose around the time he opened the padlock. And this is where I need your medical opinion. The evening dose and the aconite from the padlock spike that injured his hand, when combined...was it enough to bring about a fatal reaction?"

Fooks flicked his eyes from one to the other. Neither offered an opinion. They stared at him in wonder, and after a while, he shifted self-consciously.

"Well?" he prompted.

"I suppose it would depend on the amount of aconite in the dose Stephen took." Sullivan glanced at Martha.

"I make the batch from the flowers of aconite, one-quarter to one grain. Mixed with water and ginger for taste. I gave Stephen enough for two days at most. He had a dropper, and I advised him to take two drops morning and night. Even if he'd taken the whole quantity, it wouldn't be enough to kill him." She hesitated. "The rub is a more intense concentration and made from powdered root, which, as you're aware, is more toxic. You said Stephen scratched his hand." She swallowed hard. "Was the cut deep?"

"No, but the skin was broken, and it bled."

"I suppose it's possible Stephen's death might have occurred the way Mr. Crane suggested." Her eyes watered. "Oh, poor Stephen." She sniffed.

Fooks put a hand on her arm. "Don't blame yourself, Martha. You didn't kill Stephen. An unfortunate coincidence. Nothing more."

Martha swallowed her feelings. She wasn't dissolving into floods of tears like Lucinda had earlier. To Fooks' relief, Martha quickly recovered. Phew! No need for his services to comfort yet another sobbing woman.

"Mr. Crane."

Sullivan drew Fooks' attention away from Martha.

"If you furnish me with the source of the poison, I can do a proper test. Martha, leave this with me, and if you can let me have what Stephen took, I'll be able to give you a conclusive result."

"I can get the padlock," Fooks whispered.

"The batch is at home. Stephen should have the last dose I gave him, especially if he took some shortly before he died."

"Perhaps if you would come along with me to Stephen's office now and help identify it," Fooks said slowly.

"Yes, of course. I'll help in any way I can." She shot up. Fooks had no choice but to go with her.

A few minutes later, Fooks sat at Stephen's desk, going through the drawers. Both Tubby and Martha watched him.

"Did you ever see Mr. Mercer take anything, Tubby?" Fooks asked when he concluded his search to no avail. "Perhaps from a small bottle?"

"Yes."

"Where did he keep the bottle?"

Tubby reached over and pulled out the top left-hand drawer. After groping around underneath the desktop, he released a tray. It contained pencils, erasers, treasury tags, and the like. There, nestled in one compartment, sat a small brown bottle.

Fooks stared for a moment before picking it up. He looked the question at Martha. She responded with a slight nod.

"Excuse me," she murmured before leaving the office at speed.

"I don't understand," Tubby said.

"No." Fooks pocketed the bottle and shut the drawers. Getting up, he glanced at the chest. "I'm gonna need to take the padlock."

"But the key is missing."

Fooks pulled on his gloves and shook his head.

"I don't need a key."

As he moved to the chest, Tubby went with him, curious. Fooks knelt by the chest, and Tubby watched with interest as he took out his tools. He selected one and teased the mechanism into the opening position. Then he carefully held the padlock so the spike wouldn't snag him again. He still held his breath until the lock clicked open. The spike sprang out harmlessly.

"Mr. Crane—"

"This killed Stephen, Tubby," Fooks said, pointing at the spike. "It's laced with poison."

Tubby gasped. "No!"

Fooks smiled faintly at Tubby's reaction. "Yeah, surprising, isn't it? I'll be taking this now, Tubby."

Tubby backed away until he came up against a desk.

"Please. I don't want it anywhere near me."

Fooks clicked the shank shut with a tight-lipped smile and put the padlock in his pocket. He returned his tools to his top pocket and stood up. For a moment, he considered the younger man.

"Tubby, can you give me your permission to look in the locked room at your house?"

Tubby stared at the chest, wide-eyed. "What? I told you, Mr. Crane. It's not my room."

"It's in your house."

"I know, but I still can't allow it. Tyler rents the room from Ma, and as a lawyer, I can tell you he has the right to privacy."

"Okay, Tubby. I understand. Sheriff Bennett will decide what we do. Would a court order, do you?"

"If you think it's necessary."

"I do."

Fooks walked to the door and stopped with his hand on the handle. "Tubby, do me a favor, please?" he asked over his shoulder. When Tubby acknowledged him, he continued. "If you see Tyler in the meantime, say nothing to him. Might seriously interfere with our investigation."

"Are you close to figuring out what happened, Mr. Crane?"

Fooks pressed his lips into a tight smile. "Yes, Tubby. Very close, indeed."

Fooks dashed back to Dr. Sullivan's office and handed over Stephen's medication and the secret compartment from the padlock. The doc promised he would have the results as soon as he could.

Fooks returned to the sheriff's office to wait.

"Have you spoken to our guest?" he asked Bennett without preamble. He nodded at the cellblock.

"Took him his lunch. Collected the tray ten minutes ago."

"You tell him about Lucinda?"

"No. Figured something you might wanna do." Bennett grinned at the sour expression on Fooks' face.

"Aw, thanks."

Fooks hitched up his pants before heading for the cellblock door.

"Crane."

Fooks glanced back, and Bennett tapped the desk with his finger. Fooks flashed a grin.

"'Course, Sheriff. I was forgettin'." He laid his gun on the desk. "Where would I be without you here to remind me?" He didn't wait for an answer, and he didn't want to hear it anyway.

A few seconds later, Fooks stood by the side of Alan's cell.

"What d'ya want, Crane?" Alan said with a snarl when he saw who it was. He returned to reading the newspaper.

"Thought you might wanna know we've spoken to Lucinda Mercer. She confirmed you didn't shoot at me the other night."

"Good." Alan folded the newspaper and rose. "Then ya can let me outta here."

"Nope. Can't do that."

Alan gripped the bars.

"She told us she did the shooting."

"Ridiculous."

Fooks pursed his lips. "Maybe, but I kinda believe her." He folded his arms. "The rifle we found had LF stamped on the butt. F for Lucinda's maiden name, Francis. Bennett says he remembers she is a crack shot. And she's admitted the shots came from your place. So, it does involve you." He shook his head. "All stacks up, Mr. Long."

"Still doesn't mean I had anything to do with it."

"Not on the face of it, no, except she says you put her up to it."

Alan waved a hand dismissively and walked away from the bars.

Fooks stared at Alan's back. "She told us everything."

Alan turned around.

"Why you ask her to shoot at me. How you and Tyler Callaghan planned to intimidate Stephen Mercer. Only it backfired, didn't it? And you ended up killing him."

Alan hissed. "Stupid bitch!"

"Now, now, Mr. Long."

Alan seized the bars and shook them. "You won't get away with this!" His face reddened. "I'm not saying any more until my lawyer gets here. The law will find me innocent."

Fooks held his ground. He only moved back when Alan took a swipe at him.

"You didn't think anyone would find out, did you? You were so sure you had covered all your tracks. Well, let me tell you something." Fooks' voice became harder, and his speech faster. "What the three of you did to Stephen was beyond despicable. I hope you rot in hell."

Fooks walked away.

"We didn't kill him."

Fooks turned his head.

"You didn't mean to. The fact is, you did." He paused. "I hope, when your lawyer gets here, you make a full confession to him. Whether you go anywhere else ever again will depend on what you say to him."

Leaning against the cellblock door, Fooks slid the bolt across with a finality he knew wasn't there yet.

Suddenly a wave of weariness overcome him. He collapsed onto the spare desk and put his head in his hands.

Bennett gave him a moment.

"Are ya all right?"

Fooks rubbed his hands over his face.

Bennett went to the coffee pot, poured a cup, and set it on the desk by Fooks.

Fooks started in surprise and gave the sheriff a slight smile of thanks. "Yeah, I'm all right. Been a helluva day, though."

"Sure has," Bennett agreed, sitting back at his desk.

Fooks sat sideways, facing him. He cradled his coffee. "And I haven't even told you what I found at Tubby's house yet."

He spent the next few minutes briefing Bennett on the events since they'd last met. Afterward, Bennett reached into the bottom drawer of his desk and brought out a half-empty bottle of whiskey. He offered the bottle to Fooks for his coffee, but Fooks shook his head.

"I meant to ask Alan about the tarp again."

"Why is that important?"

"Because it involves Tubby, but he doesn't know he's involved."

"That don't make sense."

"Aw, I dunno." Fooks sighed. "I'm going for a walk." He levered up. "What time is the lawyer due?"

"Four o'clock train. Anytime from then on, I guess."

"Okay, I'll be back to see him."

CHAPTER TWENTY-THREE

Fooks glanced at Rev before opening the door to the sheriff's office. Alan Long's lawyer would be there, and Fooks expected a hard time. When he opened the door, his expression changed. With hands on hips, he grinned.

"Well, if it isn't Monroe Blair," he said.

Blair glanced around from talking with Bennett and did a double-take. He was a studious looking young man, with round eyeglasses, and appeared to be wearing his bigger brother's go-to-church suit.

"Mr.—"

"Crane," Fooks said, supplying the name he wanted Blair to use. They shook hands. "Joseph Crane. We met in..." Fooks put his fingers to his lips, feigning deep thought, and then clicked his fingers. "I know. It was Jacksonville, Colorado."

"Yes, we definitely met in Jacksonville," Blair said cautiously.

"Just got in? The long journey musta tired you out. Why don't..." Fooks put an arm around Blair's shoulders and steered him away from the sheriff. "...we go and settle you in the hotel. Have a beer."

"I should—"

"Are you hungry? Maybe a spot of supper. I'm told they do a great steak pie at the café. Is this yours?" Fooks picked up the valise from the corner.

"Yes, but I really ought to see my client first, Mr. Crane."

Rev held open the door.

"Aw, he's not going anywhere. Sheriff Bennett is looking after him real good."

"I must insist."

"Hotel is kinda full, and with the seven o'clock stage due any minute..." Unconsciously, everyone in the office glanced at the wall clock. It said ten past five. "...why, you might not get a room. Don't want you coming all this way and finding yourself out on the street."

With a last shove, Blair was outside. Rev shut the door on them quickly.

Outside, Blair shrugged off Fooks' arm.

"Are you mad?" Blair asked in astonishment. "You're preventing me from seeing my client."

"No. No." Fooks put down the valise and held up his hands in surrender. "I'm not preventing. I'm just delaying. You need to understand a few things first. Like why I'm here."

Blair frowned at him. "Yes, I'm wondering about that."

"Good." Fooks spun him around. "I'll tell you all about it, but I'd prefer to do it somewhere private. How's life in Jacksonville?"

With the valise in one hand, Fooks gripped Blair's arm, propelling them in the hotel's direction. Blair slumped. No point in arguing.

"Fine."

"And how is the judge?"

"Retired, but his wife is keeping him busy."

"Ah, yes. Wives are like that."

Blair gave him a sharp look. What did a notorious outlaw like Florian Fooks know about wives? Perhaps he was about to find out.

Installed in a hotel room, Blair sat on the edge of the bed. Fooks heaved his suitcase onto a chair.

"Phew! That's heavy, Mr. Blair. What have you got in there, bricks?" Fooks turned and stood with hands on hips.

"Books, Mr. Fooks."

"Ah, of course."

"Now, would you mind telling me what this is all about? I'm a patient man, but really..."

Fooks winced. "Yeah, I'm sorry." He reached for another chair, spun it around, and sat on it backward, facing Blair. "Look, I have to explain why I'm here, posing as a federal agent."

Blair raised an eyebrow, waiting.

"Coleman and Murphy came to see me. Asked for my help."

"I thought you'd—"

"I have, and I am. Tobias Swan and me, we took your advice after Jacksonville. You and the judge made a lot of sense."

A foolish mistake on their part had led to Fooks and Swan being recognized, hence, their capture and incarceration in the Jacksonville jail. While awaiting extradition to Wyoming, they provided information about two other men in jail with them. Their crime was murder, which was not something Fooks and Swan agreed with. When accomplices of the other men came to break them out, Fooks and Swan helped foil the escape. As a result, the judge suggested most strongly the two of them should go straight. The seed was already planted in their minds, it just needed watering. The judge gave them that extra push.

Blair smiled. "I hoped you had when I didn't hear about any more robberies credited to you. How long has it been now, two years?"

"Nearer three," Fooks said. "I'm curious. Why are you here in Wyoming?"

Blair reddened. "Love." When Fooks smiled in interest, Blair continued, "She lives in Laramie. I met her some time ago, and after the judge retired, I moved on. Laramie seemed as good a place as any."

"Women can make all the difference. I've got myself a real good wife." Fooks smiled as he thought of Mary. "And before you say it," he added, catching sight of Blair's expression, "yes, she knows who I am. I asked her to marry me, and after she said yes, I told her who I was. I wanted no mistake, and I wanted it legal. She...thought about it carefully and decided to trust me." He pressed his lips into a tight smile. "I haven't given her any reason to doubt me so far. Well..." He rolled his eyes. "Until now, that is."

"Why? What have you done?"

"Nothing *too* illegal," Fooks said with a wince. "Sheriff Bennett knows me as Joseph Crane, federal agent, because of our past association."

He told Blair about the confusion between Quinn Mooney's gang and the Guardian Wall Gang, how he and Mooney looked alike. "This time around, I've tried to gloss over the federal agent bit, but Bennett has looked at me closely a few times. I'm not on safe ground, but I need to be here. Coleman and Murphy didn't kill Stephen Mercer. Whoever did fitted them up."

"Who did?"

Fooks swung his leg over the chair and stood. "That's why I'm here trying to figure that out. I have my suspicions." He shook his head. "Haven't fitted all the pieces together yet, but I think I'm real close."

"And does my client, Alan Long, feature in your suspicions?"

"Yeah," Fooks said, surprised Blair had to ask. "Right at the very top."

"Why? Because he asked Lucinda Mercer to shoot at you?"

"Not exactly the action of an innocent man, is it?" Fooks flashed a quick grin.

"Your partner, is he here as well?"

Fooks' face fell. "No. I haven't seen Swan for a while," he said quietly. His eyes hit the ceiling. "If he'd been here, Lucinda'd probably be dead by now."

Blair stiffened. "Perhaps it's better he's not here."

"Oh, I don't mean revenge, Mr. Blair. If he had been in the street with me that night... He doesn't miss. Even at range."

"Then he would be in trouble, which is not something he can afford. Any more than you. You're here, and that can't be helped. Don't make any slips, Mr. Fooks. You don't want to give Sheriff Bennett cause to look at you more closely."

Fooks swallowed. "I know." He winced. "It's not easy, though, is it?" He didn't wait for Blair to comment. "I'm not sure I'm cut out to be a law-abiding man. I'm trying, but it's harder than I thought it would be. Now and then, something happens to remind me I'm not as free as the next man." He bit his lip. "Hard to take when I'm trying so hard."

"The judge was right to put his trust in you. We both knew you could do it."

Fooks flashed a quick smile. "Tobias and me can't thank the judge and you enough." He could still feel the knot he'd had in his stomach when he and Swan had stood before the judge's bench that night, hoping with little hope he would let them go. Truth had saved them. The elation he'd felt when he'd heard the words had been like no other. "Now I'm trying to live a quiet, law-abiding life," he said and sighed. "But I think I'm failing miserably."

"Is that true?" Blair asked in surprise.

Fooks shook his head. "No, I don't suppose it is. I'm living quietly in a small town not far away. I own a hardware store. I have a wife and a baby due any day now. I want to give them more, but I don't know how." Fooks surprised himself by revealing this much information. He looked anxiously at Blair. Had he revealed too much?

Blair smiled. "There's no perfect life. I think you're doing just fine, Mr. Fooks. Now, I really must go and see my client."

Fooks shook his head. "I should do some more thinking on this. I can't fit all the pieces together."

Fooks didn't sleep well that night. He tossed and turned, endlessly going over everything he knew, wondering where he was going to go from here. He really needed to be getting back to Mary and didn't have the luxury for a drawn-out investigation. Damn Tobias for running out on him. He'd be home by now if this had involved Tobias Swan. They didn't think alike, but Tobias had a knack for seeing things from a different angle than Fooks. That ability had served them well in the past.

He stared at the ceiling until first light, with no resolution. Staying in bed wasn't accomplishing anything. Sighing, he dressed quickly. He waited for the livery to open, having foregone breakfast. With a certain amount of relief, he was soon on his horse, riding out of town.

At first, he rode aimlessly, but the fresh morning air soon wiped the cobwebs from his mind. Before long, the rhythmic clop of his horse's hooves distracted his thoughts just enough for his subconscious mind to work. Soon he had an idea. He spurred his horse on, loping gracefully along the trail toward Thompkins Decorative Ironmongery.

"Mr. Crane," Preston greeted with a grin as Fooks rode into the yard. "You're up early."

"'Morning," Fooks said, returning the grin. "Got some good news." He winced. "Well, I think I do."

He dismounted and led his horse to a hitching rail.

"Must be for you to ride out here this early. Come in and have some coffee."

Fooks took a seat in the now-familiar office while they waited for the coffee to boil.

"News for me?" Preston asked.

"Gotta lead on one of your padlocks," Fooks said.

Preston chuckled. "You rode all the way out here to tell me that?"

Fooks squeezed his bottom lip between thumb and forefinger. "I was hoping you had a key." Should confirm Preston's ownership.

"Which one are you talking about?" Preston's eyes lit up. "Not the big one with the secret chamber?"

Fooks shook his head. Too early to reveal the part that one played in events. Fooks described the padlock he'd found at Tubby's.

"Yes, I know the one you mean."

Preston went to the filing cabinet. From the top drawer, he took a loose-leaf folder. Beautifully executed ink drawings of locks filled the pages. On the table, he flicked through until he found the page he wanted. "Is that it?"

Fooks leaned forward and then stood up to get a better view.

"Yes, that's the one."

Preston tended to the coffee.

Fooks flicked through some more pages. "These drawings are exquisite, Preston. Did you do them?"

"Yes, I trained as a draftsman before I took up ironmongery. I like to keep my hand in now and then. I do drawings of all my locks when I get 'em. Here ya go."

Preston set down two mugs of coffee. Fooks picked his cup up immediately and examined the folder again. He flicked through it with his left hand.

"You also draw the keys," he noted.

"Yes. A lock is not complete without the key."

Fooks grinned in reply as he put the cup to his lips. *All depends on whose padlock it is.*

"Are these to scale?"

"Yes."

Fooks considered as he tapped his finger on the relevant page. "Can you replicate a key from one of these drawings?"

"Hmmm. Well, I've never tried, but I don't need to." When Fooks asked the silent question, Preston added with embarrassment, "I have this."

He reached behind a chair, brought out a wooden box, and opened the lid. Keys of all descriptions filled the box. Fooks was wide-eyed.

Preston smiled at his reaction. "Every time I find a lock, I make a copy of the key and throw it in here. I usually display the original with the lock, as you saw in the house the first time you were here. And if I sell the lock, I always have a spare just in case. The copy for the key to that padlock is in here somewhere."

"You and Alan Long both seem to have a thing for keys. He has a whole cupboard full." Fooks winced. Would Preston wonder how he knew that?

Fooks knew his mistake hadn't registered when Preston chuckled. "He gave me the idea, although I'm not as orderly as he is."

Fooks laughed. "So I can see. A key for the padlock is in here?"

"Probably."

"Can I look?"

"Sure, if you've got the time."

Preston swept the open folder aside and upended the box. Together they sorted through the pile, matching likely keys to the drawing. After a while, Preston left Fooks happily working his way through.

Some time passed before Fooks declared he might have the right one.

"Let's see." Preston inspected the one Fooks held out. "The design is right for the age of the lock. Yeah, I'd say that was the one."

"Can I take it to try? If it fits, I'm sure Sheriff Bennett will agree it's yours and you'll get it back."

"Sure, why not?"

Fooks smiled, tucking the key away in the pocket of his red and green plaid coat. A few minutes later, coated, hatted, gloved, and ready to go, he said, "Before the burglary, who was the last person you showed the padlock to? The one with the secret compartment?"

Preston considered this. "A while ago now, but I think maybe Alan." He nodded. "Yeah, I'm pretty sure Alan."

"Thank you, Preston. As usual, you've been a great help." Fooks stuck out his hand.

"Anytime."

Outside, Fooks gathered the reins of his horse. *Excellent.* With Preston's missing padlock placed prominently on Tyler's door, Bennett should have just enough reason to allow a search of the room.

CHAPTER TWENTY-FOUR

Fooks returned to Bennett's office and asked to see the drawings of the padlocks Preston had supplied when reporting their loss. Quite a contrast to the beautiful to-scale drawings Preston kept for his own purposes. As Fooks expected, one drawing matched the padlock found at Tubby's house. Getting Bennett to allow him to open it was a different matter. He had to act carefully.

"Sheriff," he said, getting the other man's attention, "correct me if I'm wrong, but recovery of stolen property is a lawful enterprise, isn't it?"

"Well, yeah, I'd say so. Why?"

Fooks pressed his lips together tightly. He declined to answer, causing Bennett to shake his head in frustration.

"Tubby said he'd allow me to open the lock on Tyler's door if we had a piece of paper signed by a judge."

"And you've already asked me. The circuit judge won't be here for another three weeks."

"Yeah, you said. Yet I think the answers to some missing pieces in our puzzle are behind that locked door."

"Look, Crane, I realize it's frustrating." Bennett tapped his fingers on the desk. "There is another way, y'know? We can ask Tyler to open the thing."

"No, rather not." Bennett needed more. "This business involves Tyler, and I don't want him getting wind until it's time to go get him. Likely need a force when we do. I'm trusting Tubby not to let on to him as it is."

"You shouldn'ta told him. They're pretty tight."

"Yeah," Fooks admitted. "I was hoping to draw Tubby out on the tarp business. If he understood how important the timing is." Fooks rolled his eyes. "Didn't work. At least, not then." He leaned a hand on his fist and puffed.

"What are ya trying to say to me?" Bennett asked a moment later.

Fooks feigned surprise. "What makes you think I'm trying to say anything?"

"'Cause, sadly, I'm getting to know ya."

Fooks smiled and scratched his ear.

"The law is a flexible beast, isn't it?" he mused a moment later.

Bennett waited.

"I mean..." Fooks sat back in his chair and laced his fingers over his stomach. "We don't write the letter of the law in stone, do we? There's sometimes a gray area."

"What are ya getting at?"

Fooks leaned forward, propped his elbow on the desk, and cupped his chin. "Flexibility is what I'm getting at." If he didn't ask straight out, soon he'd annoy Bennett beyond endurance. "How far are you willing to stretch the law?"

Bennett glared at him. "Depends," he said finally. "What have ya got in mind?"

"Recovery of stolen property." Fooks tapped the drawing. "This belongs to Preston Thompkins, and I'd like to give it back to him."

Bennett examined the drawing. "How sure are you it's Preston's?"

"See this molding around the top of the body and keyhole? Almost unique. Probably isn't another like it in this part of the country." Bennett twitched his nose as he considered. Fooks smiled and held up his closed hand, concealing something. "Besides, I have this." He opened his hand to reveal the key. "I rode out to visit Preston first thing. He gave me this. If it fits, doesn't that prove the padlock belongs to Preston?"

"Suppose so," Bennett conceded cautiously.

"So, if I take the padlock off, I can give it back to its lawful owner, and if the door should suddenly swing open..."

Bennett drew himself up. "All right. But Tubby is present."

"Yes," Fooks acknowledged. "Understood."

Bennett walked to the door. "I'll round him up."

"SNAP."

Giggling and chortling greeted Fooks and Bennett's arrival at Tubby's house.

"You're letting me win, Rev," Mrs. Wilson said.

"No, ma'am. You're jus' better'n me at this game. Your turn, Lovina."

Fooks' eyebrows disappeared into his hairline as he glanced into the sitting room. He had wondered where Rev was when he hadn't joined him for breakfast. Now he knew. Rev and Tubby's mother were cozily playing cards on a tray over her lap. Rev must have been there for some time. Fooks raised an eyebrow at Tubby.

"He turned up as I was leaving for work this morning," Tubby explained. "Ma told me how much she enjoyed his company yesterday." He shrugged. "Nice to see her happy."

Bennett walked over to the door to Tyler's room.

"Is this the padlock?" he asked, giving it a tap.

"Yes," Fooks replied. "Satisfied?"

Bennett made a grand show of unfolding the drawing and comparing. Fooks stood patiently, waiting. Emotions flickered across Tubby's face, confusion and annoyance in equal measures.

"Yeah, looks right to me," Bennett said finally, folding the drawing and stepping aside.

Fooks took his place and drew out the key.

"I can't say I'm happy about this, Sheriff. Tyler can be litigious," Tubby warned, perhaps thinking of Bennett, perhaps of himself.

"If Crane's key fits, you let me worry about Tyler."

Fooks turned the key, and the padlock opened. "Ah." Once removed from the door, he studied it in his open palm.

"Guess that proves it," he said, glancing at Bennett.

"Guess it does," Bennett agreed.

With his toe, Fooks gave the door a push.

"Oops."

Now free to move, the door swung open slightly.

Fooks appealed to Bennett first and then to Tubby, seeking permission to enter. Bennett glanced at Tubby, who shrugged in resignation. Bennett gave Fooks a nod.

Fooks pushed the door open wider. The room contained a single bed, nightstand, chair, writing desk, and chest of drawers. Fooks moved to the writing desk first. On top of it lay two padlocks and their keys.

"Guess these are the other two missing padlocks," he said.

"Yeah, they look familiar," Bennett said at his side. "We're not removing anything, Crane. D'ya understand?"

"Yes. Be careful how you touch things. Wouldn't do for Tyler to suspect we've been here before we're ready."

Bennett pointed to the door.

"I'll put the padlock back." Fooks grinned. "I didn't say when I'd give the padlock back to Preston, did I?"

"No, I guess ya didn't," Bennett said with resignation.

"Wanna check through the chest of drawers? I'll take this," Fooks said, waving a hand at the writing desk.

Bennett opened the first drawer. Fooks noticed Tubby hovering in the doorway.

"You don't have to be part of this, Tubby," Fooks said. "When are you next expecting Tyler? Is he a creature of habit?" He carried on searching while he spoke.

"He comes into town most Fridays and stays the night. Sometimes more often. Just depends."

"Then we'd better hurry. I don't want Tyler catching us in his room before we're ready," Bennett said.

Fooks nodded and returned to his search. He found nothing interesting in the cubbyholes on top of the writing desk. He sat in the desk chair and searched the drawers.

"Ah! This'll do it." Fooks pointed at a bottle identical to the one Martha used for Mrs. Wilson's liniment.

Tubby came into the room. "Ma's missing liniment," he said with surprise.

"A bottle of your ma's liniment went missing?" Fooks queried, his eyebrows hiding in his bangs.

"About a month ago."

"Did you report it?"

"No. Well, y'see, we weren't sure if we'd mislaid it or if Martha had taken it back." He tailed off. Fooks and Bennett swapped glances. "Should we have done?"

"In the wrong hands, Tubby, this is poison," Fooks said.

"Ya shoulda reported it," Bennett said.

Tubby dropped his head in shame. "I'm sorry."

"Yeah, well, at the time, I'da probably laughed at ya. Don't give it no more mind," Bennett said.

"Yeah, Tubby, you weren't to know." Fooks smiled in sympathy. "I'll put it back."

Tubby sat on the bed and wrung his hands while Fooks and Bennett continued with their search. Fooks wasn't finding anything else, and he slammed the drawers with increasing frustration.

Meanwhile, Bennett contended with underwear and shirts.

"How many pairs of socks can a man possibly need?" he muttered. "The last time I looked, he only had two feet. Same as me."

Fooks smiled at the sheriff's comments and pulled out the drawer of the nightstand. He froze when he saw what was inside.

"Sheriff."

When Bennett turned, and Fooks beckoned him over. The sheriff breathed in sharply when he saw where Fooks was pointing.

"Is this it?"

"Yeah, I reckon so. The small key for the secret compartment, on a chain. Exactly like Preston said," Fooks said.

"So...Tyler Callaghan...Alan."

"Tyler's my friend. He wouldn't kill someone. I'm sure there's a rational explanation," Tubby burst out.

Fooks sat on the bed next to Tubby.

"I'm sorry, Tubby. The way things are looking..." An idea formed. "D'you wanna help your friend?"

"How?" Tubby asked.

"A few ways. You can begin by answering a question—"

"All right, I lied to you about the tarp," Tubby said. "When we brought the chest in, it was covered by the tarp. We were folding it together when Mr. Mercer came back and saw Alan. Left me to continue on my own. I-I gave the folded tarp back to Alan as he left."

Fooks smiled. "Thank you for telling me, Tubby, but that's not what I was gonna ask," he said gently. "Who gave you the padlock to put on the chest?"

Tubby sucked in a shuddering breath. "I...Mr. Crane, I-I swear I didn't know there was poison in it. I only found out yesterday when you told me. I swear."

"All right, Tubby, your reaction told me you didn't know what the padlock contained." Fooks laid a hand on Tubby's shoulder. "I'm aware you're not to blame, but I do need you to tell me who asked you to put the padlock on the chest. It's important."

"He's my friend, Mr. Crane. My best friend." Tubby's voice broke.

"I know, Tubby, and I'm so sorry."

Tubby gulped. "Tyler," he said barely audibly. "He gave it to me and said that when Alan brought the chest, I was to slip it on. That's all he asked me to do. A simple, paltry thing." He swallowed hard. "Am I in trouble? Ma—"

"No, Tubby, you're not in trouble," Bennett reassured him with a smile.

Tubby took a deep breath of relief.

"There is one more thing you can do to help your friend Tyler, Tubby." Fooks glanced at Bennett for permission to put into words a plan they'd not discussed. Bennett waved a hand. "We need to bring Tyler in, but Sheriff Bennett and me have a problem. We can't go out to his ranch to arrest him. Not with all his ranch hands there. Y'see, they're a loyal bunch, and we could be riding into a massacre." He paused for effect. "Ours. Tyler would be in a lot more trouble than he's already in if they pile in on Tyler's side. Will you help us?"

"How?"

"I want you to do something brave for me. Can you do that?"

"What?"

Fooks glanced at Bennett. "What would entice Tyler into town? Would making him think Sheriff Bennett has arrested you for killing Stephen, do it?"

Tubby looked at him, wide-eyed. "Me?"

"Yes. If you asked Tyler for his help, would he help you? Knowing you had nothing to do with it, is he a man to let you take the fall, Tubby?"

Tubby gulped. "What about Ma?"

"We can take her into our confidence."

"What will folks in town think?"

Fooks smiled. "When the dust settles and the story all comes out, you'll be quite the hero."

"Really?"

"Yes. In fact, I would say Theodore Wilson, Attorney at Law, has a very professional and trustworthy ring. Don't you think? Shows here is a man who's prepared to go the extra mile to see justice upheld."

"Oh, I don't know about that, Mr. Crane," Tubby said and flushed.

Fooks sat and watched Tubby's thinking, visible on his face.

"You're not actually arresting me for Mr. Mercer's murder, are you, Sheriff?" Tubby asked. "We're just making it look like it to bring Tyler in for questioning."

"No, Tubby, I'm not arresting you. We want Tyler to come in peaceable so Crane and me can question him. You have my word." Bennett held out his hand.

Tubby hesitated over the hand before taking it.

"You have mine, too," said Fooks, holding out his.

After shaking hands, Bennett caught Tubby's elbow and helped him off the bed.

"Let's get you all locked up in my best cell." He chuckled. "Alan's sure gonna be surprised at his new company."

CHAPTER TWENTY-FIVE

Tubby played his part like a theatrical knight. He wrote a note to Tyler telling him of his predicament and asking for his help. Bennett would send a deputy out to the Looped C with it later.

Alan looked up with interest when Bennett ushered Tubby into the cell across the aisle. Fooks flicked through the book Tubby had chosen to pass the time. Not finding anything untoward, he passed it through the bars. With a shake of his head and after giving Tubby a look of disappointment, Fooks and Bennett left.

"What are you in for?" Alan asked immediately.

"They've arrested me for the murder of Stephen Mercer," Tubby replied.

"No." Alan was incredulous.

Fooks shared a grin with Bennett as he closed the cellblock door.

"That'll make for an interesting discussion," Bennett said with a chuckle.

Fooks slid the bolt across. "Shame we can't be there to hear it."

"If you're right, things are coming to a head."

"Sure hope so. Need to be getting home soon."

Rev stayed with Tubby's mother. For the next hour, Fooks remained in the sheriff's office, sipping coffee and studying his crazy string artwork. He wasn't nervous when alone in Bennett's company now, although he noticed Pete "Dead-Eye" Dingus no longer covered his and Swan's wanted posters.

"Got time to ride out to the Thorold ranch, Sheriff?"

"Why?"

"'Cause there're some questions I'd like to ask Celia about her relationship with Alan."

"Why's that important?"

Fooks twitched his nose. "Maybe it is, maybe it isn't. I've just got a hunch there's something more than we think."

Bennett appeared to give it some thought. Finally, he snatched up his keys and reached for his hat.

"Your hunches have got us this far. I suppose I shouldn't be in a dang-fired hurry to dismiss them." When Fooks grinned, Bennett added under his breath, "Much as I'd like to."

Fooks and Bennett rode out to the Thorold ranch. They told her what happened with Alan and that he had been seen at her place shortly before his arrest.

"You think I had something to do with shooting at you?"

"No, ma'am, but your relationship with Alan is pertinent to our investigation into Stephen Mercer's murder," Fooks said.

"Oh, you're convinced it's murder now?"

Fooks turned to Bennett for an answer.

"Yes, ma'am, I'm afraid it is, and we'd be obliged if you would answer our questions. Alan is a person of interest in this investigation, and some of his actions are pretty suspicious. We're trying to understand his motivation."

Fooks tried hard not to smile at Bennett's official-sounding tone but didn't quite manage it. He tried harder when Bennett glowered at him.

Celia turned away from them, hugging herself. She stared out the window.

"Very well. After Charlie died last year, it wasn't long before Alan came around. He and Charlie were friends for a long time. Seemed natural Alan would want to look out for the widow of his old friend. I was such a mess for months after I lost Charlie. I was grateful for his help and his company."

She sat on a chair, staring into space. At first, Fooks and Bennett weren't sure if she would continue. They swapped glances, trying to decide who should say something. Before they could decide, she said, "After a while, our friendship became something more. I need not spell out to you what I mean, do I, Mr. Crane?"

"No, ma'am."

Celia took a deep breath. "Alan never discussed his financial affairs, and I didn't ask. I had enough to cope with running this place to wonder about someone else's business. I surmised his affairs are complicated and varied. He would make no plans to meet, and when he did, he often canceled. He disliked me turning up at his apartment unannounced. I accepted that because I liked the attention he gave me when he could.

"He let something slip one day. I didn't pay any heed at first. Later, when he stopped coming, I saw this might be something I could use against him."

She chewed her bottom lip. "This won't hold me in a very good light, Sheriff. I-I'm rather ashamed of myself now." She put her head down and plucked at an imaginary piece of lint on her skirt.

"Take your time, ma'am, but Crane and I need to hear this."

"I know. Thank you for bearing with me." A moment later, she continued. "Alan let slip about his investment in the Looped C. He didn't say anything more, and I didn't ask for any details. He probably wouldn't tell me, anyway. At the time, it didn't seem important." She swallowed hard. "I still had some of Charlie's business affairs to sort out. Charlie was never very good at bookkeeping. He would throw everything in a box, and once a year, he and his accountant would go through it all. I discovered a bill of sale and a receipt amongst his papers. It was the receipt for the Northern Switchback Pasture.

"Charlie purchased the land days before Tyler's father passed. Tyler still used it as his own, which made me wonder whether Tyler knew the land was no longer part of the Looped C. The more I pondered on the timing, the more sure I became that Tyler didn't know his father had sold the land. I thought about going to see him and showing him the paperwork. Then I remembered what Alan had said about him owning part of the Looped C.

"His desertion was still raw, and I saw a way to hurt him. I contacted Stephen Mercer. He'd been so kind when he'd helped me deal with Charlie's will. When I mentioned Alan owned part of the Looped C, Stephen was keen to take the case. Stephen said the land registry records supported my claim, but I don't understand how. I didn't think Charlie had gotten around to filing the paperwork." She shrugged. "I didn't ask about it. I just fenced off the Northern Switchback Pasture.

"The court upheld my claim, and Stephen and I celebrated here one night. I had more to drink than I should have, and I...well, let's say I did not behave appropriately to him. He was a gentleman, of course, and he let me down gently.

"Tyler appealed the decision, as I suspected he might, and I approached Stephen to act for me again. I-I wouldn't have blamed him if he'd refused. But I had some information that might change his mind. I felt it my duty to tell Stephen about Lucinda and Alan. He admitted he already knew from another source. "

"How did you find out about Alan and Lucinda, ma'am?" Fooks asked. He didn't know why he wanted that information, but he asked anyway.

"Lucinda told me." She turned her head and saw the surprise on the faces of the two men. "Not in so many words. I met her in the general store one day, and we exchanged greetings. She and I have never been close, and she was frosty with me. She took great delight in telling me a certain friend of mine – she emphasized the word mine – was such pleasing company. She said what a shame we'd fallen out." Celia shrugged. "I already knew about the rumors between her and Preston Thompkins. What else would I conclude?"

Bennett and Fooks pulled faces, signaling their agreement.

"Alan came here again one night. He said Tyler asked for his help and he thought given our previous relationship he could persuade me to drop my defense. He seemed desperate for me to do so, even resorting to seduction." She swallowed hard before stiffening. "I-I let him stay. In the morning, I told him I would still go ahead. The Northern Switchback Pasture is my property, and I'm determined to hang onto it. I remember telling him I had every confidence in Stephen and no doubt the appeal would fail. To rub it in, I even told Alan I would give Stephen the chest he admired as my appreciation for all his hard work. Alan left angry. Yet he calmed down enough to come again the next evening.

"If I recall correctly, that was the evening before Stephen died. Alan apologized, told me he would break it off with Lucinda, and...you must think I'm so gullible, said I was the one he wanted and asked to marry me. He's a persuasive man."

Fooks and Bennett swapped glances, and Fooks leaned forward.

"What happened, ma'am?" he asked.

A moment passed before she answered. "As he was leaving the next morning, my foreman came to tell me the springboard was ready to take the chest into town. Alan offered to take the chest for me. To save me a trip into town. I was skeptical at first, given our previous disagreement, but he assured me that was all forgotten, so I agreed. I had no other reason to go to town."

"Was appreciation for winning the case the only reason you gave the chest to Stephen, ma'am?" Fooks asked.

Celia spun to face him. "Yes. No." She sighed. "There is one thing further I should add." This got the men's attention. "I wanted Stephen to have it to say sorry for my unwelcome advances."

"And the chest didn't have a padlock on it?"

Celia shook her head. "You asked me before. No, there wasn't."

Fooks and Bennett swapped glances again, satisfied. Celia was naïve and gullible but not part of the conspiracy.

Night had fallen when Tyler Callaghan walked into the sheriff's office. Bennett, Fooks, and Rev turned around in surprise at the sudden entrance. Blair widened his eyes.

"Sheriff, have I got it right that you've arrested Tubby for Mercer's murder?" he asked without preamble. "What are you doing here?" The last question was for Monroe Blair.

"I have a client," Blair said, gesturing to the cellblock.

"You're my lawyer," Tyler said.

"I can represent both you and Alan."

Tyler sneered at Bennett. "Well, is it true? Have ya arrested Tubby?"

"Yes."

Tyler stood with hands on hips, pursing his lips thoughtfully.

"Well now, that is a shame because now I have to do..." Tyler drew his gun. "Guns on the table, please." He glanced from one man to the next, trying to work out where any threat was likely to come from. "You first, Crane. Thumb and forefinger only. Nice and slow."

Fooks' hand had frozen above his gun, and he reconfigured his fingers as ordered.

"Now, take a step back."

Fooks did as requested.

"Your turn, Sheriff."

"Tyler, what is this?" Bennett asked as he complied.

"Justice." Tyler gestured with his gun for Bennett to step back, and then he turned to Blair. "You, too, Mr. Blair."

"I'm not armed. Mr. Callaghan, I-I would strongly advise you not to do this," Blair spluttered. He held his hands at shoulder height.

Tyler grunted. "Too late. I'm doing it."

He swept his gun round to point at Rev, who had crept forward.

"Don't try it, Bible Man."

Rev stood still. Then he raised his arms and grinned. "When the Good Lord presents opportunities—"

"Don't try that again, or the Good Lord will present me with opportunities. Ya armed?"

"Only with the words of the Almighty."

"Yeah, well, I'm looking for someone more reliable." Tyler ordered Bennett, "Check him."

Bennett moved across the room. After a moment's hesitation, he made an exaggerated show of frisking Rev. He found nothing but a Bible.

"Satisfied?"

Tyler nodded.

"Now, Sheriff, I want ya to take the keys and open the door." When Bennett hesitated, Tyler cocked his gun. "I'm not messing with ya. Do it."

Bennett took the keys from his desk drawer and slid back the bolt on the cellblock. He opened the door and waited for further instructions.

Tyler ushered the four men into the cellblock.

"Well, it's about time you got here," Alan said, getting to his feet.

"Shut up," Tyler snapped. "On ya feet, Tubby. I'm taking ya outta here. Open the door to Tubby's cell, if you please."

"Tyler, I'd rather stay here," Tubby said.

"And let them hang you?"

"I didn't kill Mr. Mercer. I keep telling them. Mr. Crane is close to figuring everything out."

"Yeah, that's what worries me. Out now, or someone gets hurt."

Tubby gripped the bars tightly, and Fooks gave him a reassuring nod. Tubby returned a pained expression. "When he does, Ty, I'll be in the clear...," he said, his voice trailing off.

"Any more talking, an' I'm gonna shoot someone. We can start with Crane if ya like," Tyler said, turning to point his gun at Fooks.

"All right, all right, I'll come out. Don't shoot anyone."

Tubby held his hands up and slid out warily. Tyler gave Fooks a hefty shove into the cell. For a moment, Fooks wanted to retaliate, but he stopped himself in time. *Calm down. This is what we wanted. Sorta. The last thing you want is* him *appearing. Getting yourself killed sure won't help matters.*

"Lock him in, Sheriff."

"What 'bout me?" Alan cried. "Ya've gotta let me outta here."

All eyes turned to Tyler. "Let him out, too."

Alan pushed Bennett out of the way in his hurry to escape. Tyler ushered Bennett and Blair into the same cell. He relieved Bennett of the keys and handed them to Tubby.

Tubby fumbled with the lock. "I'm sorry, Sheriff."

"It's all right, Tubby," Bennett reassured him.

Alan ran into the office and immediately returned with Bennett's gun.

"Now, there's one man here I've got a score to settle with." He pulled back the hammer and pointed the gun at Fooks.

"Wouldn't do that, boy." Rev's hand closed on Alan's arm, pushing it and the gun downward.

"Take ya hand off me," Alan said, wrestling his arm free.

The gun went off. A wayward bullet flew.

"Yeow!"

All eyes widened.

"You shot me!" Blair shrieked before collapsing onto the bunk.

All eyes turned to Alan. Amazed at what he'd done, he could only stand and stare.

Rev made a move but stopped when Tyler swung his gun in his direction.

"I told you, don't move." Tyler laid a hand on Alan's other arm and squeezed it to get his attention. "Put the gun away. We're already in enough trouble as it is." He tossed his head at Bennett. "How bad is he?"

Bennett checked Blair over. He tore off his bandanna, wadded it up, and tucked it inside Blair's jacket. "Bleeding badly. Don't like the look of it."

"Oh, great," Tyler said with a heavy sigh.

Bennett darted to the bars. "What the heck, Alan? Tyler, let us out so the doc can look at him."

"You sure it's not just a flesh wound?" Tyler asked.

"No, I'm not sure, and that ain't the point. Men can still die of flesh wounds if left untreated." Behind Bennett, Blair whimpered in emphasis.

"You'll be out in the morning. He'll keep until then." Tyler turned to Rev. "You, why are you standing there? Get in that cell. Alan, put up the gun. Now!"

Alan continued to point his gun at Fooks. His finger twitched over the trigger. Fooks froze. The last thing he wanted to do was startle Alan into firing.

"Alan." Tubby's hands flew to his mouth, and he gasped when Alan and the gun turned to him.

Now that Alan's focus had moved from him, Fooks crossed his legs and touched his fingertips to his lips. It wasn't the first time he'd stared down the barrel of a gun, but others weren't used to it. *Calm, Tubby,* he silently urged. He met the frightened young man's eyes and gave him a reassuring nod.

The standoff lasted several long moments. Alan's eyes flicked between Tyler and Blair. All eyes were on him.

"Alan, please." Tubby choked back tears.

"Alan, enough now. Let's get going," Tyler urged.

To everyone's relief, Alan uncocked the gun and let out a long, low sigh. Fooks concealed a relieved breath. Tyler ushered Rev into the cell across the aisle. With trembling hands, Tubby locked the door.

"We'll be leaving ya now. Good night, gentlemen." Tyler tipped his hat politely and followed Alan and Tubby out.

"Well now, this is just great," Bennett fumed.

"What will happen now?" Blair asked, wincing in pain.

"Now, now, Sheriff. This is exactly what we were hoping for," Fooks said, trying to keep the tremor from his voice. To disguise it, he leaned over, and his hand slid inside his right boot. The cell door block stood ajar, and his sharp ears caught the conversation in the main office before the front door slammed shut.

"It was?" Bennett frowned. "I'm pretty sure I didn't bargain on being incarcerated in my own jail."

"Remember how I said something had to happen? To force Tyler into showing his hand. Well, that's what just happened."

"Yeah, ya did, but I didn't expect Tyler to break Tubby and Alan oughta jail."

"I don't think he knew Alan was here. Both he and Tyler are certainly in a lot of trouble now," Fooks said.

"I'll say," Blair said. He rested his head back against the wall. "Am I going to die?"

"Naw, bullet hardly touched ya. I jus' said that to make 'em think it's worse than it is."

Blair didn't seem at all relieved to hear that.

From his boot, Fooks pulled a thin-bladed knife.

"I can't believe it," Bennett said, pacing up and down. "I never expected him to do that." He shook his head.

"Neither did I, exactly," Fooks agreed. "Not with Mr. Blair here."

Bennett groaned. "Gonna be ages afore we can get after them. Patterson won't stop by until nine o'clock in the morning. They'll be long gone by then."

Fooks gazed at Rev. "Lend me your pectoral cross, if you please, Rev?" he asked politely.

"Aw now, I dunno. The last time ya used it for what you're gonna do, ya bent it."

Fooks grinned across at him. "Well, this time I'll bend it back," he said pleasantly. "We can't afford to wait for Patterson. Doc needs to look at Mr. Blair, and as the sheriff says, they'll be long gone by the time Patterson gets here. We really oughta be getting after them as soon as we can."

Rev reluctantly unbuttoned his tunic. Nestled against his rather grubby henley was a large base-metal cross. The downward member had a distinct kink in the bottom right edge. He took the cross off, wrapped the chain around the length, and slid it across the floor to Fooks.

"Thank you," Fooks said, picking it up.

"Ya will look after it?"

"'Course."

"What are you doing?" Bennett asked, having retreated to the bunk in despair, expecting a long wait.

"Er, sheriff, if you don't want me to offend your sensibilities, I suggest you look away now," Fooks advised.

Fooks selected the reverse of the point he'd previously used. He stuck it in the lock, preventing the mechanism from turning. Reaching round to the outside, he inserted the tip of the knife in the lock. Several moments of face pulling and knife wiggling followed until they all heard the click of release. Not hearing anything from the other room, Fooks, with a pleased grin, pushed open the cell door.

"I'll see if they left the keys," he said, handing Rev back his cross. "There you go, just like new." He quickly evaded Bennett's scowl.

Sometime later, when they regrouped in the office, Rev took a rifle from the rack. Bennett glanced at him before fixing his attention on Fooks.

"What now, Crane? I can raise a posse, but we've no idea where they're heading. Too dark to pick up their trail now, and by first light, they'll have a big lead on us."

Fooks pinched his bottom lip in thought. "Round up your two deputies, but we won't need a posse. I know where they've gone."

"Ya do? How?" Bennett was incredulous.

"I caught part of their conversation as they left. Tubby insisted they go to his house first. He's concerned about his Ma. He also said it loud enough so we'd hear... Well, I heard. Rev and me'll head over there. Try to stall 'em. Round up your deputies, Mark, and..." Fooks gave the sheriff a wide grin. "Arriving in the nick of time will be just fine."

Bennett gave Fooks his usual frown, shook his head, and nodded.

"What about me?" Blair asked.

"I'll wake the doc up on my way. Get ya sorted."

Fooks rolled his eyes and nudged Rev's arm. "C'mon. We're losing time."

CHAPTER TWENTY-SIX

"I don't like it, boy," Rev said as he and Fooks skulked in the bushes outside Tubby Wilson's house.

"Now you're sounding like Sid. What don't you like?" Fooks asked patiently, keeping his voice down.

"It's too quiet. Lovina is in there."

Fooks looked sideways at his friend. "Lovina?" Although dark, Fooks knew the mention of Mrs. Wilson's first name embarrassed his friend.

"Yeah, Lovina. She and I kinda...hit it off." Rev spluttered. "Now's not the time for this conversation, boy. Concentrate on the matter at hand."

Fooks grinned briefly but left it. Time enough for that conversation later.

"It's too quiet in there. Did we miss 'em?" Rev asked after a while.

"Yeah, I'm beginning to think that."

Fooks drew his gun. With practiced ease, he pulled back the barrel latch and rotated the barrel downward. Five chambers already loaded. With a glance at Rev, he balked over loading a sixth. He only ever loaded all six chambers if he was likely to use them. With a sigh, he decided not to and closed the gun.

"Okay, cover me, and I'll go look."

Rev grabbed Fooks' arm as he rose.

"No, I'll do it."

Fooks was mildly surprised. Rev was never big on heroics.

"Ya've got more to lose than me."

"I know, but..."

"I said I'd go. I need to know about Lovina. If we're right, they've gone."

Hearing a muffled sound, Rev crept closer until he discerned the cause. It was the sound of someone trying to yell for help through a gag. He had an awful feeling he knew who it was.

He scuffled around the side of the house, checking for unlocked windows as he went. He'd almost given up finding one and was contemplating smashing a pane when the latch on the kitchen window gave. He opened it, pulled himself across the sill, and clambered awkwardly over the sink. He cursed when his long tunic caught on the pump. Once free, his eyes went to the ceiling. He mouthed the benediction and sketched a hasty cross.

Certain no one else was in the house, he made his way to the room the noise came from and found Lovina gagged, with her arms and legs tied to a chair. He removed the gag first.

"They've got my boy, Rev!" she cried. "My poor boy."

"All right, Lovina. Help is at hand. Crane is outside, and the sheriff is on his way."

Rev freed her and took her in his arms. Only because she was distraught, he told himself.

"It's okay, Lovina. They won't harm him."

"How do you know?" she demanded. "I've never liked that Alan Long. All his people were bad."

"Shhh, now. Tyler will see him all right. He always has done, hasn't he?"

Lovina nodded and snuggled her head against Rev's shoulder.

A few minutes later, he raised his head.

Fooks rose to his feet when the sheriff arrived with the two part-time deputies. Neither seemed fully awake.

"We missed 'em, Sheriff," he said. "How's Mr. Blair?"

"Expected as much," Bennett said with resignation. "Aw, Doc's with Blair at the office. I told him when he felt better to stay and co-ordinate things." He shrugged at the questioning look from Fooks to show he didn't know what things, either. "Where's Rev?"

"He scouted round the back."

"I'm here," Rev said, opening the front door.

"Anyone in there?"

"Jus' Lo...Mrs. Wilson."

"Is she all right?" Fooks asked, starting for the door. He stopped. Bennett should go first. This was his town, and it his responsibility to uphold the law. He rolled his eyes at his mistake. So used to being in charge. Better watch himself. Mustn't give Bennett any more ideas.

"They tied her up and gagged her, but yeah, she's all right." Rev stood aside to let Bennett and Fooks through before following. The two deputies brought up the rear.

"Sheriff, they took my boy!" Mrs. Wilson cried when she saw Bennett.

"I know, Mrs. Wilson. We'll get him back safe and sound, don't you worry." Bennett patted her hand. "Now, did they say where they were going?"

"No. No, I didn't hear."

"They said nothing at all?" Fooks asked.

Mrs. Wilson shook her head. "It was all so sudden. I was asleep." She gasped. "Here I am, in front of you all in my nightclothes—" She sounded shocked but didn't appear to be.

"Now, Lovina, don't you worry. Ya look fine." Rev dropped into the chair beside her and took her hand. "Lovina, think. Did they say anything at all? It might help us find Theodore."

Lovina smiled at Rev. "Thank you, dear." She touched his cheek fondly.

Fooks and Bennett swapped smiles.

"Want me to get Annie, Sheriff?" asked Patterson, the part-time deputy. When Bennett glanced at him, he continued. "Y'know, to sit with her." He waved a hand at Mrs. Wilson. "Till we come back?"

Bennett nodded. Patterson sped away to fetch Annie from a few doors away.

"They said something about forty-nine. I don't understand what that means."

"Forty-nine? Does it mean anything, Sheriff?"

Bennett shook his head. "Not to me." He turned to Stoner, the other part-time deputy, who also shook his head.

Fooks crouched by Mrs. Wilson's chair. "What were their exact words, Mrs. Wilson?"

Lovina thought for a moment. "Theodore asked where they were going. Tyler answered, but that Alan Long interrupted. He's an awful man. Never liked him, not even as a boy."

"Lovina..."

"As they bundled Theodore away, he looked over his shoulder at me and mouthed something. Rev, he looked so scared."

"Mrs. Wilson, what did Tub...Theodore mouth to you?"

"Exactly what I heard before. Forty-nine." She glanced at Fooks and then at Bennett. "What does it mean?"

CHAPTER TWENTY-SEVEN

Fooks returned quickly to the jail, where he studied the county map, hoping that if he stared long enough, he would find a clue. However, the map didn't show enough detail, no more than the major towns and significant geographical features. Bennett and his deputies had gone to consult with folks in town who might have an idea what "forty-nine" meant.

Fooks glanced around when the door opened. It was Rev.

"Any luck, boy?" he asked, closing the door.

Fooks shook his head. "No. Bennett's out waking anyone who might know. Did Mrs. Wilson say any more?"

"Yeah, but again, another mystery," Rev said, standing next to Fooks. "She said Alan asked how long as they were leaving." Rev shrugged. "Presume he meant how long to get where they are going."

When nothing further came, Fooks was compelled to ask, "Was there an answer?"

"Yes. Lovina heard 'Looped C.' Is that Callaghan's ranch?"

"Yes." Fooks stood with hands on hips. "Gives us something more to go on," he murmured.

"What?"

"We now know it's a place rather than a thing, and likely on or near Tyler's ranch."

"Where's Blair?"

Fooks grinned and went to the cellblock door. He opened it and pointed in. Rev chortled softly when he saw Blair stretched out on one of the cell bunks.

"Doc's seen to him, and he was plumb tuckered out. Could hardly keep his eyes open, so I put him to bed," Fooks said.

He was closing the door when Bennett and his deputies stalked back in.

"No luck. Asked just about anyone we could think of who might know." Bennett stopped short when he noticed Fooks' face. "What?"

Rev told him what else Mrs. Wilson had said.

"How does that help us?" Bennett asked, moving to the county map. "Just about everywhere is near the Looped C. Now what?"

Fooks moved to study the map again. His index finger honed in on one spot roughly at the location of the Looped C. He tapped the spot, his eyes flicking around the rest of the map.

"Sheriff, do you have a more detailed map? One that... No. I know where..." He made for the door.

Bennett glanced at Rev, who shrugged but led the others as they followed.

Fooks stopped outside Stephen's office and selected a tool to pick the lock. He winced when the others joined him, expecting them to want an explanation for his behavior.

"The Thorold-Callaghan case file has a map of both ranches," he said. "May not give us what we need, but—"

"Open it," Bennett interrupted.

Fooks briefly pondered the irony of a sheriff telling him to break into a private office. He gave Bennett his usual tight-lipped smile and a nod.

It wasn't long before they were all crowding around the late Mr. Mercer's desk. They watched Fooks rifle through the relevant file until he found what he wanted.

"Here we are," Fooks said, spreading the map on the desk. "This is Thorold land." He pointed to the land at his left. "The disputed land up here." He waved a hand at the top of the sheet. "And Callaghan's Looped C is over here. As I suspected, not all, but maybe enough."

He raised his head to the crowd. "We're looking for 'forty-nine,' gentlemen, or anywhere Tyler might head for. I suspect he had a place all figured out before he came into town, well provisioned but accessible if you know where to look. My guess is it'll be somewhere remote and easily defended by a few men. Mustn't rule out the possibility he ordered some of his men to take part. Not all of 'em. Some, I reckon. He must realize we'll give chase once we're free. If not at 'forty-nine,' then somewhere else. He'll be ready for a showdown."

"Better raise a posse," Bennett said, but he didn't move. Instead, he sought approval from Fooks.

"There's five of us already. Many more makes it harder to hurry. A posse is never stealthy, and we should take 'em by surprise if we can."

Not to mention, inexperienced posses are not very good shots, with unruly and younger members who are downright gung-ho. Fooks had encountered his fair share of posses in the past. They usually made a mistake or two, which he would turn to his advantage. Now that he was on the other side, he didn't want any mistakes.

"We can manage, but we could use a tracker once we know where we're going."

Bennett turned to Stoner. "Go find Amos. Tell him there's money in it for him. And it's urgent."

In the next half-hour, there were a few suggestions, with several places described, discussed, and dismissed. All were held in reserve in case nothing more likely surfaced. Patterson proved to be an excellent strategist. He offered several scenarios that had Fooks nodding in agreement. He could have done with someone like Patterson in Guardian Wall.

Stoner burst in with another man in tow, a grizzled old-timer in dirty buckskins, presumably the Amos he'd gone to get.

"Not 'forty-nine.' It's Fort Tyne," he said, excited. "Amos figured it straight away." He nodded to the man at his side.

"Then what kept ya?" Bennett barked.

"Socks," Amos said.

"Huh?"

"Needed some."

"I know where ya can find a pair. Or twenty," Bennett muttered.

"Fort Tyne?" Fooks queried, bringing them back to the matter at hand.

"Yeah." Amos stepped forward and spun the map around. Fooks blinked and moved back, allowing him to continue. The stench from the older man's buckskins reminded him of Sid just before his annual bath.

Amos studied the map for a moment before tapping his finger on a spot and spinning the map back. "Right there. See where it says 'ruins'? That's Fort Tyne. Back in the late sixties, the Army set up a line of military forts all round here, first to protect travelers on the Overland Stage against Indian attack, later to protect workers building the Union Pacific Railroad. Most of 'em have gone outta use or are about to. Fort Steele over at Sinclair is pretty much run down. Fort Halleck at Elk Mountain is all but abandoned. Only used Fort Tyne for 'bout a year till they realized it was in the wrong place. Gone a long while now, but it's on Looped C land."

"That's it." Fooks grinned. "Thanks, Amos. We coulda been here all night. What's the lay of the land like?" he asked.

Amos sketched a map of the site, adding details of buildings and cover. A short while later, the posse was saddling up.

"Mr. Crane! Mr. Crane!"

Fooks wheeled his horse in the shout's direction. The night messenger boy held out a telegram. *Oh, sheesh! Not Mary.*

"It's urgent, sir. Was coming to get you at the hotel, but you're here." The man cast an eye over the posse, which pulled up when Fooks broke off.

Fooks' horse, unhappy with the abrupt change of direction and speed, pranced and tossed its head. "Whoa there, boy," Fooks said softly. He came alongside the messenger and snatched the telegram. "Thanks."

It was from Mary. Fooks scanned the few words she'd written:

New arrival imminent. Come home now.

"Sheesh!"
"Is there a reply, sir?"

Fooks stared at the telegram. What was he supposed to do? Even if he left now, he wouldn't get home in time.

"Problem?" Rev appeared at his side, concerned for his friend.

Fooks numbly handed over the telegram and watched Rev read it, hoping he'd have the answer to his dilemma.

"What do I do?"

"Nothing ya can do. However, ya cut it, babe'll be here by the time ya get there. Few more hours won't make no difference."

"But Rev, if something should happen to Mary, I wouldn't get a chance to—"

"She knows where ya are and how long it'll take to get back. Don't think 'bout anything going wrong. Trust in the Lord. In the meantime, we have the bad guys to catch. We know where they are, and right now, we have the element of surprise. D'ya want them to get away?"

"No."

"Once we do this, then ya can get on your way. Come with ya if ya want."

Fooks shook his head, swallowing hard. He glanced at the rest of the posse, all ready to ride, and then back at Rev. "I-I don't know what to do." He looked helplessly at his friend.

Rev shook Fooks' arm. "Yes, ya do, boy. Yes, ya do."

Fooks took off his hat and ran a hand through his hair. "Any reply, sir?"

The telegraph messenger boy hopped from side to side.

"Huh?" Fooks had forgotten he was there. "Er...yeah. Yes. Tell Mrs. Crane I'm on my way. No, that's not right. Um..." He scrubbed his forehead, thinking.

"How about this? Wrapping things up. Be home soon," Rev offered.

Fooks nodded. "Yes. Send that."

He clapped his hat on, tightened the stampede strings under his chin, and nodded to Rev, and they were off.

They arrived in darkness, but the stars were winking out as the sky lightened. Not much time to agree on strategy, sneak their way to cover, and hunker down.

The posse pulled up before the land dipped. Bennett and Fooks crept forward on hands and knees, leaving the others holding their horses. Flat on their fronts, they cautiously peered over the edge, into the valley below.

The complex sat at the bottom of a shallow basin, lost from sight once over the brow of the surrounding hills. A few buildings still stood, not all complete, some comprising little more than one or two walls. Doors hung haphazardly. Shuttered windows banged in the stiff wind. Weeds socialized between the rotten boards of the thresholds. Roofs had partially caved in, and their shingles lay scattered for several yards around, waiting to trip up the unwary. The middle of the complex had a large, open space, formerly the parade ground. At one side stood the remains of the fort's flagpole, now snapped off at head height.

The fort had never had a stockade, but the outline was plain. A post and rail fence around the perimeter achieved this, with a gap for the entrance. Outside the fence, on either side of the entrance, lay two foxholes, originally for the fort's defense. Nature was filling them in, and their bottoms were now mud.

Only one building was complete enough to be habitable, tucked away in the far-left corner, away from the entrance. Judging by the size of the chimney, it may have been the fort's smithy. The blacksmith was long gone, but tonight a faint glow came from the one small window to the left of the door. Next to it stood a derelict barn. Its back had collapsed, but the front appeared occupied, albeit open on one side. From here emanated the sounds of horses, which seemed to resent the cramped conditions.

More horses milled around in the improvised paddock to the right of the building. Ominously, there were more than three horses; it was more like twelve.

Sheriff Bennett peered through binoculars at the deserted fort.

"Reckon they're holed up in the old smithy. Looks like half the Looped C is there."

Beside him, Fooks shifted. "Let me see." He grabbed the binoculars, only to look round in surprise when Bennett gave a squawk. The strap around his neck had cut across his throat. Bennett growled and freed the strap. Fooks bit his lip and murmured an apology.

"Hmmm."

"What d'ya see?"

"Same as you, I reckon. Counted twelve horses, all saddled and ready to go."

"They outnumber us."

"Not necessarily." Fooks brought the binoculars down and bounced his fist against his lips, thinking. "If it was me and I was planning to go somewhere in a hurry... "He broke off and shook his head. He peered through the binoculars again. This time he swept the surrounding countryside. "No lookouts. None I can spot, anyway."

"Don't suppose Tyler thought we'd be pursuin' quite yet," Bennett said with a chuckle. "Gonna be quite a surprise when we start shootin'."

"Hmmm."

"What now?" Bennett snapped.

Fooks bit his lip in frustration. *Amateur, Mark. Do I have to think of everything?* "We need a better plan than shooting up the place and hoping for the best."

"Ya got a plan?"

Fooks nodded. "Working on it." He looked skyward. "Be daybreak soon. We'd best get into position while we still can," he said, shuffling away.

"What's the plan?" Bennett asked, and then he growled when no answer came.

They returned to the others, who were waiting expectantly for a plan of action.

"We haven't got much time, fellas," Fooks said, glancing at the lightening sky. "The aim is to take 'em alive, and there's no reason why we can't. These aren't dangerous outlaws." Fooks caught Bennett giving him a sharp look, but he resisted the temptation to meet his eye. "We've got the element of surprise here, but we should give them the chance to come in peaceable." Now he turned to Bennett. "When it's fully light and we can all see what we're doing, let 'em know we're here and what we want."

"Why me?" asked Bennett, disgruntled by Fooks' tone of 267ommand. "I don't trust those hands. Most of 'em are hot-headed and will go off half-cocked, 'specially if they think they're defending their boss."

"We'll just have to hope Tyler has a tight rein on them." Fooks turned to Bennett. "It has to be you, Sheriff. You have the authority." He paused for effect. "'Cause you're in charge."

Bennett glared at Fooks as if he didn't believe him. Fooks shrugged and turned to his horse.

"We oughta leave these here and move in on foot."

"Just a minute, Crane. What's the plan?"

Fooks turned back. Running the reins through his fingers, he pondered what to say. "I reckon they'll talk, but we'd best get into close positions just in case." He twitched his head. "I figger Tyler planned to send a hand into town to negotiate, safe in the knowledge no one knew where he was. Least, that's what I woulda done if I was in his situation. We've turned the tables right now, so we can call the shots." He turned back to his horse, and then, with a grin over his shoulder, he added, "No pun intended."

First light found Fooks squatting precariously in a foxhole. He was halfway up the side nearest the fence, avoiding the melting mud at the bottom. Rev had found suitable cover some way behind him along the overgrown trail to the entrance. Stoner and Patterson occupied the other foxhole. Bennett moved into the fort. He sheltered behind the sole-surviving wall of the barrack block, off to the right. He blew on his fingers before he took up position, his gun drawn. Amos had disappeared. Fooks suspected he was scouting around the other side of the site.

Fooks had been in his foxhole for some time, waiting for Bennett's signal to move in. He pulled the neck of his red and green plaid coat around him. Why didn't he get a new coat when he was able? When the sun came up, it would rise fully over the hills, and that was fast approaching. Any minute now, they would make their move.

But they hadn't sneaked as silently as they'd thought. The occupants of the smithy, realizing they had company, shot first. This took away any element of surprise Bennett had hoped they'd have.

Fooks ducked low. The cacophony of gunshots in his direction made it impossible for him to get a shot away in reply.

The last thing he expected was movement from his rear.

CHAPTER TWENTY-EIGHT

His adrenaline flowing, Fooks spun around, about to squeeze the trigger. The brief flash of a familiar mustache slithering into the foxhole stopped him. Almost immediately, an unsavory, but also familiar, aroma followed.

"What…! Sheesh!"

"Are them's the good guys or the bad guys who are shooting at us?" Brad asked, taking a position next to Fooks, his big Colt out and ready to fire.

"We're the good guys. How can you ask that?"

"Ya wearing a black hat."

"It's not black." Fooks sucked in a breath through gritted teeth. "It's charcoal."

"So? Charcoal's black."

Fooks sucked in another deep breath. "What the…heck are you two doing here?"

A maniacal laugh escaped Sid.

"Makes a change, Brad. Usually, it's the good guys shootin' at us."

Brad chortled in agreement.

"I can't believe I'm having this conversation here, in the middle of a gunfight." Fooks took a deep breath, summoning his patience. "What are you two doing here? I told you to go back to the Wall."

"Yeah, well, when we didn't hear nothing, we figured ya were out of ya depth, so we's here to help."

Fooks had no response. Staring open-mouthed was about the most he could do, apart from ducking his head when a shot whizzed by far too closely for comfort.

"Looks like we's got here jus' in time, too." Brad fired off a random shot in the general direction of the smithy.

"I don't believe this. I must be dreaming," Fooks muttered, shaking his head.

"Are we taking 'em alive, Fooks?" Sid asked.

"Yes."

"All of 'em?" Brad queried.

"Yes."

"Ya sure?"

"Yes," Fooks hissed, insistent.

Brad shrugged twice. Once in a not-convinced kinda way and then in a well-if-ya're-sure kinda way.

"If ya wanna get closer, Fooks, me 'n' Sid'll cover ya," Brad said, considerate to a fault.

From where they were, the nearest cover lay thirty feet away. Crossing to it would make a target a toddler could hit.

"Me! Why me?"

"'Cause that's what made ya such a great leader, Fooks. Ya never told no man t'do a thing ya wouldn't do yaself."

"Shut up, Sid," Fooks snapped. "I'm not going out there."

Fooks collected himself. Perhaps having Brad and Sid here wasn't such a bad thing. It'd even up the numbers, if nothing else. "Sheriff Bennett is in charge here. We're waiting for his signal, and then we're moving in, but you two keep outta sight. If Bennett sees you, he will arrest you."

"Ya ain't convinced him yet it weren't us?" Brad asked, sounding surprised and disappointed.

"Yes, he knows, but he'll still arrest you for being you."

Brad grunted. "Don't sound too grateful to me, considering we've come to save the day."

Fooks groaned and banged his forehead on the side of the foxhole.

"Where's Rev?" Sid asked.

Fooks shook his head, wiping away the earth he'd embedded into his forehead with a furious swipe. "Back there by the large rock. Does he know you're here?"

"Nope." Brad grinned. "Be a pleasant surprise for him, too."

Fooks shook his head and took up position again. From where he crouched, he could see that Bennett was pinned behind the extant wall of the barrack block. Bennett frowned at him, having seen the slithering twosome invade Fooks' position. Fooks took the brief break in firing to nod and raise a hand in Bennett's direction, and then a shot sent him sprawling to the foxhole's bottom, now defrosting into a muddy sludge.

"You's all right, Fooks?" Brad asked.

Fooks raised up on his elbows and glared at Brad from under his lopsided hat. Brad bit his lip to contain his mirth. Sid had no such qualms and giggled at the sight of Fooks' mud-splattered face.

"Yeah, I'm all right." Fooks sighed as he crawled out from the mud to take up his previous position. He adjusted his hat.

"They're gonna run outta bullets if they keep that up," Brad said mildly.

"That's the plan. Bennett reckons the way to minimize bloodshed is to wait 'em out."

"What kinda dang fool plan is that? I say we rush 'em."

"No. We're waiting," Fooks said firmly. "And you don't get a say. You're not here." He shook his hand, trying to rid himself of mud, and puffed.

"For all we know, they could have a whole armory in there."

"Yes, but we only have finite ammunition out here. We're making every shot count."

"What's finite mean, Brad? Is that a new kinda bullet?"

When Fooks and Brad both eyed Sid, he shuffled aside in embarrassment. He didn't see Fooks and Brad exchange fond smiles.

"Look, if you wanna be useful, circle round that way." Fooks waved towards the bushes and woodland off to his left. "When Bennett gives us the signal, creep up in the rear. Watch out for an old man with long gray hair, dressed in buckskins. He's on our side."

"What's the signal?" Brad asked.

Fooks growled. "You'll know it."

Brad snorted. "Not much of a plan, Fooks."

"I'm not in charge," Fooks replied in a tone that suggested, if he'd been able to take the lead, their organization would have been better. "Now get."

A break in the firing allowed Bennett"to yell,""We've gotcha surrounded! Come on out!"

In his foxhole, Fooks winced at the cliché. How many times had he heard that? Must be a phrase they taught at sheriff school. The bowl of the complex had the fortunate, or unfortunate, ability to enhance any sound. Fooks heard Brad's distinctive chortle from the bushes yards away.

Bennett's answer came pinging off the stone post, the cornerstone of the former barracks.

"We didn't kill Mercer!" yelled Alan.

"Someone did. And you're my prime suspects." Bennett paused. "C'mon out, an' we can talk about it."

Shooting recommenced from the smithy, but with noticeably less ferocity. This allowed the plume of gunsmoke that had enveloped the complex to begin to dissipate.

A short time later, Fooks saw movement from the smithy. He cast an eye towards Bennett. This was it. Judging by the number of horses, the defenders outnumbered the forces of law and order. He had no doubts about Rev and the surprise help. Amos had the appearance of the type of man who'd lived a hard life. You didn't come through without learning a trick or two about survival. He sure hoped Bennett and his deputies were up for this, or things could become a might tricky.

As he watched, Tyler made a run for it with five hands. That left four in the smithy, with Alan and presumably Tubby. Amos appeared from the back of the complex, rifle in hand. Tyler fired off a hopeful shot in his direction, and Amos stumbled back and went down.

Amos squirmed around, took aim, and fired. He missed, and Tyler made it to the relative safety behind the broken-down officers' quarters. The hands found refuge where they could nearby. Amos crawled behind a collapsed building. From the amount of cursing coming from his direction, he appeared hurt but not seriously.

Fooks cursed under his breath. Shots still rang from the smithy. The defenders had split their forces and were now able to attack from two directions. Tyler and the hands had the ideal places to provide cover to the smithy. Sneaking up would not work anymore. The tables had turned. Bennett and co. were now in imminent danger of being pinned down. A glance from Bennett confirmed that he'd read the situation the same way.

"Bennett!" yelled Tyler during a gap in the gunfire. "You still there?"

"Yeah, I'm still here."

"What d'ya wanna do? Looks like me and my boys are holding all the aces here."

"You can come out with your hands up!" Bennett yelled back, more in hope than expectation. Fooks rolled his eyes. If he'd had to deal with more sheriffs like Bennett in the past, he might not have given up outlawing when he had. He twitched his head. 'Course, he might also be serving time right now.

"Ah, you saw the pig flying past just now as well. Not a chance till we have an understanding."

"What's there to understand? We've come to take you and Alan in. There's two men shot already this day. I want no more. That's a lot of trouble on top of what I want ya for, which is murder, by the way."

Silence from the officers' quarters and then, "Are you saying Blair's dead?"

"No, not when we left, but Stephen Mercer is, an' he shouldn't be. That's murder in anyone's book."

"I told ya, we didn't murder Stephen Mercer."

"Then come out, and let's talk about it."

"Don't you dare, Tyler!" Alan hollered. "I shot our lawyer, and you shot the old fella. We won't get a fair hearing now."

Fooks listened to the exchanges with increasing frustration. Something had to happen to break the stalemate. Bennett appeared fresh out of ideas, so... Fooks hesitated. He sighed. Up to him, then.

"Joseph Crane here. Now, we don't have any interest in you ranch boys. Toss your guns down and come out with your hands up. You have my word we'll let you ride outta here." When no immediate answer came, he added, "What d'you say?"

"Why should we believe you?" came a shout.

"Ya can believe me!" Bennett yelled.

"There you are. You all know Sheriff Bennett. He's an honest lawman," Fooks said. *Unlike some I've known in my time.* "You've got two minutes to make up your minds, and then we're gonna start shooting. And we won't stop." Fooks shrugged when Bennett glared at him. It was a bluff, but it sounded good. Fooks took out his pocket watch. "The two minutes start now."

From the direction of the officers' quarters, they could hear voices, but they were not loud enough to make out what was being said. Fooks signaled to Rev. He wanted him to join him in his foxhole.

Keeping low, Rev crossed the distance before slithering into the foxhole.

"See some help arrived," he said as he took up position beside Fooks. He pointed the barrel of his rifle over the edge.

"Yes, what d'you know?"

"I recognize that look. You've gotta plan."

"This is not gonna be a classic Florian Fooks plan, Rev, but it's the best I can do on the spur of the moment. Once those hands give up, the numbers will look a whole lot better in our favor. They may have figgered there's six of us, but they won't be expecting Brad and Sid."

"Will the hands give up?"

"Some will. Not all of 'em, but enough, I reckon."

"Then what?"

Fooks hesitated. "Then I'll go out there and talk to them."

"What! Ya can't go out there. Ya're gonna get gunned down for sure."

Fooks considered this. "I agree. It's a risk. But I'm an odds player, Rev, and I've weighed the risks. These men aren't killers. Mercer's death was an accident."

"Are ya willing to bet *your* life on it?"

Fooks didn't answer immediately. "May not come to that. Let's see what happens in the next little while." He glanced at his watch. "One more minute, fellas!" he yelled. He took out his gun and exposed the chamber cylinder. This time he loaded six shots.

"What d'ya say, Mr. Callaghan?" a voice asked.

"Man has the right to make his own decisions in life, Phil. But know this. I need men I can rely on. Whoever takes their deal can clear their things and collect their pay."

Fooks glanced at Rev and swallowed. This could be the make-or-break moment. He glued his eyes to the watch hand as it ticked away. "Thirty seconds."

"He's not giving them much of a choice," Rev said under his breath.

"Just wait and see."

Fooks changed his position, putting his shoulder to the wall of the foxhole and drawing the opposite leg up. The stance put his back towards Rev. His friend could read him, and he wanted no more discussion about his course of action. He'd decided.

"Twenty seconds."

Behind him, Rev levered the trigger and settled into a sniper stance.

"Ten seconds. Then we open fire."

Fooks pulled the brim of his hat down low. From the officers' quarters, he detected movement. Was this gonna work? When nothing else happened, he fixed his eyes on his watch once more.

"Five seconds."

He craned his neck up to see if there was any movement.

"Four seconds."

A gun thudded onto the ground between the parties.

"I'm sorry, Mr. Callaghan, but I got family to think about."

Fooks widened his eyes. *So do I.* He shook his head. Now wasn't the time to think about Mary. He had to stay focused. "Three seconds."

"Don't shoot, Mr. Crane, Sheriff. I'm coming out."

A man rose nervously, holding his hands up.

"All right, Phil. I understand," Tyler said with resignation.

"Get your horse, Phil," Bennett said. "An' be quick about it."

The man nodded and ran to the paddock.

"Anyone else? Two seconds."

Another gun joined the first, and a ranch hand crept into view.

"One second."

From the smithy came four more guns and men.

"No!"

Alan's anguished cry was audible above Tyler's cursing.

"All right. All right." Tyler tossed his gun and rose in place, his hands up. "Give it up, boys," he said to his three remaining men. "Alan, it's over."

Bennett motioned to Stoner and Patterson to move forward and collect the guns. Conscious that Alan still had his gun, they emerged with their guns drawn.

From the smithy came sounds of scuffling, and then Alan appeared, holding Tubby in front of him for protection, gun pointed at his head.

"Alan!" Tyler exclaimed. "It's no good. Give it up."

"Listen to him, Alan," Bennett said, stepping out from behind the wall.

"No. Now you're gonna all listen to me. Tubby and me are going to ride outta here. You ain't gonna stop us. D'you hear?"

"Ya're gonna leave me to take the fall for this?" Tyler yelled.

"'Fraid so, ol' friend. You've given me no choice. Hold it right there, Sheriff. I've got a hostage and nothing to lose."

Fooks holstered his gun and scrambled from the foxhole. Rev made a grab for him, but he shook him off.

"You've everything to lose, Alan. How about your life?" Fooks yelled, straightening up.

Alan's attention turned to him. The gun moved from Tubby and trained on Fooks.

With hands up, Fooks stepped towards the pair. Behind him, Rev cursed.

Alan backed away, dragging Tubby with him.

"Don't come any closer, Crane."

"Alan, you didn't mean to kill Stephen Mercer, so I doubt if you'll hang. But you kill me or Tubby, and it's a certainty."

Fooks continued walking forwards at a steady pace. This woulda been so much easier if he'd had Tobe here to watch his back. Instead, he had to rely on Rev and his rifle skills. And he fervently hoped the situation would not allow his black alter ego a foothold.

Fooks came to a halt ten feet from Alan and Tubby.

"Are you all right, Tubby?" he asked in a calm voice.

"N-not really, Mr. Crane."

Fooks smiled faintly. "It's okay, Tubby. You just do exactly what Alan says, and you won't get hurt. Isn't that right, Alan?"

"Yeah. Back off, Crane."

Fooks held his hands higher and flashed a smile he knew would infuriate Alan. "How d'you see this playing out? What d'you hope to gain?"

"Shut up, Crane."

Alan dragged Tubby close to the paddock rails. Many of the Looped C ranch hands had already collected their horses and gone, but several remained. Alan ventured a quick look behind him, locating their horses.

"Tubby, I'd like you to listen to me carefully. Can you do that?" Fooks said.

Tubby hesitated and then nodded.

"Whatever happens in the next few moments, I want you to look down and keep looking down." He emphasized the word "down." "Do you understand me?"

Tubby nodded. "I think so, sir."

"Good." This was gonna be tricky. "How're you gonna do this, Alan? Getting yourself and Tubby mounted isn't gonna be easy."

"You leave me to worry about that. Back off, Crane, or so help me... " Alan waved his gun wildly in Fooks' direction. "You've been asking for it since the moment we first met."

"Asking for what?" Fooks' voice took on a hard, eerily quiet tone. He kept Alan's eyes locked with his. "Down, Tubby. Now." He said it quietly, and Alan narrowed his eyes, unable to hear. Alan raised his gun at Fooks.

All movement narrowed into a sharp focus. All noise from around the site retreated to a distant hum. Yet here, tension magnified the moment.

Turning sideways, Fooks presented a smaller target. Then he went for his gun. He was no fast draw, but he wasn't a slouch, either.

With Alan distracted, Tubby wrenched free and hurled himself to the ground.

Fooks fired, relying on the accuracy of his gun rather than any skill on his part.

Alan pitched backward, and his gun flew from his hand.

Fooks gawked in genuine surprise. Swan had always told him the Schofield would save his life one day. Today his friend's superior firearm knowledge had come true.

Fooks raced to kick Alan's gun away and pointed his gun at the writhing, moaning man on the ground.

"Ya busted my arm!" Alan yelled, and he followed this with a string of expletives.

"Yes, I did. Better than killing you. Although..."

Fooks broke off abruptly as adrenaline and stress overwhelmed him. Something was happening. *No!* His dark persona flared into life. He tried to fight it. His body shook with the effort. He'd have no control if Florian Fooks fully emerged. Tobias Swan usually mitigated the effects, but he wasn't here. He gasped in panic. He couldn't do it. Sweat ran down his back, and his face heated at the effort of trying to stop...

The tidal wave of Florian Fooks submerged his milder being. He was calm. He was in control. He was at his most ruthless. He'd taken over completely.

Fooks stood over Alan, pointing the gun at his head. He cocked it with masterful skill.

"Gimme an excuse," said Florian Fooks, outlaw leader, cool and calculating.

CHAPTER TWENTY-NINE

Alan gaped up, fear stark in his eyes.

"No!" he screamed, his bloody hand reaching up, imploring.

Everyone stopped. Their focus on Fooks and Alan. Silence amplified the sharp sounds of the injured man gasping and Fooks' measured breathing. His finger tightened on the trigger.

"Think of Mary, boy."

Rev's voice rang clear and bell-like in Fooks' head. The loudness and proximity caused Fooks to take a sharp intake of breath. It was enough. The distraction jolted Fooks back to himself. He blinked once, twice, taking a moment to realize where he was, what he was about to do.

Stunned by how close he'd come to disaster, he relaxed his finger, releasing the trigger. He breathed hard for a few moments before stepping away. Gulping air, he waved his gun at Alan, disguising how much his hand was shaking.

"Get up," he ordered, emotion making his voice catch. Alan sat up slowly.

Fooks, dazed, scrubbed a hand over his forehead. Overwhelming tiredness followed these events. *Can't give in. Still much to do.* He blinked several times and stood back to allow Alan to get to his feet.

Fooks handed a pale and shaky Alan over to Stoner. He appeared to have some medical knowledge and took Alan away to tend to his arm, leaving Fooks to view what was happening elsewhere.

Tyler was secure, and Bennett was crouched by Amos. From the amount of cursing, Amos was doctoring himself. He didn't need any help from Bennett, who stood and scanned around until his eyes fell on Fooks.

Fooks licked his lips but held his ground as Bennett made his way over to him. *Don't want this right now.* He couldn't meet Bennett's eye, and he expected difficult questions.

Fortunately, the return of three ranch hands provided a distraction. Fooks narrowed his eyes when he saw two men on horseback, one tall, one short, following them.

"Get in there," the taller one commanded.

The three pulled up on the edge of the parade ground and dismounted.

"Caught 'em circling around," Brad said. "Thought we'd best apprehend 'em so they wouldn't jeopardize ya operation."

Brad tipped his hat, Sid gave Fooks and Bennett a cheery wave, and then the two men galloped away.

Bennett raised an eyebrow at Fooks for an explanation. Fooks, not completely back to himself, pulled a face and shrugged. Bennett grunted before saying, "Let's tidy up here an' get on back."

Patterson and Rev dealt with the three ranch hands.

"What happened to you?" Bennett asked quietly, eying the mudlark beside him.

"Lost my footing," Fooks replied softly, still shaken by his own actions.

"Who were those two guys?" Bennett asked.

Fooks swallowed and twitched his head. "Just two good Samaritans," he said, hoping Bennett would buy that as an explanation.

Bennett grunted, but prudence told him to leave it. A subdued, taciturn Crane was unsettling. There'd be time for a fuller account later.

Tubby lay on the ground, face up. Fear still showed in his eyes, and it didn't lessen when Fooks and Bennett crouched beside him.

"Are you all right, Tubby?" Bennett asked.

Fooks went to put his hand on the younger man's arm, but Tubby recoiled in a panic.

"Are...are *you* Mr. Crane? For a moment there, I thought—"

"I'm sorry I scared you." Fooks let out a weak laugh. "Scared me, too."

"What happened?"

Fooks shook his head. "Caught up in the situation, I guess. It's over now. C'mon, up you get."

Tubby, still regarding Fooks warily, allowed him to help him to his feet.

"Let's get back," Bennett said, sweeping his hand around the site, including everyone. His eyes fell on Tyler and Alan, now side by side. "I've got a lot of questions for you two." He turned back to Fooks. "Might have some for you as well."

Fooks rolled his eyes, and he took Tubby's arm. "Let's get you home. Bet your ma is out of her mind with worry."

They found Blair waiting for them at the sheriff's office. His arm was in a sling, and he showed signs of discomfort as they brought in the prisoners.

"Sorry, Mr. Blair. It was an accident," Alan said contritely. Pale and in pain, he managed a faint smile. "Got an injury of m'own now."

"Yeah, I'll get the doc to ya as soon as ya're locked up," Bennett said.

"You'd better be quick. I've lost all feeling in my hand."

"Quicker ya stop complainin', the quicker I'll get him. In ya go, Tyler."

"Sheriff, might I talk to my client here first?" Blair asked. His eyes flicked to the cellblock door after Alan walked through. "Under the circumstances, Mr. Long will have to make alternative arrangements."

"Oh, great."

Alan stomped inside.

Bennett gestured for Tyler to take a seat. He waited for Stoner and Patterson to finish locking up the three ranch hands and Alan before he slid the bolt on the cellblock door.

"Patterson, go get the doc. Stoner, stop by the I and have them fix breakfast for…" He made a quick count. "Eight." Blair shook his head. "Seven, then. And tell 'em the town'll pay."

"Very generous, Mark," Fooks said, pulling out a chair.

"Waal, we've been up all night, an' we ain't finished yet." Bennett rubbed a hand wearily over his face. "Let's get on with this, and then we can all get to bed."

When they settled, Bennett glanced at Fooks, expecting him to lead Tyler's questioning. Fooks shook his head. He was still wrestling with his actions of the night before. It would be a while before he came to terms with it. He gestured to Bennett to go ahead.

"Why don't you start at the beginning? We'll chip in with questions as we go."

Tyler sought permission from Blair, who nodded. "I guess it all started when Pa died. He left me in a hole financially. If I could just get over the first few months, then I wouldn't have to sell the ranch. My home." He hesitated. "So, I approached Alan for help. He agreed to bail me out. He owns fifty percent of the Looped C as a silent partner. We kept it between the two of us. Way we both wanted it."

"Your pa died three years ago. How have things been since?" Fooks asked, determined to pay attention and stop himself from dwelling on earlier.

"How are Mr. Callaghan's financial affairs relevant?" Blair asked.

"Money and the lack of it are powerful motivators, Mr. Blair. Believe me, I know," Fooks said with hidden meaning, perhaps talking about himself, too.

"I don't mind answering the question. I wanna be honest."

Blair nodded.

Tyler hesitated before he continued. "This ain't easy to admit, but I don't have the head for business Pa had. I made some mistakes, which cost me. Things are looking pretty dicey right now, and when Celia fenced off my land, having cows die on me, it was the last straw."

Fooks glanced at Blair from the corner of his eye and phrased his next question neutrally. "What did you decide to do?"

"I didn't know exactly. I had to do something. When I spoke to Alan, things kinda got worse."

"In what way?"

"There was me thinking Alan was gonna be my savior again. Turns out Alan isn't as wealthy as he appears. He may own a lot of properties, but some of 'em make very little profit for him. He got mad. He'd overinvested, and if the Looped C went under, then so did he."

"Explains why Alan was so concerned about Celia's claim on the land," Bennett said.

"Sure does."

"Alan said he could persuade Celia to change her mind. I didn't ask for details, but knowing Alan...women kinda like him, if ya know what I mean." When they nodded, Tyler continued. "I guess it didn't work how he'd figgered. He came back with an alternative plan. I didn't hold with it at first, but I could see Alan was as desperate as me."

"So, what happened was all Alan's idea?" Blair asked.

Tyler pulled a face. "I'd like to tell ya yes after what he did to Tubby and you, Mr. Blair. But in all honesty, I can't. It was a chance remark by Lucinda Mercer that got us thinking."

"What did Lucinda say?" Fooks asked.

"Like I said, Alan has this way with women. Sleazy, I'd call it, but they seem to fall for it every time. Lucinda did." Tyler took a deep breath. "She said she wished Stephen would get ill so he would have to take a break from work."

"Wait a minute. Are you saying Alan deliberately cultivated a relationship with Lucinda Mercer in order to do harm to her husband?" Fooks eyes popped.

"She's a lonely woman...good-looking one, too. I don't think their relationship took a lot of cultivating." Tyler shook his head. "Ya need to ask him about the details. I wanted to stay out of it."

"Oh, we will," Bennett said.

"So, let me get this right," Blair said. "Lucinda Mercer said to Alan, 'Wouldn't it be nice if Stephen got ill—'"

"I don't think she said it quite like that."

"Were you there to hear it said?" Fooks asked.

"No."

"Then how d'ya know?" Bennett asked.

"Look, I don't know the exact words," Tyler spluttered. "I only know what Alan told me."

Fooks and Bennett swapped glances.

"All right. What happened next?" Blair asked, breaking the silence.

"I was at Tubby's one day…long before all this. Martha Pickering called to tend to Lovina's legs. I remember her saying how dangerous the stuff she used was."

Fooks bit his lip. Probably best if Blair asked the question. He wasn't disappointed. "What is it called?" Blair asked.

Tyler waved a hand. "Ak-something. I dunno. Nothing I've ever heard of."

Both Fooks and Bennett turned to Blair. If either mentioned the name, Blair might construe that as leading the witness. They had to get Tyler to say it without prompting. Easier said than done.

"What does it look like?" Blair asked.

"It's clear, kinda gloopy, like glue. Comes in a bottle 'bout yay big." Tyler held his fingers apart, indicating the size was the same as the aconite bottle they'd found in his room.

Blair nodded and made a note. He winced. It was difficult being right-handed with his right arm in a sling.

"Anyway, when Alan pondered what would make Stephen ill enough to stop him working, I remember the ak-whatsit. Alan grinned and said he knew how it could work. Celia was gonna give Stephen a wooden chest. Alan reckoned it needed a padlock. He asked me if I knew about Preston's padlocks. I laughed and said of course. He'd shown just about everyone those damn padlocks."

Fooks rubbed his forehead. "So, Alan stole the padlock, and you stole Mrs. Wilson's liniment to put inside."

"About the size of it, yeah."

"How did events unfold?" Blair asked.

"Alan contrived to be with Celia before she sent the chest into town. Said he'd take it. We just had to get the padlock on. He persuaded me to ask Tubby."

"Did Tubby know what the padlock contained?"

Tyler shook his head. "No, he had no idea. Which is why, when I got his note that you'd arrested him for Stephen's murder, I had to do something about it." Tyler smiled ruefully. "Which is what you'd figgered, huh, Sheriff?"

Fooks tried not to look too smug.

"Lucinda made sure Stephen opened the padlock, hurting his hand. While she was in the office, I kept Tubby out of the way, and when Lucinda left, I slipped in." Tyler allowed Blair to keep up with his notes. "Alan let himself in the back door. Together we planned to take advantage of Stephen's incapacity, put pressure on him to withdraw his defense of my appeal. Things went wrong. Stephen was far more ill than we'd banked on. Nothing we could do."

"Shoulda run for help," Bennett barked.

"We didn't know what to do. Stephen died right in front of us." Silence descended on the jail as they took it all in. Having started, Tyler wanted to finish. "Alan was all for leaving him there and have Tubby discover him in the morning. I wouldn't hear of it. I didn't want Tubby getting into trouble. Alan remembered the conversation with Emmett earlier. Seems two of the Guardian Wall Gang, Coleman and Murphy, were in town."

Tyler pursed his lips. "So, we set the livery on fire to set 'em up. Two men already wanted. Seemed the ideal solution to our problems." He shrugged.

"I went off to my poker game as usual. Alan waited until the last possible moment to go tell the sheriff about Coleman and Murphy. I came out of my poker game early. With Bennett outta the way, searching for 'em, Alan and me moved Stephen's body into the alley. We started the fire. I raised the alarm. Then we waited until all the animals were out. Only moved Stephen's body in when folks stopped coming and going. Easy enough to sneak in through the side door, leave Stephen, and sneak out again. No one would be any the wiser. Everyone would think he'd died in the fire."

"Until I came along and found oil on the lock of the unused side door," Fooks murmured.

"Yes."

"Sorry 'bout that."

CHAPTER THIRTY

Late afternoon found Fooks pacing in the sheriff's office. Bennett had released the ranch hands with a telling-off. He'd dispatched Tyler to the hotel under Deputy Patterson's guard, leaving Alan alone in the cellblock. Bennett, along with Alan's new lawyer, was in there now, questioning him. As the man responsible for Alan's injury, Bennett thought it inappropriate to have Fooks present. Fooks had huffed and puffed before finally accepting that his exclusion was just. Bennett would likely find out more without him anyway.

So, here he was, pacing the office and running his fingers through his hair. He came to a stop and, with arms folded, stared at the crazy stringing, which had been no help at all. Rev had disappeared, no doubt keeping Lovina company again.

"Lovina." Fooks rolled his eyes.

He stalked to the noticeboard and glared at the wanted posters.

"I know you and you. Don't know you. Thought you were dead. Not sure about you. Think I know your brother."

Fooks turned and puffed.

"Bored. Bored. Boring."

He craned his neck to view the papers on Bennett's desk. Nothing remotely interesting. He moved to put his ear to the cellblock door in the hope he could overhear something.

He jumped back as Bennett opened the door. Bennett looked surprised, and Fooks couldn't control the furtive expression crossing his features.

As Bennett glared at him, Fooks swallowed hard. Bennett catching him wouldn't do anything to allay his suspicion of him.

"Well? What has he said?"

Fooks' frustration mounted when Bennett didn't answer immediately.

Instead, Bennett went to his desk, sat, and pulled out a whiskey bottle and two glasses from the bottom drawer. Fooks had to be patient, hopping from foot to foot, while Bennett poured two drinks. One glass, he pushed in Fooks' direction.

Fooks pulled up a chair, waiting. Bennett downed his in one gulp and then reached to pour another. Fooks watched him until he could bear it no longer.

"Well?"

Bennett rubbed his bristled cheek.

"Like Lucinda told us, Alan got her to shoot at you and Rev to frighten ya off. His lawyer an' I am satisfied there was no attempt at murder. Lucinda is too good with a rifle to make a mistake."

Fooks nodded. That's what he'd thought, and he hadn't planned to take things any further. "Okay."

He leaned forward to catch what else Bennett would say.

Bennett rubbed his forehead. "Alan wanting to do improvements to the house Martha rents from him has nothing to do with this. Turns out it's just a coincidence."

"Did Alan confirm he stole the padlocks from Preston?"

"Yes. See, he knew when Preston would be out. Seems he used to own the property and still had a set of keys."

Bennett held up a hand to stay Fooks' questions. "I know. I didn't see 'em, either. Guess he musta got rid of 'em." He paused. "Alan broke in when Preston was away. Took several items to disguise what he was really after."

"Makes sense," Fooks said, pursing his lips.

Bennett gave him a sharp look. At that point, Doc Sullivan interrupted them. He stood with his hand on the door.

"Is now a good time, Sheriff?"

"Yeah, come on in," Bennett said, beckoning him to enter.

Fooks positioned another chair around Bennett's desk.

"I've finished my analysis of the aconite," Sullivan said when everyone had settled. "The amount of aconite from the padlock is potent, and it would kill a person ingesting even a small quantity. But from what you tell me, Mr. Crane, and coupled with my own findings from examining the cut on Stephen's hand, the amount entering his body in that way was not enough to kill him.

"I also analyzed the aconite in Martha's headache potion, which Stephen took just before he died. Martha is correct. The amount and frequency he took were not enough to kill him, either.

"However, as Mr. Crane rightly surmised, the two forms of aconite administered in quick succession were enough to kill him."

He looked at the two men for their reactions. Bennett frowned. Fooks chewed his bottom lip.

Sullivan continued. "I shall provide a full written report for the trial, Mark. No doubt, the lawyers will want to have my findings independently verified."

Bennett and Fooks said their thanks and goodbyes.

"I suppose whether they try Alan and Tyler for murder or manslaughter depends on whether they knew about Stephen taking aconite already," Fooks said a few minutes after Doc Sullivan had left.

"Same result. How the legalities play out is something the court will decide. Far as I'm concerned, we've done our bit."

Fooks found sleep hard to come by. He was tired, having only snatched a few hours of sleep during the day, yet his mind wouldn't stop buzzing. In desperation, he dressed quickly and, in stocking feet, walked across the landing to Blair's room. He knocked gently and put his ear to the door. When he heard sounds of movement within, he stepped back.

Blair, dressed in a snowy white nightshirt, opened the door warily.

"Good, you're up," said Fooks, pushing into the room.

"Not really..." Blair said. After closing the door, he turned to see that Fooks was already taking a seat. "It's the middle of the night. Is there some emergency?"

Fooks briefly glanced at Blair before shaking his head and gnawing at his thumbnail. Sensing he wouldn't find out by asking, Blair sat and waited, feeling his injured arm.

"How do you do it, Mr. Blair?" Fooks asked, finally. "How do *you* defend someone who's guilty?"

"It's difficult sometimes—"

"How can you justify it to yourself and the victims if they get off?" Fooks shook his head. "How can you bear to be in company with criminals, day in, day out?" He ran his fingers through his hair.

"How did *you*, Mr. Fooks?"

Fooks shook his head. "I'm not talking about me," he muttered. "You're a decent man."

"And you aren't?"

Fooks rubbed his forehead. "Not really."

"It seems to me you are. Otherwise, why are you here in Angelworth? I know you're acquainted with Coleman and Murphy, but this was none of your affair. Yet you solved a case when there wasn't a case." Blair paused. "Through your tenacity, you proved their innocence."

Fooks flopped his hands into his lap and shook his head. "Did you know Stephen Mercer?"

"Not personally, but I'd heard of him before I came to Wyoming."

"Yeah, he was getting quite the reputation."

"Why did you come here tonight, Mr. Fooks?" Blair asked after a moment's silence.

"I'm not sure." Fooks frowned. "Alan Long and Tyler Callaghan killed Stephen Mercer, a man I liked and admired. He didn't deserve to die."

"No one does."

"I'm finding it difficult to understand how you can defend the men responsible for Stephen's death. That's all."

"It's my job. I will work with Alan Long's lawyer and see what we can do."

Fooks nodded. "I know."

"Stephen wasn't entirely blameless, though. He encouraged Mr. Woodward to take action against Mr. Thompkins—"

"He defended Celia and Martha against two..." Fooks struggled to come up with an adjective for Alan and Tyler, so he left it. He rubbed his forehead. Probably best not mention that he suspected Stephen had forged the record of the disputed land.

"Mr. Fooks, do you regret your involvement in this investigation? Especially now you've proved the innocence of two men." Blair smiled faintly. "In this matter, at least."

Fooks felt a flush creep across his cheeks. "No. I guess I don't."

"You've done your part. Now let me do mine. I have to defend Tyler because he's my client. Some of my clients are victims; others may not be. Some cases, I will win;

others, I won't. It's something I have to accept, but I will always do my best. Try to get the most favorable outcome for my client as I can."

"Yeah." Fooks sighed. "I'm sorry, Mr. Blair. I'm tired and not making any sense."

"I'm not surprised. The last few days have been trying for all." Blair took a deep breath. "Look, Mr. Fooks, whatever the reason you become involved, you did a superb job. Something any law-abiding man with a profound sense of right and wrong would do."

Fooks groaned, but Blair carried on regardless.

"You did what your conscience told you had to, and you did it well, to the best of your ability. Your considerable ability, I might add. I've no doubt that if you used those abilities on the right side of the law, you would be a formidable advocate. I admit some of your methods were unorthodox, but you got the right result. Something to be proud of."

"Rev said that to me not too long ago."

"He's right."

Blair studied the despondent ex-outlaw.

"Mr. Fooks, it seems to me you've given yourself a second chance at life. My advice to you..." Blair grinned. "...and I won't charge you, is to seize the opportunity and make the most of it. Whatever the future holds for you, your actions here must stand you in good stead."

"I want to." Fooks rolled his eyes. For the first time, he felt he was truly committed to a law-abiding life. "I'm not struggling with finding Stephen's killers. That's a good thing. What happens next is what's making me uncomfortable. You'll defend Tyler, and I don't think you should. I don't understand what defense he thinks he's got. Tyler deserves the same fate as Stephen. Alan, more so." He hesitated. "Although, that may just be my dislike of the man talking."

"And that's what's bothering you? The law decides by due process what happens to them, not I. It's not your concern anymore. Try to separate the investigation and the legal process in your mind, Mr. Fooks. That..." Blair lent forward. "...is what law-abiding citizens do."

Fooks rubbed his forehead. "Yeah, I know." He raised his head to the ceiling, and his voice caught when he next spoke. "For a long time, I took the law into my own hands. Metering out justice in my own way. Now I'm within the law. It's the hardest thing I'm struggling with. I can't just do something without considering the consequences." He smiled. "Mostly."

Blair returned Fooks' smile and rose, prompting Fooks to do the same. They shook hands.

"Goodbye, Mr. Fooks, and good luck."

"Goodbye, Mr. Blair, and thank you."

Fooks reached the door and opened it. He looked back. "There's one more thing. Lucinda Mercer will need a good lawyer. I think losing her husband is punishment enough, and I'd hate to see her suffer any more. Will you represent her?"

"Yes," Blair said with a nod. "I'll see her in the morning."

Fooks smiled. "Thank you. Good night. I'll be away in the morning. Gotta long ride ahead of me. A wife and a new baby to see."

CHAPTER THIRTY-ONE

"So, there you are." Fooks grinned and stood with hands on hips, regarding Rev. "Been looking for you everywhere."

He climbed onto the hotel porch and took a seat next to his friend. He'd been packed and ready to go for ages. Looking for Rev had cost him time, and here Rev had been all along.

"Morning."

Fooks wanted an explanation for where Rev had been for the last two days. He couldn't fail to notice Rev no longer wore his black tunic. Suspenders held up his black pants as usual, but underneath he now wore a crisp white collarless shirt. He'd shaved and, if Fooks wasn't mistaken, submitted himself to a haircut.

"Bennett has withdrawn the murder warrant on Brad and Sid. When you go back to the Wall—"

"I'm not going back to the Wall." Rev paused and licked his lips. "Least, I've no plans right now." He shrugged. "Who knows? Mebbe later at some point."

Fooks didn't answer immediately. He nodded slowly. "All right, send a telegram to Sticky. He can give 'em the good news when they're next in town." He narrowed his eyes at Rev. "What are *your* plans?"

Rev sniffed. "Kinda like Angelworth. It's a nice little town. People are friendly. Thought I might stay for a while."

"What will you do? Is now the right time to go back to ministering?"

"Not exactly. Reverend ain't my denomination, y'understand, but he can use some help with running the church an' all. Thought I'd stay an' give him a hand."

"And where will you live?" Fooks asked, trying to keep his face straight.

Rev ran his tongue around his teeth. "Heard about a room going over at the Wilson house. Thought I might apply."

Fooks gave Rev a wide grin. "Good luck to you, Rev. I hope it works out." He stood and offered his hand. "Gotta go. I've got a daughter to meet."

Rev took his hand and smiled. "Thanks. Good luck."

Fooks stopped by the sheriff's office before he left. He knew he was taking a risk. If Bennett was going to do anything, this would be the time, but he didn't want to just leave.

"Well now, that's all wrapped up. There's just the trial. Blair has arranged a transfer to Cheyenne 'cause of the complexity of the case. Will ya be around to give evidence, Crane?"

Fooks stood with hands on hips, looking thoughtful. "No, Sheriff, I don't think I will." He smiled. "In fact, I'd rather you kept me out of it. I'm happy for you to take the credit for this investigation."

"Ya sure? Man like you—" Bennett stopped abruptly and chuckled. "What am I saying? Of course, you can't give evidence at the trial."

Fooks frowned. "What d'you mean, Sheriff? I have business elsewhere. Won't wait."

"Sure. Or is it 'cause ya don't want anyone looking into who you are?"

Fooks stiffened. Surely, not now, when he was so close to getting back to Mary. Bennett went on. "You ain't a federal employee, are ya?"

Fooks wiggled his nose and sniffed. Then he tried an unconvincing laugh. "Whatever gives you that idea?"

Bennett thought for a moment. "Something tells me Joseph Crane is not ya real name."

Fooks grinned. "Oh, now, Sheriff—"

"In fact, I don't believe there is a federal employee with that name."

Fooks kept silent.

"Now, er, as far I'm aware, it ain't illegal to impersonate a fictitious person."

Fooks pursed his lips. "True enough." He folded his arms. "What are you getting at, Sheriff?"

Bennett smiled ruefully and settled himself on the edge of his desk. "Well now, I'm not exactly sure, but I do know there is something not quite right about ya. Thought that the first time you were here. Gotten to know ya better this time around, but the feeling hasn't gone away."

Fooks smiled, and his hands returned to his hips. "I guess I've got that sorta manner about me." He shrugged before turning to go. "Well, I'll be taking my leave now."

"Goodbye." Bennett smiled. He waited until Fooks had opened the door before adding, "Mr. Fooks."

Fooks didn't turn back. He stopped with his hand on the door.

Bennett's grin widened. "Weren't sure my suspicions were correct until just now."

Fooks looked around. He wasn't about to confirm anything unless a direct question required an answer. *Is Bennett about to arrest me? How should I handle this? Let's try brazening it out.* He turned to confront Bennett, his thumbs hooked into his gun belt.

"What are you going to do, Sheriff?" His voice was low, with an edge hard as his look.

Bennett hadn't moved. He still sat easily on the desk.

"Is it true you have a wife?"

Fooks blinked, surprised by the unexpected question, one he could answer truthfully.

"Yes."

"What kinda woman is she?"

Not really any of your business, but all right. "Respectable. Owns and runs a ladies hat shop."

"As a front?"

"No!" Fooks squeaked, and he cleared his throat. "Ran it long before I met her. She's the daughter of a former sheriff, if you must know." *Careful, Fooks, calm down.*

"You tell her who you are?"

"Yes." Fooks swallowed hard. What was Bennett getting at? "I'm making a new life for myself away from crime. Sh-she trusts me." He winced at the uncharacteristic stutter.

Bennett didn't move. He stared at Fooks for the longest time.

"Heard rumors about you going straight. Reckon that must be good news for all concerned, all things considered." Bennett rose to his feet. "You did fine work here, Fooks, but I still don't want ya in my town." He shook his head. "You'll be gone soon, I expect."

Fooks nodded, giving Bennett a tight-lipped smile. "Going right now."

"Safe journey, Mr. Fooks."

Fooks closed the door and started along the boardwalk towards the hotel. He puffed out his cheeks. *Bennett figured it out, did he? Phew, close one.*

Before he rode away from Angelworth, Fooks stopped by the cemetery. A thorough man by nature, there was something he needed to do before he started for home. Anyone would think he was deliberately delaying getting back to Mary. He didn't know if he would be back this way again, if ever, and he needed to do this.

He stood at the side of Stephen Mercer's grave, gazing down at the piled-up earth.

"Well, I guess you won't thank me too much, but I found out who killed you. Hope you understand I couldn't let two innocent men take the fall, even if they are already outside the law."

He crouched and laid a hand on the earth.

"You were a good man, Stephen. I'm sorry you had to die the way you did." He glanced around and dropped his voice. "Just so you know, I was Florian Fooks."

He rose to his feet. "Rest in peace, Mr. Mercer."

With a tight-lipped smile and a nod, he settled his hat and then walked to his horse and mounted up. He gave the grave one last acknowledgment before whirling away, urging his horse into a fast lope.

If this trip had told him anything, it was that the other fella was long gone. He was Joseph Crane now, and he had things to do in his new life. His wife, a baby daughter hopefully, and his hardware store were all the things he wanted right now. All law-abiding, ordinary, everyday things. They would start when he got home.

EPILOGUE

Fooks drew up outside his home with a skid of hooves, his horse blowing hard. A light burned in the house even at this late hour. Fooks fell through the front door in his haste.

Inside, Janet Turner let out a gasp of surprise. Wash grinned and rose quickly.

"Mary? Is she?" Fooks glanced at the bedroom door and moved towards it. The Turners stopped him.

"Mary is just fine. She's sleeping."

Fooks stared at Janet.

"Is she all right?" He unconsciously surrendered his saddlebags to Wash.

"She's perfectly fine. And so is your daughter." Janet smiled. She patted his arm, nodded at Wash to deal with him, and went to the bedroom.

"Daughter?"

Wash just grinned and, catching Fooks' arm, propelled his dazed-looking friend to an armchair.

"Yeah, you have a daughter."

Fooks sank into the chair with a whimper. "A daughter? I wanted to *be* here."

"There was nothing for you to do. You'd only be in the way. Believe me, this is one situation where it's best to let the womenfolk get on with it and stay outta the way."

Fooks, not so sure, shook his head. Wash put a hand on his shoulder and gave it a reassuring squeeze.

"Did you take care of that business to your friends' satisfaction?"

Fooks remembered the tough conversations they'd had before he'd left. Wash was far from stupid, and no doubt, he'd guessed who the friends were whom Fooks had gone away to help.

"Yes. All worked out well," Fooks said, keeping out of Wash's eye line.

"Good. Mustn't let these things slide. Best to nip 'em in the bud."

"Yeah."

Fooks relaxed into the comfort of his chair, glad to be home. His gaze landed on the mantel. There was a letter. He couldn't make out the postmark, but he would know the untidy handwriting anywhere. It belonged to his partner, who'd run off while he and Mary had been on their honeymoon. At last. News.

Fooks was levering himself up to go look when Janet came back into the room. She was carrying his daughter, wrapped in a blanket. As she came closer, Fooks swallowed nervously and sank back into the chair, letter and Tobias Swan instantly forgotten.

"Here, darlin'. Let me introduce you to your pappy," Janet said, preparing to put the baby into Fooks' arms.

He gave her a horrified stare.

"Um, no... I mean, I'm not..." He indicated his disheveled state.

"She won't notice. Here."

"Er..." Fooks swatted away his hat and frantically pulled off his gloves. "I don't know how. I've never..." A moment later, he was awkwardly holding a baby.

Janet teased back the blanket so he could see the baby's face. "Oh!"

The baby, closely swaddled, had a little round face, a button nose, and tufts of brown hair.

"She's beautiful," Fooks gasped, instantly in love. The baby yawned and smiled. "Oh, she's got my..." He grinned at Wash and Janet. The baby had his dimples, which were much in evidence as part of his joyous grin.

"Yep," Wash agreed dryly. "I reckon she'll break hearts with those when she's older."

Fooks tore his eyes from his daughter and looked up at them. "Does she have a name?"

"No, not yet. Mary wanted to wait until you came home."

"We talked about a name before I went away. Pretty much decided, if the baby was a girl, we would call her Susan Eloise, after our ma's." Fooks stared back at his daughter. "Hi, Susan. What d'you think of your name, huh?"

Susan blew bubbles, and Fooks laughed. "I guess that's a yes."

He tore his eyes away from her and looked at the Turners.

"Mary's okay?"

"Yes, she's fine," Janet laughed. "I was with her all the way, and I've been here ever since to help."

"Thank you," Fooks breathed. "When did...um...she..." He grinned. "My daughter. Ha!" He chuckled. He liked the sound of that. "When did she arrive?"

"Two days ago."

He couldn't take his eyes from the bundle in his arms. "I'm sorry I missed you, sweetheart, but I'm here now," he whispered. His eyes widened when the baby squirmed. "Um? What do I do?"

Fooks relaxed as the baby settled, and he sat back in the chair. He swallowed hard and smiled. "Thank you for being here." Wash put his hand on Fooks' shoulder and gave it a shake. "I can't believe she's here. I'm a father,"

Fooks squealed, his voice several octaves higher than its usual baritone.

"Hey, sweetheart, I'm your..." Fooks glanced at Janet. What had she called him? Pappy? Hmmm, he liked the sound of that.

Fooks and Mary had already spoken about what their child would call them when old enough to talk. Mary had no objections to Mama. Fooks was undecided about what he wanted to be. He didn't want to be Pa. It reminded him too much of his own father. He'd wrinkled his nose at Papa, and Father was too formal. Yes, he liked Pappy.

"Pappy," he said to the baby.

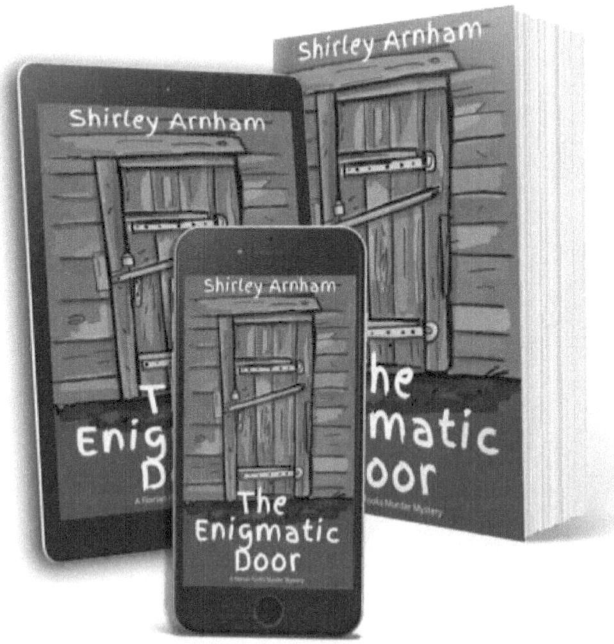

If you enjoyed *The Enigmatic door*, please share your thoughts by leaving a review on Amazon.

ABOUT ME

Shirley Arnham always enjoyed writing and flirted with fan fiction over the years. Once retired from a career in accountancy, she thought what now? With plenty of stories in her head, why not try her hand at writing a book. Shirley lives in Norfolk, England and is looking forward to traveling the world with her husband.

The Enigmatic Door is her first published novel and is the first in the Outlaw Detective series.

Discover more at:

www.shirleyarnham.com

ACKNOWLEGMENT

I would like to thank my beta readers Fliss and Sue for wading through this text even though this is not their genre.

Also Gin and Niki for helping me sound more American.

My editor, Kristina Stanley, for being patient with a newbie writer.

To Jefferson at *First Editing,* for removing commas where they shouldn't be and for adding them where they should.

Most of all I would like to thank my husband Murray for NOT reading any of my drafts and keeping our relationship sane.

IN THE PIPELINE

His partner's life at stake. No dilemma. This time he has to go.

Nearly a year has passed since Joseph Crane, hardware store owner, husband and father to a small daughter has left the safety of Bronze Canyon. Hearing that his old partner is wanted for murder and is missing, Florian Fooks as he is uncomfortably known outside Bronze Canyon, crosses the Mississippi for the first time.

Way outside his comfort zone, in Boston, he discovers that the murder victim was the uncle of the woman, his partner Tobias Swan, ran away with. With Tobias as the last person to see the victim alive and the police closing in on him, Fooks is in a race against time to prove his partner innocent. The more he discovers about the dead man's murky life, the more convinced Fooks becomes that there is more to his death than appears at first glance.

www.ingramcontent.com/pod-product-compliance
Lightning Source LLC
Chambersburg PA
CBHW061556190726
48288CB00007B/2047